Dead People Don't Make Jam

Sean Crawley

Dead People Don't Make Jam

Dead People Don't Make Jam
ISBN 978 1 76041 859 5
Copyright © Sean Crawley 2020
Cover image: Victoria Chen at Unsplash

First published 2020 by
Ginninderra Press
PO Box 3461 Port Adelaide 5015
www.ginninderrapress.com.au

Contents

The Track

Davis and I are making a track. We're doing it with our feet, no tools needed. It's the path we take each day as we wind our way from the back gate down to the rock platform up the north end of the beach we call our own. Our footprints on the sand rarely last a day, but the ones across the grass, and through the low heath, and under the forest canopy, are doing their work. The track gets more obvious, little by little, day by day.

We take this route because if we go by the road way we have to drive, or, if not drive, wear shoes on the hot tar, and we end up down the south end where the people are. We also like the birds and the lizards and the snakes we come across. Nature is healing us both.

I call him Davis because he once was my boss and Paul sounds weird to me for some reason. He's always been Davis and he seems OK with it staying that way – even after all the shit that went down. We've changed the setting, not our relationship.

When we do hop in the car, to drive to the shops for food, the locals wonder who the fuck we are. Davis is a heap older than me and even though I'm quite androgynous, I am clearly a young Asian woman, so the usual conclusions are made. If you look closely, though, and if you have what some people call a 'gaydar', you'll know there's nothing going on between us – well, not in that sense anyway.

We work on our track every morning unless it's storming. And if the wind's not too wild in the afternoons, we go again. Davis sometimes brings a torch when we do the afternoon beach thing. The sunsets can be so nourishing that we sit on the dune and just bathe in the dying day. Davis teaches me astronomy.

'Is that Mars?' I ask.

'No that can't be Mars, it's not on the ecliptic. Remember the ecliptic?'

'Oh yeah, the line the sun takes from sunrise to sunset.'

'That's her.'

Davis has a gender for lots of things. Bottles are always a he. Trees are always she. And cars, well they can be either, but you'd never guess which ones he assigns as girls and which ones get the boy names. It's purely arbitrary, he explained to me once. The ecliptic is female by sheer randomness. I don't think he's ever called the track male or female, it's just the track.

Davis used to talk a lot about politics and history; it was why I hung out with him at work. The tea room was full of ladies comparing lunches and waistlines. Out the back, he and I sucked hard on full-strength cigarettes and vented our anger at the craziness of everything. Food could be scoffed at your desk later. He has an amazing knowledge, broad and general, big-picture stuff, but when he needs a detail like a number, or a date, or a scientific name in Latin, he's got it – right there in that bald head of his. Work was great fun back then, with Davis.

After he blew the whistle, after he'd been chewed up and spat out by countless hearings and court cases then sent on his way with a suspended sentence, he almost stopped talking completely. I tuned into events on the computer at work, sneaking onto the alternative news websites. Some commentators cheered him on while others saw just another opportunity to propose a conspiracy theory. That was a tough eighteen months. He texted me to say it was best if we ceased all communications for the moment. I texted back 'K', and cried.

The day after the judge handed down the final verdict and it was clear that he was not coming back to work – not here anyway, that was for certain, nor anywhere else perhaps – he texted me to say he was leaving the city. He had a house lined up down the coast. Miserable and lonely at work and sick of trying to find comfort with a woman –

funny how I hate lesbians even though I am one – I asked him if I could come.

Does everyone wake up earlier and earlier as they get older? I'm now getting up regularly not long after sunrise. I remember having to set the alarm to wake any time before nine. Davis gets up in the dark. I asked him once, 'So what time do you get up, Davis?'

'About fourish.'

I didn't have to ask what he did. I knew that. He was reading and making notes in cheap exercise books that he bought from the smelly two-dollar shop in town. The third bedroom was his space, a study of sorts, and it was a girl.

'She likes books and paper and pens,' he said one morning out of the blue as we worked on our track and got wet in a drizzle.

'Who's she?' I asked.

'The study. She's a bibliophile.'

When we first moved in, I asked him if he wanted to talk about all the madness that erupted after he blew the whistle.

'I'm a good listener, Davis, you know that. I can smoke three Camel before I get a word in.'

'All talked out, Lily, all talked out. Let me just say, I wasn't prepared…not by a long shot.'

I gathered our stay in the bush down the coast near the beach, with his pre-dawn sessions in the female study, was preparation. Books came by the score in the post every week, and I helped Davis make shelves out of fence palings and bricks that we found lying around the messy yard. The study, she was looking good; one whole wall ended up as books from floor to ceiling. I took some pride in the fact that I introduced Davis to 0.7-gauge gel rollerball pens.

'Nice. Nice flow. Nice opaqueness… I mean, opacity,' he said. He stuck with the cheap exercise books, though. 'He's a bit fancy,' he said when I gave him a blank journal with thick paper, hardbound and all. 'Not sure what I'll write in that.'

At least it stayed sitting on his desk. Waiting, maybe, for when he was prepared.

It took about a year for me to exorcise the raciness that the city had planted inside me without my consent. Davis reckoned he got rid of most of his poison during the eighteen months sitting by himself on benches outside hearing rooms and court houses.

With the raciness gone, life began to fill with the simplest of things and moments.

I collected stuff from along our track and from off the beach. The beach was different everyday and you never knew what the sea would offer up.

When he'd see me stoop and pick up something, Davis would say, 'He's a goodun,' or, 'She'll work well on that necklace you're stringing.'

Who needs raciness?

After two years, our track to the beach was bare dirt in some places. The chocolate-coloured patches in the green and yellow grass were cool in the mornings and warm on the sunny afternoons.

'She feels good, this earth,' said Davis.

The day he said that, we went into town. We never really got to know anyone there. And Davis and I, the bald bloke in the sarong and that funny-looking Asian dyke, were still a mystery to the locals – but at least they'd given up gawking and silently guessing. After we got our usual supplies, Davis headed down to the local electrical appliance store that surprisingly had not closed down like a lot of the other shops. He bought a radio. It was a plug-in one. So the batteries he bought as well must have been for the torch.

When we got home, he put the radio on our op-shop dining table. He plugged it in and tuned it into the ABC.

'He's a bit crackly, but she'll do,' said Davis.

Never thought I'd be introduced to a hermaphroditic radio and not even blink an eye.

Davis then went into the study and came out with the blank journal I had given him and a gel rollerball pen.

Basim, Tyson, Betty and Ted

Everyone wants to know what happened in carriage three that day. The hullabaloo surrounding the events of carriages one, two and four has died down. Now the attention has turned to us lot – that mob of free-loving peaceniks, they call us. They can call us whatever they like, we don't care, we've all become best friends, some of us even lovers.

They're calling us all in to meet with the experts. They want to work out why the humans on our carriage didn't degenerate into panic, violence and hatred, like what happened to the others. I mean the public address system told the whole train that the issue would be fixed as soon as possible. And the air conditioning and water bubblers kept working the whole time. So I don't wonder about us, I'm more worried about all the mayhem that erupted in them other carriages.

I still can't get my head around that rape on carriage one and the numerous other assaults. One commuter is still in hospital, and some are in psych wards, for goodness sake. It's too easy to say that human nature showed its true colours that day, and us lot in carriage three are posing bit of a problem for that view of humanity. I've given it a heap of thought and I'm going to tell them experts. I ran it by Trudie and she reckons I've nailed it.

When the train came to an unexpected halt that day, Tina, all four foot ten of her, jumped up and started shushing everyone. She was pointing to Fadila, who had young Basim asleep in her arms. Tina and Fadila have now become best friends. Fadila is helping Tina with her English skills.

None of us disputed the need to keep quiet, so we whispered about our transport dilemma. Basim did wake later, his smile and his wanting to feed us all rice crackers was hell cute. There was a collective desire to keep the young fella from fear, and I'm sure that was a factor, but that initial agreement to keep our voices down was crucial.

It's my point number one. I'll tell them experts, 'There was a sleeping toddler, so we all kept our voices down.'

About fifteen minutes later, Enzo had to change Tyson's colostomy bag. Tyson was only nineteen when a police car hit his pushbike. The poor bugger's future as a professional triathlete was smashed along with his C5 vertebrae. Confined to a wheelchair and needing the help of others for life, we were all humbled down big time when Tyson told us, 'It was the best thing that ever happened to me. I was totally up myself before the accident.'

Tyson has one of those real contagious laughs that got us able-bodied folk joining in and forgetting our woes. Some of us would be late for stuff; Roger had a job interview for an attorney's position in a big city firm, and Robyn was meeting her daughter at the airport. Gwyneth's claustrophobia was playing up, but Tyson's great attitude kept it all in perspective, let me tell you.

And that's my point number two. I'll tell them, 'Nothing like a quadriplegic in the midst to keep things real.'

The love and care shown by Enzo touched our hearts, and it got us wondering if we'd give up a high-paid job to be a disability worker, like he did. I really believe now that we all have the capacity to help others. Enzo said it was the best job he'd ever had, and we didn't doubt him for a second.

Ted and Betty were holding hands and all dressed up. They were going out to lunch at a fancy restaurant in town. We all thought they must've been married for decades. Turns out they met just six months ago in the retirement village.

'I've been married twice before,' Betty said. 'One was a mongrel bastard and the other carked it with cancer, but Ted is the love of my life.'

Tyson laughed and Basim gave Betty a rice cracker and a hug. Imagine that, ninety-bloody-three and meeting your true soulmate.

I'd been checking Trudie out since she got on at Strathfield, but had been too scared to talk to her. She had this big textbook with the word 'psychology' standing out on the cover. By now, though, I'd lost all fear and I went straight over and introduced myself. We've been together everyday since.

And that's my point number three. I am going to tell them experts, 'Love is possible at any age and at any time. Hang in because you never know what's around the corner, or, in this case, when your train will get stuck in a tunnel.'

They better let us go then, because we're all going out to lunch to celebrate Ted and Betty's one-year anniversary and Tina getting into uni. And that's why I'm all dressed up.

Werzy

Most people think that Werzy is my twin sister. I did too, until Mum told us both the truth when we needed our birth certificates for a history project in Year 8. It was bit of a shock to find out that Werzy was my aunty and one month younger than me.

See, my mother is the eldest of thirteen and when her mum, Nanna Cornelia, had Werzy, her thirteenth, it was all too much. We took her in as one of our own and moved, quick-smart apparently, from Adelaide up to Brisbane.

Werzy took the news a lot better than I expected; my surname, date of birth, star sign and parentage hadn't changed, but Werzy's whole world was turned upside down. So her nonchalant attitude seemed odd to me at the time. What I didn't know then was that she had a much bigger secret hidden away in her fubsy body.

Werzy got her nickname in primary school. Her first name, Wilhelmina, drew the attention of Brad Cunningham, a bully who was prone to a bit of rodomontade, which I thought was to cover up his bad case of haplography. I found out later, though, that his dad was a blue-singleted wife-basher who drank every day until he became catawampus. Poor Brad, no wonder he couldn't spell. Anyway, Willy, as we called her at the time, always carried a dictionary around with her. She was a logophile, and if you think I'm a bit verbose, it's actually all her fault.

'Wilhelmina, Wilhelmina, she grows on a rock and couldn't be meaner,' sang Brad one little lunch, when we were made sit under the camphor laurel trees to drink the free, warm milk.

'He's suggesting I'm rupestrine,' said Willy, unperturbed.

She showed me the word in her dictionary and I laughed. Brad didn't take too kindly to my cachination, so he stood up, walked across the cracked asphalt and punched me in the nose. I'm ashamed to admit it but I cried. Wilhelmina stepped in and kicked him in the groin. Brad dropped to the ground like a sack of starchy tubers and the whole of Year 5 sat stunned with opened mouths.

After all the kerfuffle, the principal called a school assembly. He gave a ten-minute lecture on bullying, and appropriate and inappropriate responses. Then in front of us all, he gave Willy – yes, Willy – two cuts of his cane and then Brad got six. The assembly was dismissed and I was trying to be as apatetic as possible because by now the whole school knew my sister had stepped in to defend me. If I knew then what I know now, maybe I would have cried out, 'She's my aunty, not my sister,' but I'm sure it wouldn't have made a difference.

For some reason, Brad spent the rest of Year 5 trying his darnedest to get on side with me and Willy. I didn't mind, since I figured that if I could be seen joking around and even rough-housing a bit with the boy who got six cuts of the cane without even a wince, maybe the humiliation of being the boy who needed his twin sister to step in for him might wane. Brad even tried to use big words to gain our favour. He consulted with the librarian and together they found the word lexicomane. He started calling Willy 'Lexi Comane', but my twin sister, once again, stopped him in his tracks.

She said, 'Brad, lexicomane is not a real word. If you desired to attribute a word to me to characterise my propensity to use big words, you could have scrutinised the thesaurus a bit more thoroughly and found sesquipedalian. Now that is a real word.'

Brad was without word. For a moment anyway. He picked up a stick off the ground and threw it at a noisy crow in the tree. 'Did you know I can throw a rock from the top of Mt Gravatt all the way into the Brisbane River?'

'Your mendacity metagrobolises me,' said Willy.

'I give up,' groaned Brad. 'You win, Willy Wordsworth!'

And that was that. Out of sheer frustration, Brad the bully, trying to ingratiate himself with the master of the lexicon and swift kicker to the testicles, had popped out a nickname that stuck like the proverbial mud. Like wildfire, the name Willy Wordsworth swept through Sunnybank State Primary School.

In the weeks ahead, it got trimmed and morphed. Willy Wordsworth was truncated to Wordsworth, then that was transmogrified into Wordsy. And then finally, in true-to-form Australianisation, it ended up rolling off our tongues as Werzy.

After Mum told us that we weren't twins, Werzy and I grew apart a bit. It wasn't really because she was now my aunty, which we decided to keep as a family secret for the moment, nor that she was still a word freak quick to violence, it was more that in high school the boys hung out with the boys and the girls looked down on us as immature and despicable. Werzy was fine with me one on one, but at school, even though she was quite a tomboy, she hung out with all the pretty girls in our year; the very same girls that us immature and pimply boys used to fantasise over.

Brad Cunningham and I would watch them from the other side of the quadrangle.

'Why doesn't Werzy invite us over to hang out with her mates?' Brad would ask from time to time.

They would laugh and hug each other, even hold hands as they walked to period five after lunch. It was then that I first thought Werzy might be a lesbian.

'Did you know Tina Westbourne is intimately allied with that young and hirsute PE teacher, Mr King? It's ridiculously clandestine and she has unmitigatedly succumbed to limmerence. It's quite disconcerting,' said Werzy one afternoon after school as we divided up the rest of the milk left in the fridge. 'He's a certified philanderer. An interloper of the worst kind,' she continued with spittle forming a line of ebullition along the lower labium of her mouth. She was optically verdant and beastly, and clearly jealous of Mr King's success.

By the time we reached Year 12, Werzy got over Tina Westbourne by having several sexual dalliances with other girls – and I was still a virgin! On the night of the graduation formal, she called Mum and Dad and me into the lounge room to announce that she was a man trapped inside a female body. I was discombobulated, and didn't know whether to say, 'Sure, bro!' or ask, 'So now you're my uncle?'

Inside my busy mind, I was reconstructing the world. I realised that Werzy wasn't gay after all – she was a he, and therefore as hetero-sexual as *moi*. I took it all in my stride, and in the car as Dad drove us to the formal it dawned on me that Werzy was now uniquely and perfectly placed to help me crack onto Tina Westbourne. Howzat that for serendipity?

Busting a Rhyme or Two
on a Lovely Spring Morning

I promised Nina I would bite my tongue and just nod.

Last time we visited my wife's mother, things went pear-shaped – excuse the cliché. The old bird claimed that a comet was circling the Earth, and I asked her if she meant the comet was orbiting the sun.

'No,' she said with authority. 'It's a new comet and it's orbiting the Earth.'

'Bullshit, Elsie.' I couldn't help myself. I recalled a similar exchange when she claimed that chickens don't have a brain. That time, I agreed to disagree; this time I would not back down.

'How dare you speak to me like that!'

'I'll call bullshit bullshit when I hear it, Elsie. You don't get off the hook just because you're my mother-in-law. Facts are facts.'

Elsie faked an angina attack and we had to leave.

The next day, she phoned Nina to warn her about me. 'You know what they say, dear. A dimple on the chin, the devil within,' she said.

'Don't be silly, Mum. Now, have you heard back from the doctors?' My wife can deflect like a pro.

'So where is Jason at the moment, dear? Is he at work? What is that new job of his? It's in Darlinghurst, isn't it? Does he ever work late? You know there are a lot of temptations for a man in that suburb? Don't be surprised if he strays, Nina.'

'Mum! Jason's business is Jason's business. Now those results… from the doctor?'

Elsie took about two months to calm down and recover from my outburst before inviting us over for a cuppa and some of her burnt scones. I mean, they weren't burnt when she invited us. They would be, though, when we sat down on her precious Sanderson print lounge suite to listen to her latest ravings.

As you can see, I'm maybe not quite ready to go back there, yet. But for my wife, I will do it. I will bite my tongue and just nod. I will detach myself and float above as a remote observer. I will laugh in the face of insanity – to myself, that is.

When we arrived, Elsie decided to have tea and scones on the deck outside. It was a lovely spring morning, the sun was shining and the wisteria was in flower. The scones were baked to perfection and the conversation, though superficial, was pleasant and devoid of false astronomy. Apart from saying hello on arrival, I remained tight-lipped. I nodded in acknowledgement and occasionally dared to offer a 'mmm' in affirmation.

'Did you see the sunset last night?' my wife asked her mother.

'Oh yes, dear. That's why it's such a lovely day today. You know, red sky at night, shepherd's delight. It's never wrong.'

I choked and some scone flew out of my mouth and landed on the table next to the green depression-glass butter dish. Everyone pretended not to notice.

Nina asked if I was all right.

I nodded, took a swig of tea, patted my chest and said, 'I'm fine. Go on, Elsie.' My wife smiled at me, I was doing very well indeed.

Elsie went on, and on and on. The old wives' tales and pseudo-science polluted the crisp morning air. She was obviously fishing for a bite from her son-in-law. I just nodded in agreement and ate scones. Lots of scones.

My wife must've been too relaxed, possibly because of my exemplary behaviour, when she let out, 'Jason has had some issues with his oesophagus lately. He's seeing the doctor on Monday.'

I nearly choked again. I could sense that things were likely to crash and burn real fast. Again excuse my cliché – they must be contagious,

I tell you. Nina, my beautiful and caring wife had slipped. Her usual tactic of being a grey rock just flew out the window – even though we were on the deck outside. A tactic taught to Nina by her counsellor specifically to cope with the mother, it entails being bland and not giving away too much information.

I looked at Nina, she looked at me. She said sorry with her eyes. I reassured her with a wink and a nod, and a big smile. I could handle this; I was prepared. I would not take any bait offered by Elsie, the old fisherwoman.

And, by George, Elsie was off. The titbit of information about my oesophagus was like the starting gun in the hundred-yard dash.

'Well, if you ask me, an apple a day keeps the doctor away.'

I nodded.

'Nina, go inside and get an apple from the fruit bowl on the kitchen bench. You know, a stitch in time saves nine.'

I nodded.

Nina wouldn't normally obey her mother's army-like orders, but I figured that she was kicking herself for feeding the beast, as I called it. She went inside to find an apple.

'I once had a friend who always used to stay up late and sleep in all morning, she got oesophageal cancer and died at fifty-eight. Early to bed and early to rise, keeps one healthy, wealthy and wise. That's my motto, Jason. Couldn't be a more sage piece of advice if you ask me.'

Despite no one asking her anything, Elsie ploughed on. 'Beatrice was her name. She was a dancer, and you know what that lot are like! Birds of a feather flock together, no truer a word than that.'

I nodded. I was tempted to point out that her rhyming aphorism was actually six words and not one, and that I knew a dancer who bluntly refused to socialise with the troupe she was in.

Nina returned with an apple, from which I quickly took a massive bite.

'Now, what time do you go to bed and when do you get up in the morning, Jason?'

I pointed to my full mouth and held up a hand to indicate I couldn't speak.

'Mum! Leave Jason be. He has good sleeping habits, don't you worry.'

'But I want to worry, dear.'

I choked on my cancer-preventative apple. A small piece took flight and landed right next to the small piece of scone next to the butter dish. Everyone pretended not to notice.

'Talk about worry,' said Nina, 'Auntie Mary rang me last week and told me that Frank was likely to loose his superannuation due to his business partner gambling it all away.'

I love my wife. Not only can she deflect and be a grey rock, but when her long fuse runs out, she can give as good as she gets. Nina knows that her mother hasn't talked to her sister Mary for years. Apparently, Mary gave Elsie the flick when she grew tired of her sister's flirtatious ways with her husband Frank.

'Oh, poor Frank.' said Elsie. 'Mary has no place telling this kind of private information to the world. You know, loose lips sink ships.'

I nodded and thought, takes one to know one.

'I know. I'll send Frank a lovely card and a lottery ticket. You know, a friend in need is a friend indeed.' The old biddy looked straight at me.

With my mouth purposely refilled with apple, I simply nodded.

'Mum! You're kidding, aren't you? Don't you think that would be an insult to Mary?'

'No, I don't! That woman is as hard as nails and a mean one to boot. You know, when we were young…'

Nina interjected, 'Yes, Mum! I've heard it many times. Mary, on her way to school, used to step on the cracks in the pavement and sing, step on a crack, break your mother's back. That's right, isn't it?'

Go, Nina!

'That is right, Christina. And your dear grandmother died a broken woman. These things should not be fooled around with. They have a truth to them.'

'Bullshit, Mum. Nan died of emphysema caused by fifty years of smoking.'

Touché, Nina.

'Well, that's what the doctors say,' said Elsie. Never a backward step from this old battleaxe. 'I hope for my sake you didn't step on any cracks in the pavement when you were young.'

Nina looked over at me with eyes wide open in frustration. I nodded. Inside, I laughed out aloud at the insanity.

'OK, Mum, we have to go now. Thanks for the tea and scones, have a lovely day. I'll take the tray inside for you.' Nina needed to get away from this irrepressible matriarch – quick smart.

Elsie looked at me and said, 'Well, you've been very quiet today, young man. What, the cat got your tongue?'

With Nina gone, I was very tempted to let loose. The saying, empty vessels make the most noise, came to mind, but I held my tongue.

'Come on, speak up for yourself. Has the wifey got you on a promise?'

I took a deep breath. Elsie was champing at the bit for a reaction. A reaction that could be used later as evidence in the Family Court of Recriminations. I was a bit at sea, so I took a second deep breath.

Perhaps it was the thick fog of rhymes that was hanging around, perhaps it was just plain good fortune, but whatever it was, thankfully, a poem from my distant childhood came floating like a life raft into my reach. 'Elsie,' I said. 'I've been admiring all those wonderful wisdoms that you have been espousing this morning. And they rhyme so eloquently. It gives them a much greater authority, don't you feel?'

My mother-in-law, for all her conniving cleverness, is a total sucker for flattery. 'Oh yes, I have always used those sayings to guide my own journey.'

I continued, calm and resolute, rubbing the devil cleft in my chin, 'I'll never forget a poem I learnt in fourth grade at school. It went, A wise old owl lived in an oak, The more he saw, the less he spoke, The less he spoke, the more he heard, Now, wasn't he a wise old bird?'

Nina returned, ready to escape. She'd missed the poem but could see her mother convulsing and choking on something. She quickly went around behind her and smacked her fair and square in the middle of the upper back.

Elsie's dentures popped out of her mouth, flew through the air in slow motion, and landed on the table, right on top of the small pieces of scone and apple that I had deposited there earlier.

So Long, Sixteen

The last of the ham and pudding is given to the chickens. You think how disgusted Jesus would be at the waste generated in honour of his birthday. Now there's just the New Year to get through. The thought of resolutions and reflections on the year that was is sickening. Maybe January will bring peace. Lazy summer days: holiday novels, stone fruit, salty skin, sleep inducing televised sport, no work, no commitments.

Yet the truth is that you want it darker. You scour the internet to find threats of war, financial collapse, political scandal and broken celebrity marriages. You polish off gifts of beer, wine and spirits, not for the euphoria, but to relish in the hangovers. It's a slow and tortuous suicide – a coward's exit for sure. Care factor zero. Watching and waiting for some real drama, no bullshit day-to-day histrionics, but the real deal. And not over there somewhere, but right here, right now, on our doorstep, with an ineluctable battering ram. Something to wake you up from the nightmare that this is as good as it gets.

From the ashes of the desire for violent revolution, you dream up the required treaty. It is only words – yes, that is true. Words are all we have to define ourselves and our place in this cosmic mix. The human world is built of words. Words are everything. Perhaps an anthem and a flag will accompany your attempt to articulate a fresh, more eloquent expression of the human condition. A complete package to keep us vigilant against the blinding glare of shiny new gadgets made by the third world slaves to sedate the first world sheep for the sole benefit of the one per cent in their gaudy gated palaces. Yes, we need a treaty.

'Darling, the Joneses have invited us over to watch the fireworks from their terrace.'

You despise the Joneses and their terrace, their phony friends and the whole concept of fireworks. The fact is you'll have to take something, even though they said to bring nothing, and what you bring will be placed to one side and ignored. You may as well go down to the yard, shoo away the chooks, retrieve the ham and pudding, wrap it in recycled gift paper and let Richard Jones deal with it on January One. That would be being on the level. But you say yes to the invite and will spend your dwindling holiday pay on an acceptable bottle of wine that won't be acceptable at all.

Your submissiveness, born from a fear of saying no despite an irrefutable right to decline, eats away at the pathetic remains of your once healthy identity and integrity. You pray for Armageddon and then remember you're an atheist.

Your family and friends can see that you're leaving the table. They don't understand. They are searching for a label to describe your condition. The spectrums of autism, anxiety and depression are discussed in your absence. Yet you hear every word; it is written on their eyes.

Even the vibrant colours of the rainbow, when mixed haphazardly, will make a dull brown. The only sensible response is to discard the old, worn-out palette and start again with charcoal on white paper. Can't they see that? Can't they see that brown won't do? Or grey, for that matter. Everything is so grey these days. Nothing is right or wrong; relativism gone mad. And everyone can feel the nausea – if they listen to their gut, that is.

'Where are you, lover?' she asks.

'I'm lost,' you manage to reply.

'Talk to me,' she offers.

'I can't tell you what it's like, only that if I didn't have your love I think I would simply disappear and be nothing.'

She lets you be lost. Just like she let you change your career midstream, like she let you buy that guitar and let you stop the number of kids at two. Letting you be is her greatest gift. Even after her affair, there was no thought of going solo. Your imaginings of her naked and wild with Richard Jones hurt like nothing else; not even the ruptured duodenal ulcer compared. The revenge infidelity – a seedy *ménage à trois* with Mrs Jones and her maid – only added trauma.

Time and brutal honesty did the healing. And you can't help but think that the whole sordid affair, the absolute violations of marriage vows made in the maelstrom and ignorance of passion and youth, were needed to set things right. Your love has never been stronger. You are lost in the world, not lost from her.

After years of accumulation, there were years of shedding, and now you're travelling light. No God, no philosophy, no goals, no desire for unnecessary stuff. For a while, it seemed the better way. Now, doubt with a capital D has struck again. Existential terror. Uncertainty running feral, indecision rife, January looming. Waiting for it all to break, for cracks to let the light through.

A reluctant man with a deep and rich voice strums simple chords to ask the universe for guidance. We dare to call him spiritual and he backs away again. This time for good. We cling to an idea that if we steer your way, Mr Cohen, we will be delivered from all pain and suffering. And yet we know that is a lie, like all the lies that weather us down to dust.

On New Year's Eve, you pick up your one remaining guitar and strum F# minor – your very own string reprise treaty.

'It's nice to hear you play again, lover,' she says.

'Hallelujah, Suzanne,' you cry with a smile.

Tall Tales and True

Bluey 'Cod' McCallister has a shock of red hair and can talk under wet concrete. He has long legs that stick out the bottom of a pair of Stubbies pulled up so high it would be no surprise if one day his family jewels popped out to say g'day. And it wouldn't be an issue, because the old codger can get away with murder, and he'd tell you the story of how he did in fact do exactly that – got away with murder, that is – and he'd suck you in so good that you would've have forgotten about those two hairy nuggets hanging out with more front than Myers. He has the gift of the gab, and that is why his great-granddaughter, Janey McCallister, called upon him: she needed a hand in a time of need.

'Two schooners of Resch's, love, and whatever the old fella's having,' ordered one keen-as-mustard punter.

Janey looked over to see the crowd hovering around Bluey like blowflies. The pub's corner table had become his office and no one could say that a McCallister ever shied away from an honest day's work. Bluey was on fire. Janey smiled and wondered how long it would be before she was paid a visit by the new café owner. This recent blow-in was putting a dint in Janey's takings by offering fancy-pants high teas at eighty-five bucks a pop! Of all things.

'No wuckers, Janey,' said Bluey when asked if he could do a bit of chin wagging down at the local rubbidy.

'Just keep it clean, eh, Poppy?'

'Cross the old ticker, Bob's your uncle. I'll keep it as clean as a whistle…or you can give me an early mark.'

This could go one way or the other, thought Janey. But she had to do something. That ex-well-to-do-politician, Bronwyn B, was certainly proving to be a drawcard. High teas seemed to be all the rage these days. Hasn't she got something better to do? Obviously not.

Today, Bluey had the crowd hanging on every word as he told the story of how he caught the biggest Murray cod on record in the southern hemisphere.

'Do they have Murray cod in the northern hemisphere?' asked one foolish listener.

'No, Einstein,' cracked Bluey quick as a flash. 'That's why the record's for the southern hemisphere. Crikey, you're as thick as two short planks.'

The crowd laughed and the would-be heckler pulled his head in. Which was a relief for the others. They'd been hearing this bloke's smart Alec cynicism all the way on the bus from the big smoke. The city day-trippers only wanted to have some fun, and hearing a few tales from a fair dinkum bushie in a country pub was just the ticket.

'I used three whole wombat for bait and when I hooked onto her, she took me barefoot waterskiing from Albury to Renmark and back again…with a detour up the Darling to Walgett. It took me three weeks to land her, and, with a knife as blunt as old Harry, four weeks to butcher the bugger – 'scuse me French. She was big as Uluru, and twice as cranky.'

More cashed-up punters went for drinks at the bar.

Janey pointed to the menu board and informed them, 'Bistro's open in ten minutes for lunch.'

Bluey went on, 'It was worth it, though. The cod meat was packed in ice, which was towed back from Antarctica after the prime minister wired Douglas Mawson. I went to school with Dougie. He was bit of a mummy's boy, likely a horse's hoof, if you ask me. And think about it, he was pretty cluey, I reckon, going to such a cold, dark place for months on end with just men for company. Put two and two together, folks? But anyway, he was an old China of mine, so he didn't hesitate to bring back an iceberg so we could pack all that nutritious fish and send it off to Biafra. See, ever since me mum used to get us to scoff down everything on our plate because of those poor starving kids in Africa, I vowed one day I would do something about it. So I did. That cod fed a nation for six months! And tell me if you've ever heard of Biafra lately…nah, I didn't think so. But don't get all in a flap 'bout not eating all your peas today after you order lunch from Janey over at the bar. No one's going do their nana. Janey'll just feed any leftovers to the chooks out the back.'

Bluey was in fine form. 'Anyways, the fish fillets saved Africa, then we shipped the bones up to Sydney, because I heard that Utzen, that long streak of Danish misery, who officially I claim to not know from a bar of soap, was having some engineering problems with the sails on his fancy razzamatazz opera house design. I figured that the length, strength and curve of me Murray cod's rib bones would do the job in a jiffy…and save a lot of fart-arsing around for those head-in-the-cloud architect types who were running around Bennelong Point in a tizz. Turns out I was bang on. So when you look at the old girl now, you can tell your tin lids that the whole shebang is held up by the ribs of the largest Murray cod ever caught.'

Another bunch dashed over to the bar for their favourite tipple and one for Bluey. It's a wonder the old boy doesn't get pissed rotten, thought Janey.

'Now, the last issue with such a big fish is what to do with all the bloody scales. The pile of them was so bleeding high that the Bureau of Meteorology sent me a letter claiming I was changing the weather patterns across the whole eastern seaboard! For the life of me, I couldn't think what I could do with these six-foot-wide, two-foot-high, slightly curved, tough as nails, transparent fish scales. Use your scone, Mum would say. Then it dawned on me. Der, I said to meself. "They're windscreens, plain as the nose on me face!" Toyota snapped them up like hot cakes. They used them for the first Corona they ever built here in Australia. Dead set, not a word of a lie. Don't you remember that slight fishy smell you'd get in the old Coronas? Especially when you were getting toey as a Roman sandal with your best sheila at the drive-in? You know the smell. Yeah, you do, don't ya? Well, sorry about that. It's all my fault.'

The crowd laughed a mix of disgust and sweet nostalgia.

Bluey pushed on, 'But the best thing by far that happened when I caught that fish was finding a small foal inside its stomach. See, I was getting out all the fish gut I could, 'cause Rod Laver wanted me to come up with a superior tennis racket string for his next crack at Wimbledon. He needed an edge, 'cause he didn't want to give up beer to be the best. Can't blame a man for that. So, lo and behold, as I was stripping out that fish's comic cuts, I come across what I would soon name Archer. And if ya know your history, that little beauty went on to win the Melbourne Cup. I loved that horse. And what most people don't know is that the prize for the cup back in those days was the largest pumpkin grown in the state of Victoria. Well, did we all get sick of pumpkin soup and pumpkin pie that decade? Yep! Ridgie-didge, it took us ten years to eat half of that monster. The other half we couldn't bear the sight of, so we took it down to Tullamarine and flipped it over and carved her out a bit to make the airplane hangar for the new international airport being built down there.'

The story was in full swing when the sound of a helicopter came from out of nowhere. A gust of wind and dust blew in through the front doors. Bluey looked over to Janey at the bar and winked. The time had come. The old battleaxe Bronny B had had enough and was dropping in to see the reason why her thriving high tea retirement venture had suddenly fallen arse over tit.

The hair and the attitude walked into the main bar. With rat cunning instinct, she spotted the mob of now slightly pissed tourists in the corner, and she zeroed in on the man with the mouth and the shock of red hair and the long legs that his mates call lucky legs – lucky-they-don't-snap-off-and-stab-you-up-the-bum legs.

The crowd parted, some whispering to each other, 'Isn't that… what's her name?'

The ex-speaker of the house, the madam of the high tea, the one dropped like a sack of potatoes by her old-school-blue-tie-born-to-rule chums, stood square in front of Bluey and demanded, 'Just who do you think you are?'

'Just your honest Joe Blow, spinning a tall tale or true for the sake of a laugh and to help out a mate. Howz about you, pet? What's your John Dory?'

'Pet! How dare you refer to me in that derogatory manner, young man. I will have this filthy establishment closed down if it's the last thing I do.' Bronny was getting all hot and bothered, that was obvious.

'Young man? You're too kind, Bron. You obviously don't remember me, do ya? I wet nursed you when your mother needed to go play bridge with all her royally connected fake friends. I never got to thank you for that. See, at the time I was a guinea pig for the CSIRO trial on soya protein. And were my boobs bursting, or what? Remember the CSIRO, Bronny?'

The once honourable – well, never really honourable – member turned on her expensive heel and in a flash of pearl and houndstooth disappeared out the doors even quicker than she arrived. The chopper rotors revved up and she was gone.

'She'll no doubt have to deal with a shit-load of cucumber sangas,' said Bluey.

Janey called out from the bar, 'Bistro's open!'

'What would you recommend, Bluey?' asked one day-tripper who had already Facebooked Janey's pub as a destination not to be missed.

'It's all top grub, and the mixed grill will put more than just hairs on your chest, even with no soy in it. But I recommend the Pack a Jumper Cause It Can Get Nippy.'

The crowd was fascinated, wanting to know more.

'Yeah, it's a bush tucker version of the surf 'n' turf. It's got a wallaby steak, fresh as. I know 'cause I knocked over a couple of the blighters yesterday with a boomerang given to me by Albert Namajira. And on top are some juicy yabbies that I caught in my beard as I slept in Black Wattle Creek last night. Can't beat sleeping in an icy cold creek, let me tell you!'

From behind the bar, Janey smiled at her great-granddad. She just hoped she had enough yabbies.

Walking That Path

The road to self-improvement runs all the way up to the top of that mountain over there. The path gets steeper along the way, but the peak remains as distant as the day you started out.

Whatever happened to all the rewards you were promised for taking on that journey? The enlightenment, the inner peace, the freedom, for God's sake. What about even a glimpse of God, or the Avatar, or your higher self, or whatever? And what about the lie that the ashram is the place to meet people of like-mindfulness? No one even asks you your name, let alone does the karma sutra with you. For a bunch of people committed to the self-is-illusion dogma, they seem pretty obsessed with those mirrors on the wall. The guru's well tended robes and dreadlocks reek of patchouli and ego.

The mountain of universal love stays distant but the war comes closer everyday. The lone wolves are amongst us now; the crack teams with the smart weapons will be next. If the world is what we create in our minds, why is it the way it is? All that work in meditation we're doing and what? We create violence and streets of blood? Have we gained nothing?

What about the whole month when you left the TV off, when you walked past the bottle shop with perfect restraint, when you banned everything animal from stomach or skin, and when you went full-hog Brahmacharya? How was the inner peace for those thirty days? Where was the oneness with all things? Who came along with compassion to soothe your weary soul? When did the wave of well-being wash through you? Why did you expect anything? Why?

You wake for another day. The bathroom floor is cold and you put it out of your mind. The coffee is wrong with almond milk, and you put it out of your mind. Your company is doing well courtesy of free trade arrangements and the low wages of distant humans, and you put that out of your mind too; you have to. The dream of selfless service in a gift economy remains hidden in the mist somewhere up on that ever retreating mountainside. You fill in your monthly performance evaluation and email it to HR. They know you lie, but you tell the right lies and they are fine with that.

The family is all gone now. And with their leaving went all shape to life. Gone are the social circles, gone are the love triangles, gone are the three square meals. The love triangles seemed so right at the time, so modern and liberal, so mature. We are not prudes, not conventional nor oppressed by societal norms, that's what we said to each other. You do not foresee jealousy and betrayal in something so open. The final explosion shattered all trust and respect beyond repair. No new promises could ever undo what was seen first hand in the orgasm eyes of others. Forgiveness also up on that mountainside.

The weekend comes with no invitations, again. Community, an illusion like the self and the universe. The park waits for you. Waits for your bum to warm its bench in the shady corner where no one goes. Waits for your bread roll crumbs to be had by noisy miners and bush turkeys. The paperbark trees watch the children dressed as superheroes and princesses controlling their parents every moment. Look at me, give me tea, fix my toy, I don't like that boy, take me home, I need your phone. The boot camp mob, all sweat and Lycra, lust for the instructor and dig deep and pump harder to gain just one word of favour. Dog shit in plastic handbags is carried by responsible walkers. The smell of Friday night's prawns and beer cooking in council bins is the highlight of your get out of the house and into nature adventure.

Sunday, you have one lotus left to be punched out on your ashram card. The competition to hold the warrior pose longest or to go into scorpion deepest is pathetic, can't anyone see that? The gold coin donation request for a cup of chai is the final insult. You thought there would be so much to gain here that the mountain might seem possible for a change.

There is a woman with no make-up and baggy shorts. You've seen her once or twice; she comes and goes. She is oblivious to the beautiful people and the striving and the mirror on the wall. She sees your desperation and somehow knows you have deemed this to be the last time.

She asks why you will not return. Her eyes are green pools.

You tell her you have made a mistake, that you have gained nothing from your experiment on the spiritual path.

She nods, then asks, but what you have lost? She turns and walks away.

You look at the beautiful people sipping chai and see the ugliness of all that grasping.

You laugh. You have lost so much.

The mountain moves closer.

The Quiet Man Who Fed the Octopus

2…beep. 5…bip. 5…bip. 2…beep. 4…barp. #…blip.

The door bolt clunked open and buzzed. The subject, head down and hands in pockets, pushed through with his hip and walked into the foyer. He didn't notice the lady watering the aspidistras, but she saw him. Later to be known as witness D, she was often fussing around in the foyer and she didn't miss a trick.

'They always wore hooded jackets and most of them had beards,' she answered. Could she single out the subject, though? 'He always opened the door with his hip and he never ever looked at me. All the others looked and smiled.' And then, 'Yes, he was definitely wearing a blue hoodie, black jeans and fluoro green runners on that day…that horrible day. I will never forget it.'

At unit 7A, the subject removed the leather thonging from around his neck and, with the key threaded on it, opened the door. The apartment was clean and sparsely furnished. A table and two chairs occupied the dinette. The kitchen had a fridge and a kettle, and six small glass tumblers sat inverted on a tea towel next to the sink. Everything else was bare. One bedroom door was closed but the second was open to reveal an assortment of rectangular mats arranged in neat rows facing one corner. The bathroom and toilet doors were closed. The lounge room had one sofa and on the wall opposite hung a large white sheet. A video camera on a tripod stood in the middle of the room. On the wall adjacent to the sofa, in stark contrast to the rest of the place, was an aquarium. It was a six-footer, illuminated and humming. On the gravel sat an octopus.

'Hello, Ahmed,' said the subject to the mollusc.

Ahmed blinked and unfurled one of its tentacles – a greeting of sorts. The subject smiled and proceeded to the freezer. He withdrew one pilchard and returned to slip it quickly under the tightly sealed glass lid. Except for its pulsing siphon, Ahmed remained motionless, watching as the pilchard sunk to the bottom corner.

'It will be thawed soon, my friend.'

From a built-in cupboard, in the hallway that led to the toilet and bathroom, the subject removed a black backpack and placed it on the dining table. In the meshed side pocket was a piece of paper with a mobile phone number written on it. He took out his mobile phone and punched in the number. He hit SAVE, looked up to ceiling for a moment, and then punched in PARADISE. He hit SAVE again.

Noting the time, the subject twitched and reached into the back pocket of his jeans. He removed three warm creased envelopes. He placed them on the table, arranging them neatly like the mats in the bedroom. The first was labelled Mum, the next Kelly, and the third envelope was labelled Yousef, with 'not to be opened until 12' written in brackets underneath. He looked up to see Ahmed changing colour and moving from his corner towards the pilchard.

The subject placed the key on the leather thonging next to the envelopes. He slung the backpack over his right shoulder and left the unit.

Witness D would later respond, 'Yes, when he left he was carrying a black backpack,' and, 'No, I did not notice anything different about his demeanour.'

The train was more crowded than usual for a Friday afternoon. The regular commuters, in various shades of workplace, pretended not to notice the dozens of noisy young people. Their uniforms, worn to blend in at this weekend's music festival, were much more vibrant. The subject sat on a bench seat facing inwards in the vestibule section of the carriage. The backpack was nestled between his knees, and he looked straight ahead without expression. It was hard to ignore the many nubile female buttocks hanging out of the bottom of denim short shorts at eye level, but the subject remained poker-faced. Jostling, giggling, and a cocktail of modern deodorants and perfumes assaulted his other senses.

A member of the party crowd spotted the subject, 'Hey, Brad. Is that you?' He edged over to squeeze in on the bench seat. 'Man, you look so different. Haven't seen you in years, bro. Hey, have some calamari.'

The seafood eater, though at least ten years older than the other punters, sported a dozen assorted festival bands on his left wrist.

'Hey, come on, Brad, have some calamari. It's the best stuff to line your stomach. You're going to the festival, aren't you?'

'Thank you, but I can't eat that type of food,' replied the subject.

'Allergy, eh? My old man blows up like a balloon if he even looks at a prawn.' The man boy pointed at the backpack. 'You know they'll go through that with a fine tooth comb. Pretty hard to get anything in these days. You've got to drop the pingers, and skull down as much as you can, before you get there. You know, pre-load. So, Brad, you going or what?'

The subject shook his head. He twisted his head and squinted to look through the scratched window. The harbour and late afternoon sun disappeared with a whoosh of changing air pressure. The fluorescent lighting became apparent.

The subject took out his mobile and hit CONTACTS. He scrolled down and stopped at PARADISE.

'So, where you going then, Brad?'

The subject held up his phone to show his long-lost mate the name on the screen.

'Paradise? What are you on, Brad? I'd like to give that a try.' The hyped-up calamari-eating hipster laughed.

'Yes, paradise, my friend.' The subject hit the green call button as he kicked the backpack out under the legs of the excited party crowd.

My Friend, the Essay

If you ask Andre how he is going, he will answer with a carefully thought-out thesis statement: 'Considering all the pressing and competing concerns of modern life in a post-modern world on the brink of collapse, I, like most human beings at this point in history, am applying a range of coping mechanisms, including, for the sake of sanity, occasionally burying my head in the sand.'

If you are his friend, this statement would come as no surprise. In fact, it would likely be a reason why you are a friend of Andre's in the first place. I am his friend. And I usually stick around to hear his main body and conclusion, if I have the time. But as Andre himself has pointed out, there are 'pressing and competing concerns', and, 'applying a range of coping mechanisms' is both a popular and valid response.

A lot of people cope by steering well clear of Andre. It's not only his predilection to address all of life's questions in essay format, but, unfortunately, he has both chronic halitosis and a seriously disconcerting case of strabismus. I've never asked, but I assume his wife must have no sense of smell and knows intuitively when her husband is looking at her, and when he is not.

The latest news that Andre has been sacked from his position as head teacher of English at that posh bloody Church of England secondary college for 'lewd conduct' with a Year 12 girl and that Cecilia – his psychic anosmiac wife – has left him, is why I'm driving six hours north-west out to the back of Woop Woop on a Friday night. Andre is my friend.

There are three reasons for my friendship with Andre. He taught me essay theory and structure. He is my second cousin once removed.

And he once risked his own life to pluck me from a swollen river and certain death. Education, kinship and a debt incurred for saving my life – all sound foundations for mateship.

Notice how that last paragraph of mine is an essay. A mini essay, yes, and possibly only a C-. Regardless, I owe it all to Andre.

The auto tune on the car radio is furiously cycling through 87.5 to 108.0 megahertz, over and over and over. Orange LED numbers changing faster than the eye can cope with. You'd think a top of the range Pioneer car stereo system would be able to suck out at least one radio station from the country atmosphere. I wind down the window, cold air rushing over the face, probably a better no-doze substitute than country music anyway. Don't want to crash and die. Don't want to prove all those FATIGUE KILLS signs correct. Got to see Andre.

Come to think of it, essay structure is pretty much a metaphor for life. Birth, Life, Death. Introduction, Main Body, Conclusion. Big Bang, Expanding Universe, Big Crunch. And shouldn't every story have a beginning, middle and end? Aristotle started all that, I think, the three-act drama. Sure, the modernists and the postmodernists and now the post-postmodernists like to flip conventional structure on its head, or tear it to shreds. Don't know about you, but when I pick up some postmodern book, be it stream of consciousness or metaliterature, or whatever the latest theory or fashion is deemed compulsory reading, I invariably get so lost that I wonder: was I sick, or wagging, on the day that advanced literary appreciation was taught at school? Whatever happened to story?

I'll have to ask Andre.

Three hours to go. Must get a coffee when I stop for petrol. Maybe buy a ten-dollar CD for my Pioneer still looping through the frequencies.

Surely he didn't do anything inappropriate with a student? He's been a teacher for years, and he adores Cecilia. A Year 12 girl? What about Andre's crossed eyes? The bad breath?

Maybe she's a sucker for a comprehensive and concise thesis

statement supported by logically structured and clearly expressed arguments. Not to mention extensive references to peer-reviewed literature from impeccable journals published by reputable institutions of higher learning.

Andre, you cad, you. Was she good-looking? Perky? Nubile? Was it worth it?

Forgive me. I'm trying to stay awake at the wheel.

I don't believe he did it. I'll ask him, of course. But I don't believe it. Not Andre, not the Andre I know. Not my older smarter relative who saved my life and helped me to matriculate.

That's it! Matriculate! Indoctrinated children, filled with fear of failure, lied to about how the Year 12 exams will determine the quality of the rest of their lives, yes, these poor kids, they'd do anything to get into a course at university that guarantees a six-figure income. Can't blame them really. That girl didn't really want to learn the fine art of writing the perfect essay. She just wanted the marks. They all just want the marks.

Poor Andre.

Petrol station machine-delivered cappuccino and a Keith Urban CD; can't complain, not at this hour at this latitude and longitude.

The final stretch. I'm coming, Andre. See you soon.

Everyone has to pay their way. I remember one Christmas, years ago now, after the kids had fallen asleep and the strong liquor given as presents was unwrapped and taste tested; back when the Bing Crosby *White Christmas* album was only available on vinyl and when striving to get ahead seemed like a good idea. I recall someone that muggy Yuletide night, someone a bit full of it, describing aspiration and hard work as the ethical path.

Yes, I remember well: How to get ahead was the question up for discussion that night.

'I've got a head,' quipped Uncle George as he topped up everyone's Drambuie.

Andre posed a thesis. 'In a capitalist world where everything has a price, one is forced to pay their way. Pay attention first and the bills will take care of themselves.'

It was perhaps not his most eloquent thesis statement. But he was younger then, and so was I. And despite the excess of alcohol accumulated in my circulatory system from a long hot day of indulgence celebrating the birth of Christ, or the mystery of Santa Claus, or the reality of the summer solstice – whatever be your fancy – I have never forgotten it.

Pay attention first. How true. Thank you, Andre. Whatever has happened, I am with you, friend.

I am closer than I think. I pull into Andre's driveway at ten thirty-seven. The Pioneer indicates I have listened to six out of the ten Keith Urban tracks. All of them, so far, have been twanged-out variations on the themes of love and loss, accompanied by twanged-out guitars strumming predictable country-blues chord progressions. Not too bad, actually. It suits the scenario.

Andre opens the door. He looks at me. At least I think he is looking at me. He doesn't look good.

'There's been a horrible misunderstanding,' he answers to my what's-going-on-Andre? shrug.

I give him a hug and smell that old familiar breath.

'It's like someone has changed the curriculum without telling me. I haven't got a clue what I'm meant to be doing. It feels like everything is finished. Everything. But it's the wrong conclusion.'

'Is it too late for a drink?' I ask.

'It's too late for me, I fear. But I have nothing on tomorrow, so no, I'll get the Scotch.'

As we walk down the hallway, I rack my mind for a solution. I desperately want to save Andre. It sounds trite, I know. You no doubt recall how he once saved my life. Is my desire to save his life a bit histrionic? A tad clichéd?

What to do? What to do? I need a thesis statement. My kingdom for a thesis statement.

'They'll never believe my word over a seventeen-year-old girl's.' Andre hands me a Scotch. 'And Cecilia wants a divorce.'

Then it dawns. Friday night dawning, post-long drive, post-petrol station coffee dawning. I wonder if Keith, Mr Nicole Kidman, the expat-boy-done-good-in-the-US-of-A, deserves some credit for my enlightenment?

No. Don't be silly.

It is Andre that has taught me well. Settle down, don't jump the gun, it's all in the planning. Thesis statements don't come cheap. Can't just pick one up from a bargain bin in a country roadside 7-Eleven. I know what to do.

Swollen river, no problems. New curriculum, no problems.

Pay attention. Brainstorm. Do a mind map. Propose a thesis. Pump out a first draft. Reassess the thesis. Then edit, edit, edit.

My friend, the essay.

Jazzy Jazz Jaz

The sound I get out of my Ibanez GB10 George Benson hollowbody electric guitar run through a Vox AC15 hand-wired amplifier is pure liquid sunburst. That, and my ability to improvise in all modes from Ionian through Mixolydian to Locrian gets me plenty of gigs, and women.

Smooth, they call me.

Riga is different to the others. I met her at TAFE, and not at some seedy venue somewhere in the greater Sydney metropolitan area. She's seen me struggling with coding, whereas the others have only seen my expertise on the fretboard. It's nice to have someone see you through different eyes.

Did you know that Indians have been in Scandinavia for centuries? Riga speaks Hindi at home, is fluent in Norwegian, and her English is the cutest thing you've ever heard. She struggles with plurals and leaves out articles like you wouldn't believe.

'Too many car,' she said when we dodged our way across Fort Street to get to my house for tea with honey. 'In Norway, car must give way to walker.'

This Saturday, I'm sitting in with Pistols in the Piano at the Governor's Pleasure in the Rocks and later, doing a set with Abbey C and the Suspicious Dees at the Rest Hotel in Milson's Point. With a good hour between gigs, I'll cross the bridge on foot.

Since meeting Riga, I've been reflecting on my wayward ways. She is such a contrast to the women I have been frequenting. Riga is down to earth and genuine; whereas the barmaid at the Governor's Pleasure, for example, is always high as a kite and has fake boobs. Riga is complex yet pure; juxtaposed to Abbey C (note to self: split up with this Saturday) who is complicated and mixed-up. Then there's Julie, the horn player in the Suspicious Dees; Fatima the belly dancer with the hashish hookah; Bernadette the Catholic girl who likes it rough; Dang with the dubious story as to why she left Thailand; the list goes on.

I've had some fun but can't say I've ever been sated.

The suspended fourth chord, say F# minor sus 4, for example, is so intoxicatingly alluring, yet so unfulfilling. Riga's like a major 7th, C major 7th to be precise. Solid and in the middle, with just a hint of jazz, spice.

All the other women are songs; Riga is music.

Time to take stock. Loose ends to tie off. Bad habits to quit. I can't keep saying I'll cross that bridge when I get to it. I'm standing at the bottom of the Cumberland Street stairway for goodness sake. And Riga's breaking her parents' curfew and coming out to see me play at the Rest Hotel with Abby C and the Suspicious Dees.

No dilly dallying tonight as I lug my guitar and amp across the old coat hanger. The new me has some serious business to take care of, before the show, before Riga arrives.

Out of the Box

It arrived in the mail in a plastic satchel and wrapped in bubble wrap. The postmark was smudged and there were no sender details, its origin a mystery. It was matt black and seemed to reflect no light at all. But it wasn't made of matter from a black hole because it was virtually weightless. It was the same shape and size as a cigar box and it had a seam around it and two hinge-like structures indicating it could be opened.

We could never open it. Neither Linda nor I could move the lid at all. And our friends and family who visited couldn't make any impression on it. It was tempting to smash it with a hammer. Someone suggested an X-ray as a way to explore what was inside. But how do you organise an X-ray? It's not like the police forensic teams do custom work for curious black box owners. And we didn't know any doctors or radiographers to call upon for a special favour.

It wasn't the box's odd, black, non-reflective finish that aroused such a strong desire to solve the problem of what the hell was this thing, or who on Earth sent it. Nor was it the fact it felt cold to the touch. Even when left out in the sun on a hot day, an experiment I couldn't resist performing, it stayed icy cold. It was so cold you couldn't hold onto it for very long. I thought about using it in my esky to keep the bait and beer cold on my next fishing trip. Visitors thought that Linda and I were lying when we swore blind that we hadn't put this thing in the freezer for a joke.

And you couldn't scratch the thing. I found that out one day after I tried unsuccessfully to prise the lid open with various tools in my shed. Out of frustration, I got a bit heavy-handed and ended up trying my darnedest to scratch or leave any sort of mark on the surface of this strange box. Even my sharpest, hardest, steel chisel wouldn't leave a mark. So it didn't need bubble wrap to be mailed, that's for certain.

It wasn't any of these things that awoke the deepest desire within me to find out what was going on here. It was how it affected children. That's what really freaked us out.

When my brother, Brendan, dropped in one Sunday with his tribe on their way to soccer, he, like everyone else who attended our house over that period, was handed the box and asked what he thought it was. In his inimitable fashion, my brother, after a short period of examination, claimed it was colder than Antarctica, darker than Africa and harder than Chinese geometry. Then his eldest, George, who was ten at the time, asked for a look. Brendan handed his son the box.

Immediately George asked, 'Why is it moaning?'

'What are you talking about, George?' I asked my nephew.

'It's moaning. Can't you hear it?' George was known to be a bit cheeky at times. A joker like his dad.

'Righto, George. You can cut out the silly buggers,' my brother ordered. 'Give your sister a look. Hey, Claudia, come over here and have a look at this, will ya?'

When Claudia held the box, she could hear the moaning as well. She said it sounded like an old lady.

'You guys are good,' said my brother. 'Elisa will tell the truth.'

Elisa was only six, and had not yet acquired the family tendency to pull legs and spin a yarn for fun. The moment she took hold of the box, her face changed. Linda reflected later that she thought our youngest niece was going to cry. I agreed. But then her expression changed again. She smiled and then laughed.

'What is it, Elisa?' my brother asked his youngest daughter.

'She says she loves us all. She's a nice lady.' Elisa handed the box back to her father.

'See, Dad? Lisie heard her too,' said George.

'It's definitely a lady,' added Claudia.

Brendan had to go. Soccer coaches don't tolerate lateness, George reminded him. The box was placed back on the antique sideboard where for some reason it had always been placed since day one. Linda and I went out the back and sat on the deck and talked about the box and the strange reactions it evoked in the children.

Later that day, my brother called to let me know that the kids all reckoned that the box was warm, and not cold at all. We tested the box out on some more children. Not random kids from off the street of course, but kids we knew through their parents. And our own grandchildren. We made sure the parents were present and let them hold the box as well. After a period of data collection, the results were clear. Adults thought the box was cold and dull and silent. Children invariably felt the box to be warm, described it as shiny and could hear a woman's voice when they held it. The results were clear but a conclusion seemed to be out of this universe.

I was going a bit crazy. Linda handled the whole box issue much better than I. She was open to supernatural possibilities. I wasn't. I started having dreams about the box. They were vivid, but manic and unable to be described on the morning after. I could feel the taste of these dreams throughout the days that followed. I asked my wife if we could take the box up to Crackneck Point and throw it off and into the ocean.

She laughed and said, 'Don't be stupid.' She said that perhaps there was some reason the box came to our address and that maybe I needed to work that out.

I did a lot of Yahooing – it was 1996. 'How to trace mail with no legible postmark' and other similar queries yielded no useful answers. And after a succession of search phrases and keywords such as: 'moaning black box', 'non-reflective materials', 'unscratchable surfaces', and even 'ghosts', for goodness sake, I gave up trying to solve the issue by any rational means.

Physically, as well as mentally, I was a mess and getting run-down.

Linda was getting worried too. She booked me an appointment for the doctors and even though I prided myself on not having been to the doctors for ten years – which was pretty silly considering I was over fifty and should've been getting my bowel and prostate regularly checked – I agreed. She made me a warm milk with Ovaltine and I managed to make a joke by reciting a few lines from the movie *Young Frankenstein*. She laughed and said I would be fine. 'Get some sleep,' she said and I curled up in the bed in the spare room as she needed a rest from me and my nightmares as much as I needed a rest from the mystery of the box.

That night, I awoke in a freezing home. Ice had formed on the inside of the spare bedroom window. I could hear a woman moaning. I got up and walked out to the sitting room, where the box lived upon the sideboard. It was open. White light was streaming out of the box and illuminating the ceiling. As I approached the box, the moaning settled down and all I could hear was breathing. I touched the sides of the box and felt warmth. Then I leaned over the box and looked down into the light. And then I felt it. Pure love. Motherly love. The love of every mother for her child. A love that I had shut out from my own mother when she was dying a painful death all those years ago. When I was trying to save her, to fix her ill health, to reverse the natural processes of ageing and death. When I was trying to be practical above simply being loving.

The old woman in the light started humming a lullaby and all my pain, all my nervous uncertainty about the reality of the universe and how that box was turning my world upside down, dissolved. I stood upright and walked back to bed.

I thought about my mother and her last days. I apologised for being so clinical. Then I felt her love for me. And the greatest thing of all was that I felt my love for her. It washed through every cell in my body. Warm and cold at the same time. Light and dark at the same time. Complete. Whole. Then I fell into sleep.

In the morning, the box was closed. It was dull and cold again. But

I was warm and shining with enthusiasm. I told Linda about what happened and she listened, patient and uncritical. After I had finished, I started to sob and my beautiful wife held me tight. I felt that a new dimension had opened up inside me. I looked at my wife, my lover and my best mate, Linda. And I saw the mother in her. I had seen it before after childbirth when she lay with our babies on the hospital bed in all that mucousy mess. But back then I dismissed it and got on with practicalities, like keeping over-keen relatives and friends at bay for a few days while mum and bub rested and bonded, and organising secure and legal baby capsules for the car trips home.

That night, the night of the epiphany, the night the box opened, as did I, Linda had a dream. It was an address. It was so clear in her mind, this address, that when she woke she wrote it down on a piece of paper. With hardly any discussion, we wrapped the box in bubble wrap and dropped into the post office on the way to my doctor's appointment. Yes, I went to the doctors, I let them prod and measure and sample. I wanted to live a long life. I wanted to learn more about everything. Especially since my latest and totally unexpected lesson on how much I didn't know. Or should I say, how much I didn't feel.

There I was: a man, a practical man, a scientific man, competent and rational, mailing a box with a ghost inside it to an address that appeared in a mother's dream.

Epilogue

Ten years after this event, my brother called me. Elisa was sixteen and, as Brendan noted, she was still immune to, and unaffected by, the sarcasm, practical jokes and silly buggering that had infected her elder siblings, George and Claudia. We both agreed that was probably a good thing, or at least a pleasant change. Apparently, Elisa came home from school and told her dad that she had watched a video in Art about Frida Kahlo. In one part of the documentary there was some old black and white grainy footage of Frida. Elisa felt she knew this woman. She'd seen her before, but hang on, she couldn't have. She couldn't place it until later when on the bus coming home from school. It all came back. The warm black box at her uncle's place on the day she scored her first goal ever in soccer – Frida Kahlo was the ghost in the box.

Needless to say, or perhaps it should be said, I welcomed this new titbit of information seemingly from the other world. And I was glad I did go to the doctor that day. The tumour in my bowel was operable; they got it early enough.

I wonder where that box is sitting right now.

Broken

There is a broken spoon in my coffee jar. It is one of those thick ceramic soup spoons that you get in Asian restaurants. This one has a delicate blue design around its rim and its handle is snapped off. Because it fits inside the jar and can still scoop, it survived the purge that I inflicted upon everything in my life about three years ago.

It's hard for me to say, but that was back when my daughter committed suicide. There, I said it. Every time, it's a bit easier – only a little bit, though.

She threw herself out of a window at her workplace in town. It caused more than the usual chatter and horror. Not because it was suicide – that was happening all over the place – but no one could remember anyone jumping out of a building recently – certainly not a female doing something like that. Girls were prone to pill eating or wrist slashing, and the boys, well, they either hanged themselves or drove their cars at terrifying speed into sturdy roadside gum trees.

Teresa was my only child and only twenty when she took matters into her own hands to end her suffering for good. I couldn't understand how a mood could be terminal. It was the ten years of sexual abuse perpetrated on her by her aunty that did the damage. But what do you do about that? The string of counsellors she saw all tried different ways to fix her. One therapist, for $150 per hour, watched her play in a sandpit in a fancy glass-walled room overlooking the bay.

'It's a recognised therapeutic modality,' the stiletto-wearing psych said when I flinched at the bill. Guess sand's not so cheap these days.

Countless times she had to repeat all the sordid details – each and every expert wanted to hear it for themselves. From the initial and supposedly innocent brushing of nipples, right through to the penetrative abuse, Teresa reluctantly told it over and over. I don't blame her for giving up.

When Teresa's mother, my ex – and I say that with extra exness – found out about the atrocities, she refused to believe any of it. The perpetrator was her sister, Teresa's aunty, my sister-in-law, the artist. By the way, her art is pretentious crap. The bitch eventually admitted to the nipple stuff but denied anything else.

'I was only being affectionate. It was just tickling. I love Teresa so much. How dare you think I could ever do any of those other things!'

At first, the deniers claimed that the counsellors must have planted this pornography into Teresa's mind. Later, they recalled the fact that Teresa once took an ecstasy pill at a musical festival – undeniable proof that the silly girl was not to be trusted. 'It was probably laced with LSD!' they said.

For fuck sake, give me a break. I believed Teresa.

When the school's year advisor told all of Year Ten about how the parents' authority over their children expires at sixteen, Teresa must have felt empowered. She blew out the candles on the birthday cake and announced that Aunty Silvianne was a lesbian who had been raping her for years. By the way, Silvianne is not her real name, it's her artist's name. Her real name is Cheryl and, when the truth came out, I used to call her by her birth name and watch her go ape-shit. How could anyone believe such a phony? Sadly, a lot of fools do. The police, well, they mightn't actually believe Cheryl, but without physical evidence it's a case of one person's word against another's. Frankly, I don't think they could be bothered.

Teresa was scared of her mother. I'm ashamed to admit it but so was I. But that night when the candle smoke was still twisting in the air, and when Teresa's mother responded to her own daughter's plea for help by calling her a liar, I found some balls and kicked my wife out. The hugs I got from Teresa confirmed that I had at last done something right.

I have to thank my daughter for teaching me the greatest lesson of my life: you can't fix everything; sometimes you just have to let go. I realise now that I had hung on to Teresa for too long. I couldn't fix her, and neither could anyone else, no matter how much I paid.

Why didn't I let her go, even if that meant having to kick her out of home? Maybe, just maybe, she would have survived. I will never know.

Three months after the funeral, my brother came and picked me up from the hospital. Somehow, I woke up one day and could feel the sun and hear the birds again. A drug and alcohol counsellor who did the rounds said something about surrounding yourself with decent people, and throwing out all the rubbish. And he didn't just mean the empty sherry bottles. So that's what I did, and boy, did I do it with gusto.

The ex was long gone; she was back in England. I heard on the grapevine that she had turned lesbian. Go figure that if you want; personally, I don't bother. And Teresa…poor Teresa….she is buried under a tree at my brother's acreage by the Macleay River. She asked for that in a letter that I found under her pillow two days after she jumped. The house was now all mine and ripe as hell for a good going over.

I couldn't believe just how much broken and useless stuff was hanging around. Old phones with no cameras, cameras with no phone, cassette-based stereos, floppy-disked computers, superseded gaming consoles, VHS video gear, burnt-out hair straighteners, face-lacerating electric razors, and unrechargeable electric toothbrushes, all became one big tangled pile ready for the e-waste depot.

Stained, ripped and embarrassingly once fashionable clothing, undies with no elastic, unmatched socks, see-through bed sheets, tired brownish pillows, moth-eaten blankets, thin frayed beach towels, two thousand coat hangers, and dozens of dusty pairs of assorted footwear, were boxed for the Vinnie's volunteers to sort through.

Busted furniture, scratched CDs with no cases, CD cases with no CDs, yellow-paged books falling apart at the binding, mildewy picture frames, chipped crockery, aluminium cookware, all the stuff nobody wants, all that crap ended up on the footpath out front. Good luck roadside collector nerds.

After I unburdened the house, I focused my new hobby onto humans. Friends, relatives, work colleagues, neighbours, local shop assistants, business owners, telemarketers, every member of my species that I came across was run through my broken-or-not filter.

About half my so-called friends needed scuttling. I was Captain Ruthless. Anyone who didn't float my boat was ceremoniously scuttled to become an artificial reef for some other species of fish – my days as a sucker fish were over, that's for sure.

Then the relos got the once over. How could I have overlooked such familial psychopathy? It was right there in the family photo album that my sister made for my fortieth birthday. Only four relatives remained. That's plenty, I thought. By the way, sis, the album went into the fire, sorry, but it was a book of sideshow freaks really.

At work, I began ignoring or standing up to the arseholes. I laughed at my department manager's attempt to pull me into line. He went and chucked a tantrum to the big, big manager. Now she, who I always liked, she had her shit together. She came and saw me. I spoke frankly, she nodded a lot, and then she said, 'Leave it to me.'

Later that day, we all stood around and watched our department head pack up his desk into a Reflex copy paper box and walk out the back door – which of course set off the fire alarm. Best day at work for a long while, let me tell you.

In less than two weeks, my life had been stripped down to contain only good stuff – no crap.

Simple, uncomplicated, real.

Teresa, I am sorry. I should have let you go, it would have hurt but it might have been better for the both of us. When you jumped that day, I know you fixed yourself the best you could. Rest in peace, little one. And I thank you – you fixed me. It is the wrong way around that a daughter fixes her dad, but so much is upside down these days. I will come as often as I can to your tree by the river. You picked the most magic place and your uncle is a good man; he was good to you and good to me, and that can give us all some hope.

The spoon without a handle that fits neatly in my coffee jar slipped from my hands and smashed on the floor. It will have to go in the bin now, but not before I punch the fridge and scream at the cobwebs swinging from the ceiling.

Every Story Has a Beginning, Middle and End

The day after the Anzac Day public holiday, the girl from HR told me that, according to a new policy, I had to use up at least four weeks of my annual leave before the end of the financial year.

She must've seen the darkness in and under my eyes. 'Hang on,' she said and dashed out only to come back with a glossy brochure detailing a 'Ten Day Luxury Health and Well Being Retreat in a Tropical Hideaway – Ubud, Bali'. I nodded and before I knew it she had booked both the flights and retreat.

'You can work out what to do for the rest of the month,' she said. 'Maybe go to Nusa Lembongan or Lombok. Stay away from Kuta, though. It's gone to the dogs and you'll undo all the good of the retreat.' HR wants us in top nick to meet the ever increasing KPIs.

You can smell Asia as soon as you step out of the sanitised aircraft cabin. It's that exotic mix of tropical foods, equatorial spices, religious incenses, rice paddies, burning plastic, open drains, and human excrement, all lightly steamed at thirty degrees Celsius for 365 days of the year. Fortunately, after about six hours, the brain switches off to this scent; it's some sort of highly evolved and sophisticated olfactory survival mechanism that has allowed humans to remain in close proximity to each other and populate the world beyond carrying capacity. In a modern sense, without it there'd be no tourism trade in south-east Asia or anywhere else in the third world where they haven't managed to master the art of hiding the outputs of human consumption either deep underground or way out to sea.

Colonial currencies are exchanged into millions of rupiah and the process of redistribution of first-world wealth begins. You can go nuts haggling over the best price for a Bintang singlet, a pair of fake Ray Bans or the cost for a car to get to Ubud from Denpasar. No matter how well you think you have bartered, deep down you know you have paid more than a local would pay. You justify being ripped off with a patronising arrogance that you're helping the less well-off. Which all falls apart when the driver tells his mate in Bahasa Indonesian how much he got you for and they laugh their heads off and smile with those big, white, all-natural teeth.

It was about two a.m. by the time I got into the room at the retreat. The concierge told me in broken English that orientation would be in the yoga shed at six a.m. I should've have run then. I should've realised that the girl from HR had sold me up a polluted creek. Sure, it was green and lush, and what they do architecturally with bamboo and stone is impressive. And yes, tropical fruit for breakfast while the hired help makes up your room and you book your massage time all sounds indulgent and rejuvenating. But here are some facts: the papaya and salad greens are washed in that same polluted creek, so in effect the detox everyone raves about hits on day two and is exactly the same as a solid dose of Epsom salts; the girl who cleans your well used toilet also massages your back and calves to a pulp no matter what you say after she asks, 'Excuse me, how is my pressure?' and the German yoga instructor, who has at least a fortnight's worth of your holiday pay in his *ikart* bum bag and has tied everyone up in excruciating knots while screaming how weak and pathetic we all are, refuses to speak to any of us lowly unenlightened participants – but he does sleep with the best-looking girl who is here from Portugal with her fiancé who consequently nearly committed suicide in the Monkey Forest on the one day we were allowed into town.

After ten days of holistic hell, I looked up an old mate, Tezza – Terry McCarthy to be precise. When Tezza came to Bali in 1974, his name caused so much delightful confusion that he ended up never leaving.

Tezza: 'G'day. I'm Terry McCarthy.'

Balinese person: 'Yes, thank you. *Terima kasih.*'

Tezza can surf like a demon and tore up the mountainous Indian Ocean off Ulawatu. With that, and his grateful name, he became a legend. In no time, he married a girl called Mali and was running a *warung* on the beach at Seminyak. He's still there and still as humble and down to earth as ever. He took me into his home, put me onto the Bintang diet and organised me a proper massage.

Needless to say, my enforced month-long holiday had a happy ending.

Wake Up and Smell the Humans

He was a lot older and drank too much. But there was no doubting his passion and sense of fun. Plus, he owned a house or six.

She was young and beautiful, legs up to the sky. But she had a brain. Plus, she was a renter with no hope of getting into the housing market.

His invitation to Paris didn't require much thought.

They stayed the night before at the airport hotel. He ordered oysters and champagne and wore a purple G-string when he answered the door to room service. The young girl attendant was not amused. People were such prudes.

One dozen oysters and ten thousand bubbles later, the night duty manager appeared at the door to inform that a complaint had been registered.

'Thanks for the update, captain. Please duly note my attire.' He did a pirouette. 'See? No genitalia visible.'

'Enjoy your stay, Mr and Mrs Leadsworth.' He bowed at the hip and shuffled backwards.

The couple laughed.

'You wouldn't marry me! Mrs Leadsworth? Pull the other one.'

'The future is a mystery!' he said. 'Come here, miss, and we shall see.' He was crude, rude and oddly desirable.

Nobody questioned the current population of fourteen billion. Why would you? That whizz kid from Kiribati, Jinny Jaackson, with the ocean up to her knees, had single-handedly reversed climate change with her ingenious nano-tech carbon-scrubber that could be constructed from coconut fibre and bleached coral. And North Korea's answer to Einstein, Hong Gildong, didn't he change the game when he discovered in the bottom of his mother's rice cooker bacteria that could produce petroleum from human poo?

Need another car? Have another baby. Everything solved.

The Club of Rome was outlawed, any members still alive were publicly shamed. Limits to growth, how limiting!

Edward Leadsworth was wealthy. One of the one per cent of the one per cent. Champagne, oysters, male lingerie and a trip to Paris for two was spare change kicking around in the bottom of his wallet. For the plebeians, though, this sort of extravagance would keep you in debt till retirement at ninety! Edward was fifty-three when his parents, aged ninety-five apiece, gassed themselves in the Bentley. He got the houses, the shares, and was doing his darnedest to spend the lot or give it away before he tumbled off this mortal coil. And wasn't that pissing off the establishment.

His poetry thinly veiled his rage at the machine. Art was now the only way to speak out against the enslavement of the masses without getting locked up for treason. There was a clause in the law that exempted any such limits to free speech. Desiring total control, the oligarchs were bribing the politicians with free trips to Paris, amongst other things, in an attempt to slash this clause from the legislation. It would be the final victory. The silencing of all dissent would keep the sheeple ignorant; just as the whip of debt kept them bound to the grindstone.

She wondered why he, or anyone else for that matter, would want to go to Paris. He'd been there before. She'd seen the photo of him and that other woman on the Eiffel Tower.

'Who is she?'

'Her name is Vivian. She didn't like Paris and she didn't like me… in the end.'

'Was it the drinking?'

'No, I think it was my age. She wanted someone older, someone closer to death.'

The Eiffel Tower had only just been reopened. Now that the hot decades had been conquered – praise be, Jinny Jaackson – the old metal frame was deemed safe. Edward booked the trip to the city of love two years ago. This was about the same time Fujitsu collapsed due to falling world temperatures. Their stockpile of air conditioners stored in that trillion-dollar underground bunker became worthless overnight.

France had bucked world trends and put a limit on the number of people that could be in the city at any one time. Thus, the two-year waiting list. It proved to be a good move. New York, London and Rome ended up following suit. Especially after the crush at the Colosseum that killed ten thousand at first and then two hundred thousand in the ensuing riots. Rome was only just recovering. Ironically, as only the Italians could do, they left the bloodstains on the steps of the old amphitheatre – a new history, says the tourism marketing spiel.

On their first night in Paris, when they talked about the tower, she made what she thought was a connection. 'Do you only date women with names starting with V?'

'No. What do you mean, Virginia?'

'Well, I know about Vivian, and wasn't your fourth wife Veronica?'

'That's just a coincidence. You've heard about Ursula. And, I once dated a Tanya.'

They went out and dined on the Champs Elysée. Even with the tightly regulated crowd control, the city was aswarm with humans. The night was cool, only twenty-nine degrees.

In 2032, '33 and '34, Jinny was the most popular name for baby girls internationally. Hong never caught on for boys, though.

'Do you want to walk to the Seine?' Edward asked Virginia.

'No. Sorry. Can we go back to the room? I'm getting a bit panicky. Too many people. I'm scared, Edward.'

He agreed. They went back to their suite and drank themselves slightly silly on Pernod. Edward got up on the bed and recited what he claimed to be one of his first poems. It was about a boy eating alphabet soup and how he was disappointed that every letter tasted the same. The boy was incredulous, which he rhymed with Pegasus, and he vowed if it took him till seventy, with no heed for brevity, he'd find that one noodle that would satisfy his doodle.

The next day, the city was still cool and people thronged about. It was so busy that Edward had to buy the services of two burly men wearing striped muscle tees and red neckerchiefs to part the crowd so they wouldn't miss their booking to ascend the iconic tower.

'We made it. Look at that, Virginia.'

'It's just like on that bank ad offering loans to poor people for that well earned escape.'

He liked her cynicism. It was a breath of fresh air.

'Will you marry me?' It came out of the blue, just like that.

She laughed. He explained he was serious, not delirious. She laughed again.

'I'll sell that unit in the Cross and buy a pretty patch down south. We can have room to move. You can quit your job…get you off that stupid housing list.'

She hesitated. He was a drinker and had been with maybe two or three girls from A to V. He only let on back to T, but she'd answered his phone one night when he was passed out on vodka. The conversation with Sarah about Rachel and Rita was revealing, to say the least. She never let on about it. She'd even forgot about it until she heard that alphabet soup poem.

'You don't have to answer now. You can take your time. Go back to work and think about it as you punch in and punch out each day. I'm sick of the crowds. Paris stinks.'

They went back the room and played music and dress-ups. Edward stayed relatively sober and performed like he was decades younger. She slept and dreamed of snakes, millions of them.

In the morning, he was sitting on the balcony and writing. He used a pen and paper, it was quaint. Virginia liked it, and she loved his poetry. It was raw and honest and clung to you long after he read it out aloud in his passionate way.

The streets were still full of people, the economy was thriving, buzzing. Worker bees racking up astronomical debt. The cool wave, as they called it, was aspirational.

He saw her coming out of the bedroom. He stood and faced her, naked. Totally uninhibited, despite such attire being absolutely prohibited, he held out his arms to greet her. 'Wake up and smell the humans!' he declared at full volume.

She had not responded to his proposal yet. But the unsettling hum of humanity down below and the stench of the species thick in the air was forcing her hand. She wondered if there were any Wendys or Winifreds in the wings. He was approaching the end of the alphabet and there, in the full regalia of nothing, he was stunning in his uniqueness. That pretty patch down the coast with this wealthy lunatic poet might just be the ticket.

Foundation Song

A gang of noisy miners squawk incessantly as she rests on the collapsing veranda.

'What do you think I am, a snake?' she asks the birds.

She stands and walks into the desiccated garden. Birds swoop, clacking their bony beaks.

'Go and find a cuckoo,' she yells.

She stoops to pick up the iron mattock, the most valuable thing she still owns. A withered beetroot is dying in the cracked earth. The squawking grows. She swings the tool wildly. Humanness and iron scares the avian flock away. She drops to the ground, regretting her actions – already missing the company.

Everything is going away, except for the sea, that is. The children were the first to go. How quickly they expired under the brand-new purple sky. Men retrieved hidden guns and marched away, taking those who believed an enemy must exist out there somewhere. Now the plants are leaving, back into the ground, once the best, volcanic.

She has felt it before, but today it grabs her whole. The urge to go under, below, deep down into coolness, away from sky, towards the core. The metallic, magnetic core.

At the edge of the house, she digs with purpose.

'Look, I'm a wombat,' she cries to the empty sky. 'Come back and sing to me, sing me goodbye.'

Doing Nothing Out the Back

It's been over thirty degrees for eight days running. That's nothing for the folk out at Bourke or Nyngan, but here in Port Macquarie, down by the coast, it's causing a lot of chatter. The worst part of it, many agree, is that the overnight minimum hasn't dropped below twenty for the whole time. You wake up, if you manage to sleep at all, smelling your skin and sweat on the pillow.

One reason why Brian and Marilyn retired to this place on the mid-north coast of New South Wales, was because they'd heard more than once, 'Port has the best climate in Australia.' They sold off the house in the big smoke after they agreed that work had become too stressful for the both of them. Time to enjoy life.

In the oppressive heat, Brian sits out the back. It's a large screened-off area that looks out over a rainforest reserve. Veranda? Patio? Deck? Outdoor living room? Paradise room? He doesn't know exactly what to call it, so he settles for simply 'out the back'. He has just about everything he needs out there. Except maybe a ceiling fan, he thinks. Might pop down to Bunnings after the heatwave's over.

'I'm going shopping, Brian,' says Marilyn. 'Don't really need anything, but at least it's air-conditioned there.'

'Righto, sweetie.'

'Can I get you anything?'

'Nah. All good here, love. You're putting on the lotto, aren't you?'

Brian and Marilyn are comfortable but a lotto win would be a nice little bonus. She fantasises about a trip to see the French Open at Roland Garros. He figures they could buy each of their children a home so they can extract themselves from the crazy cycle of debt and work and consumerism. No mortgage or landlord is true freedom, he surmises. And he hopes the kids would see it that way too. He hopes none of them would sell their hypothetical gift of a house to pursue some other bullshit dream; like a bigger house in a better postcode, or as finance for some shot at making it big. Some mad venture for so-called success. But he knows he couldn't buy them a home with conditions, they'd have to work it out for themselves, like he did at fifty-eight when he finally pulled up stumps.

Success. He writes the word down on the open page of his note book on the table out the back. He circles it and under his breath says, 'Fuck success. What a joke!'

Marilyn has given up trying to get Brian, in his retirement, to join a club, or a group, or to take up a sport. She is loving her tennis, she can feel the benefits in her bones. And the social interaction from the weekly game, plus her involvement in the local musical theatre group, always gives her something to look forward to.

One day she asked him, 'You're actually perfectly happy and content to just be at home and on your own everyday, aren't you?' She had stepped out of her own skin and had seen, with some surprise, his joy at doing nothing.

'Yes, dear. I'm having a ball, best years of my life.'

The day before Marilyn's revelation, they'd had an argument. It was rare. They were well suited in temperament and, apart from their differing needs for social contact, they liked the same sorts of things. Importantly, they still enjoyed regular and vibrant sex, above average for a couple in their sixties, according to some statistics that Brian found on the internet.

Marilyn had her phone on loudspeaker on the kitchen bench so that she could talk while shelling prawns. Brian overheard Marilyn's tennis buddy, Denise, ask, 'Is your hubby still sitting around doing nothing all day?'

'Nothing? I do nothing?' Brian was furious. 'How does Denise get that idea into her head?'

The discussion started with considerable heat and only escalated. Both sides became emotional and defensive. After about fifteen minutes, there was a break in the torrent of wordage. Some breathing needed to happen. The couple looked at each other and Marilyn started to tear up.

Brian closed the gap and hugged her. He too sniffled. 'This is stupid,' he said.

'I know. Stupid, stupid, stupid,' agreed Marilyn.

They sat down out the back and had a cup of tea. They talked sensibly and respectfully and reaffirmed that their relationship was as solid as ever.

Brian explained that he felt busier than ever, even busier than when he worked fifty-hours-plus a week. 'Just because I'm not out and about, rushing around like a chook with its head cut off, doesn't mean I'm not doing anything.'

'You're right, love.'

'I guess, also, I don't have a title any more.'

Reading, writing letters to the newspapers and politicians, brewing stout, watching and identifying birds, solving cryptic crosswords, play-ing harmonica, recording late-night foreign movies on the telly to be watched during more civilised hours, researching on the internet, sketching orchids, carving gourds, and building model boats and doll houses for the grandkids, kept Brian busy most days from four-thirty in the morning. It just happened that a whole lot of this busyness could be done, on his own, in his screened-in outdoor area – out the back and at his own pace. He even had a daybed out there, for a nap at noon, if needed.

'And oh yeah, I forgot. Don't I go to the library every Thursday? And what about about the walks we do every evening after dinner?'

'You're right, Brian. You're actually a busy beaver. I just need to get out and socialise more than you.'

'I had my fill of other people with over forty years of work. The solitude is bliss for me, darl.'

They kissed. Brian took the teapot and cups back into the kitchen. Standing at the sink he looked out the window and could see his wife sitting at his favourite spot out the back. A blue-faced honeyeater was getting into the bananas just on the other side of the flyscreen.

'Hey, Marilyn, do you want to have Denise and her husband over for dinner one night? I'll cook.'

Brian and Marilyn host dinner parties about once a month. They even get the occasional return invite as well. Brian enjoys himself but he has to be strong to avoid being roped into a whole range of other stuff. In all, he has politely refused to play a round of golf, turned down a fishing trip, declined meeting up for coffee, put off a jam session with a keen blues guitarist, and rejected an offer of part-time work doing the books for a florist.

'He's too busy,' Marilyn would say.

After unpacking the groceries, getting the perishables from the blue cooler bag quick smart into the fridge, Marilyn comes out the back and hands Brian the lotto tickets.

'Thanks, love,' he says.

She plonks down next to him and breathes out loudly. He tells her about his idea for a ceiling fan.

The sky is turning grey-green and distant thunder can be heard.

'It did this yesterday and nothing happened. Wonder if it'll break tonight?' Brian fans Marilyn's reddened face with a folded-up copy of the local paper.

'I hope so. It's too hot to do anything,' says Marilyn, holding her head back to get the full benefit of Brian's breeze. 'Denise called.'

'Oh yeah.'

'She's called off dinner tomorrow tonight. Apparently Allan got heatstroke playing golf yesterday.'

'You're kidding! He played yesterday?'

'He's a driven man, Brian, you know that.'

'That fellow needs a good dose of doing nothing.'

They laugh.

'Yes, like you and I will doing tomorrow night in bed because the dinner party's been cancelled.' Marilyn winks at her husband.

Brian smiles. He knows all about that brand of doing nothing.

An Old-fashioned Girl

'Good grief,' she said.

Yvonne's peers were used to her odd manner of speaking and other idiosyncratic ways. They agreed that she must have come from another era. An Elizabethan era, they decided, because frankly that was the only period of history they could recall – they were studying Shakespeare at the time.

Yvonne's 'good grief' reaction was to the news that Philippe, the French exchange student, would be asking her to attend the school dance. Philippe himself had not purposely started the rumour, but he had mistakenly, not knowing of the down-under bush-telegraph phenomenon, asked Penelope, another phenomenon of sorts, for the name of that girl. The one with the longest tunic in Year 11, the one with the Shirley Temple curls, who crocheted at recess and helped in the library during lunch. The one who also wrote sonnets and played the harpsichord.

'Why do you want to know?' asked Penelope.

'To the dance, I want her to ask,' he managed with his Gallic syntax.

Penelope was flabbergasted, meaning: shocked, angry and disappointed all at once. In this state, she couldn't think clearly and actually told the gorgeous French boy the girl's name.

Philippe walked off. Penelope texted the hot gossip to her gang, the cool girls, in less than ten seconds flat. The text was littered with three-letter acronyms such as ATM, IMO, WTF, FFS and LOL, and was finished with an emoji vomiting green stuff.

Yvonne did not have a mobile phone. She carried coins and knew the locations of the last remaining payphones around the district.

In complete contrast, Yvonne's mother, Gillian, was the epitome of 'now'. She was 'on trend', and had a severe case of FOMO – fear of missing out. The forty-something yummy mummy looked and sounded like every second woman you see on television or at the gym. She wore sexy, expensive corporate clothing to her workplace, where she would brag about her next holiday destination that was of course on everyone's bucket lists. And when not at work she would don a fluoro-lemon singlet top that accentuated her augmented breasts, slip into, or perhaps spray on, a pair of black leggings that showed every crevice back and front, lace up a pair of three-hundred-dollar cross trainers for her pedicured feet, pull her hair up in a high, tight, easily swung ponytail, and strap her iPhone to her arm. Deep in music and pseudo self-confidence, she would look at no one as she strutted her stuff along the concourse that threaded itself between the beach and the row of cafés where the hoi polloi would sip lattes and pretend not to be concerned if anyone had spotted them or not. Gillian would always be seen. If her body or her swinging ponytail did not gain the desired attention, the thick swirling wake of pop-diva perfume she trailed behind would certainly turn the most stubborn of heads.

Gerard was Yvonne's father and in the race to be ahead of the pack he ran a close second behind Gillian, his trophy wife. Gerard was forty-five going on nineteen. He surfed, played oz-tag, sported a continual three-day growth, attended all the music festivals and drank beer with a wedge of lime stuffed into the neck of the little bottles of bonhomie. He spent a fortune at the local surf shop buying his weekend wear and a similar amount on cologne and skincare products at the shopping centre where he liked to chat up the casual retail workers of the female variety.

Gillian and Gerard were a power couple. They actually hated each other and flirted voraciously with other people, but neither had ever had sex outside of wedlock. They were cowards at heart.

Yvonne, their antithetical offspring, had perhaps one thing in common with every other seventeen-year-old around – she was acutely embarrassed by her parents. What was different in this respect was that her parents were similarly embarrassed by her.

Yvonne turned down Philippe's invitation to the dance. She explained to him in fluent French that she only danced the waltz or the polka and only to an orchestra or string ensemble under the light of a candelabra. It wasn't a sarcastic jibe, it was the literal truth.

Dejected but undeterred, Philippe attended the dance alone. In what could be considered a consolation prize, the young exchange student, with his irresistible accent, convinced Penelope to leave the bouncing mass of sweaty teenagers, to accompany him outside to the unlit COLA – covered outdoor learning area. It was just one more easy step for him to convince her to give him a head job. Or in his words, 'Fellatio, perform.' The big mistake was that Penelope's number one hanger-on, Misty Greenhill, came along and all three of them agreed it would be totally cool for Misty to video the fellatio on her phone. Yes, the foolhardiness of hormonally disrupted youth. Just one word need be said now – VIRAL.

By three p.m. the next day, Philippe was on a plane back to Paris, proving that when something has to be done ASAP, minor miracles can happen. Penelope and Misty were suspended for a week, but they simply boasted that they missed out on having to write the in-class essay on *A Midsummer Night's Dream*, and their popularity soared.

Henry Wilkins's mother taught harpsichord and that is how he came to the attention of Yvonne. While waiting in the anteroom for her weekly lesson, she could observe the young man in action. She noticed that Henry was a keen student of insects and flowers, and that he pursued this interest with a neat set of naturalist's equipment – a butterfly net, a flower press, a leather satchel containing vials of what she surmised was formaldehyde, and an ancient-looking pair of binoculars that hung around his neck. He wore a khaki safari suit and a pith helmet and explored the backyard and the adjoining nature reserve. Yvonne knew that the bruises on Henry's legs, arms and even face were not a result of his zoological or botanical activities. They were the badges he wore for daring to be different in Year 10 at an all-boys' school. Yvonne knew this because one day a police officer interrupted the harpsichord lesson and asked if Mrs Wilkins would like to, this time, press assault charges against the culprits.

'No thank you, officer,' she replied, 'Henry is not bothered by those thugs. And he has informed me that his weekly sessions of Queen's Rule boxing are beginning to pay dividends.'

Yvonne used a fountain pen and her best vellum stationery to compose a letter to Henry. In it, she expressed her admiration of his courage and confessed her ignorance of the local flora and fauna. She suggested that one day he might take her on a field trip with the purpose of enlightening her about nature's wonders. She of course would reciprocate by bringing along a blanket and a basket of refreshments that could be enjoyed as a picnic after the excursion. It didn't matter that he was younger than her: age is a state of mind, she wrote.

Yvonne did hesitate for a short moment about whether or not to include a rather brash postscript, but then she recalled a quote by Emily Bronte:

> He is more myself than I am.
> Whatever our souls are made of, his and mine are the same.

PS, she wrote, if things proceed well, a marriage proposal by the man would not at all be out of place.

Mrs Wilkins called out, 'Henry. A letter has arrived in the post for you. It's from a young lady. Come downstairs and get it if you wish.'

Henry left the pond water wriggly under his microscope lens and bolted downstairs. His heart was pumping blood to regions of the body that had over the last few years been transforming in spectacular fashion. 'How do you know it's from a young lady, Mother?' he panted.

'Why, her name, and address, are on the back of the envelope. Which I need not have read since the letter exudes the distinctive fragrant notes of bergamot, lily-of-the-valley and sandalwood. *A la Soir de Paris*, I presume. It can only be from Yvonne.'

Henry blushed. He had been watching this unusual client of his mother's for some while now. He had even been making notes in his nature journal. An exquisite specimen, he wrote.

Not embarrassed at all by his mother, Henry opened the letter without delay and read it right there in the anteroom. His eyes were darting from left to right, from top to bottom. Then his mouth opened up.

'What is it, Henry?' asked his mother.

'Good grief,' he said.

Cowrie Dice and Lizard Handles

It glistened in the gentle wash of the intertidal zone. He stooped down and picked it up. For a man approaching ninety, he was remarkably agile.

'Here, check this out, George,' he said as he handed the shell to his stepgrandson, who was now an adult and a parent himself.

'Nice cowrie, Door?' Funny the nicknames that stick.

'It certainly is. How shiny is that one, eh?' George went to hand it back.

'No, keep it. Maybe give it to your daughter.'

George put the shell in his pocket. He had a jar full of these shells at home; most of them given to him by Door, back when he was just a kid. Back when they all lived up in Queensland. It would be a competition at times to see who could find the best cowrie shell – the one that had been subjected to the least amount of sandpapering by the perpetual motions of the ocean on the shoreline. He also had a jar filled with shiny black sea beans that also show up occasionally on the beach. They'd been given to him by Door's wife, Moo. She made bracelets and necklaces from them. Moo was his blood grandmother, or whatever you call the relations that are not step or in-law. Moo was his mum's mum. Families can get complicated

Door and Moo live on an acreage down on the south coast of New South Wales. It is a special place that their offspring, and their offspring's offspring, and so on down the generations, come to visit, sometimes for a weekend, sometimes even for months – there's plenty of room. From their place, you can walk to the beach through a national park, or you can hop into the blue canoe and paddle it down a tannin-stained creek and across a shallow lagoon over to the beach's sand dune. Maybe once every two or three years, the lagoon will empty out into the sea. You need a lot of rain for that to happen, and when it does break through, to be flushed clean, releasing fish and getting new stock, Door will inevitably say to Moo, as they stand and watch the power of nature, 'Do you want to paddle over to En Zed?'

And she will smile, but not encourage him.

'Door, can you find cowrie shells everywhere in Australia?' asked George, ever curious.

'Yes, you can. And you can find them all over the world. They were once used as money in parts of Africa and in India as well. And did you know if you have six of them, you can use them as dice?' Door explained the method. 'When you roll a cowrie shell, it will land either shiny side up or the other way, showing its aperture, the side like a toothy grin. So you roll six of them and count the grins.'

George smiled, but did not encourage him. Door could go on and on if he got started. His head was full of all sorts of stuff. But if you didn't ask too many questions, Door was equally happy just being good company, no words needed. Today, George just wanted to be. To be at the beach, the beach deserted of other humans. To be with Door, the zany old stepgrandfather who he can't remember ever not being around. Door and Moo had been a constant in his life, a comfortable constant. They never had expectations and possessed a zest for life that seemed so rare these days.

They continued in silence, walking along the length of the beach down to the rock platform.

Many years before when Door and Moo first moved here from the Sunshine Coast, Door took George and his brother Harry, and cousin Kate, out onto the rock platform at low tide to get some cunjevoi for bait. George and Kate were about ten – just old enough to go beach fishing later that night with Door. Harry, only seven, knew he was not allowed to go. He was dirty about that and started smashing limpets with a rock. George remembers the fury in Door's eyes. It was the only time he'd seen a hint of anger in the man.

Harry saw it too and dropped the rock. 'This sucks,' he said and he walked off.

'Let him go,' said Door to the other two. 'He's old enough to walk home by himself.'

George was worried. He thought his mum would be annoyed that Harry was let to walk off alone. But this was not suburbia, and a long way from where the recent abduction of a ten-year-old had struck fear into the hearts of the nation and young parents alike. George watched his brother disappear over the dune as Door cut open a sea urchin to share some roe.

'Here you go, kina, bush tucker. Better than caviar!'

The two ten-year-olds watched with disgust and amusement as this crazy man sucked out the bright orange slop with relish. There was no way George was going to give it a try but cousin Kate tried it.

'That's not bad,' she said. Then she turned to Door and pulled a face indicating that she didn't really like it but was in on the caper to get George to try it. 'Come on George, it's bush tucker. One day it may be all we have to eat.' She was a smart one, that Kate.

George broke the silence. 'Remember that day we got the cunjevoi and you ate that orange stuff inside the sea urchin?'

'Yes, I do. You wouldn't have a bar of it but I recall your cousin Kate gave it a shot. I remember too that that was the day Harry chucked a wobbly and stormed off because I wouldn't let him come night fishing.'

'Yep. It was. And he stubbed his toe on the way home.'

'That didn't help the whole hullabaloo.'

'No, it didn't.'

The two men without speaking further mulled over the memory of a rare moment of disagreement in the extended family's south coast history.

Rachel, Harry's mum, was not happy about her son being left out from the night fishing trip, nor about him being let walk off by himself. 'But it's not fair if the other two kids are going,' she said.

'Sometimes things are not fair, Rachel. But it's not really about fairness. Harry isn't ready yet. If anything, it wouldn't be fair on the older kids. He'll have plenty of chances to go fishing in his life.'

The issue of age appropriateness got thrashed out well and proper that afternoon. Rachel and Door debated the matter from every which way. There was some heat, but thankfully a fundamental respect prevailed. Moo stayed out of it and decided to take the grandkids into town for an ice cream. She was relieved when she got back to find her husband and daughter laughing as they stood side by side in the kitchen, preparing a big salad for dinner.

'Hey, Door. What about that house you and Moo used to stay in up at Alex Heads?'

'Oh, that place. That was a real treat for us.'

'There were plenty of cowrie shells on that beach. I remember that house. It had a centipede on the toilet window that I thought was real. And the hall cupboards had lizard handles.'

'Yes, that's right. They're lovely memories, George. Thank you. You know the woman that owned that house, she hardly knew Moo and me, but she was so generous to let us stay there whenever she was away. She had absolutely no expectations of us either. Purely unconditional. I'll never forget her. Jane Major was her name.'

George quizzed, 'Wasn't it Jane Minor?'

'No, it was definitely Major.'

At first, George thought Door's memory must be going. But he thought again and laughed under his breath – Door was just as likely being cryptic. The two men, with nearly fifty years age difference between them, walked back to the blue canoe.

As they paddled across the lagoon to the sound of a whistling kite, George thought about showing his daughter how to use cowrie shells for dice and Door thought about the many beautiful sunrises he had shared with Moo at Jane's house by the beach at Alex Heads.

Pillow Talk

Come and lie down next to me on my bed. Place your head on the pillow so we can talk in confidence. Or should I say, lie with me and just listen – let me talk with impunity.

Did you notice the large file on my writing desk?

No?

I'm not surprised. There's crap everywhere, isn't there?

You wouldn't suspect from my impeccable grooming and business attire that I'm such a slob. But I do hope you like my clean linen. No dirty sheets here. All the filth is in that file.

Did you notice the suitcase next to the door?

If you picked it up, you would be forgiven for thinking it empty – just some undies, two T-shirts, one pair of shorts, my swimmers and a pair of thongs. That will keep me going for a while. Don't worry, I won't be cold, I'm heading north, way north. There'll be some op shops along the way, so I'll pick up other stuff as it comes to mind.

Not sure if you saw the old beaten-up Holden Kingswood parked out front, the blue one with a red bonnet?

Bit different to the BMW you've seen me cruising around in, eh?

The Beemer's staying here. See, when I disappear, it's got to look like foul play, suspicious circumstances, way out of character. Because when I start to drip-feed the media with the contents of that file, I want to be well and truly dead in certain people's minds.

I wish you were my wife. We used to pillow talk about all sorts of stuff. It kept us connected, it was great comfort for us both.

Have you heard the saying, great minds talk about ideas, average minds talk about events and small minds talk about people?

Well, in bed at night, after our long days at work, we did talk about the big-picture stuff and what was happening in the world, but sometimes we indulged ourselves and gossiped our heads off. I like to think we did it without too much judgement. I do know we kept it in the bedroom. But when my whole world changed, I had less and less to share. I just couldn't tell her what was going on. At first, I tried to make up stuff, to pretend that my work as an accountant was just the same as usual, but it wasn't – not by a long shot.

'You're so quiet lately. What's going on?' she would ask.

I couldn't answer. I'm not sure I had an answer even for myself. All I knew was that I had become caught in a web, and paralysed. It all started with good intentions – but aren't they what paves the road to hell?

Can you please turn around?

I can talk more frankly if I don't see your face. The shame I feel chokes me nearly to death. So please, face the window so I can tell you what I hid from my wife until she couldn't bear it any more and left.

Thank you.

One of my regular clients, George, was in a spot of trouble. Over the years I managed his accounts and got to know him well. How a person deals with money can tell you a lot about them. George always was honest about his income and expenditure and was proud that he paid his fair share of tax.

He would say, 'We should all make a contribution. Me, I'm fortunate enough to be able to make a big one. Tax pays for the things we all benefit from. I can't understand why people want to cheat the system.'

George's wife got ill and she needed treatment in the USA. The procedure and the drugs were not approved over here, the costs were astronomical. I agreed to help George out by doing some creative accounting and, under the circumstances, I felt it was justified. Betty died anyway. George later made a huge donation to the local hospice that at least made her last days bearable. That's the sort of man he is.

I thought the whole affair was over, that this venture into unethical waters would be a one-off. But then, George's brother Stan, at the wake after Betty's funeral – at the wake, for God's sake – told me that I had been spoken highly of by his brother. Then he asked, 'Can I come and see you? I'd really like to give you my business.'

I swallowed a cucumber sandwich and said, 'Yes, of course.'

It was not long before I discovered that brothers of the same mother can be totally different creatures.

Stan was a property developer, with his finger in a lot of pies. What I found out early on in the piece, after he reminded me with a wink of how I had bent the rules for George, was that his biggest pie was as a silent partner in a brothel. It was in one of those industrial estates and it was semi-legit, but the drug trade taking place under its roof certainly wasn't. The problem of bucketloads of cash suddenly became my new project.

'What was the shelf company you set up for George?' he said. 'Coast and Country Consulting, wasn't it? I'm sure you don't want anyone knowing what that was really all about, do you?'

I resigned myself to having no choice but to do this bastard's dirty laundry. But it didn't stop at Stan. Once the word got out, in all the wrong circles, let me tell you, the roster I accumulated included the who's who of bloody Whoseville.

My wife, in our bed at night, continued with her tales of the patients and staff at the hospital where she worked as a nurse. But I couldn't tell her what I was up to at my place of employment. I couldn't lie to her. She was too good at spotting my micro-gestures, the ones she learnt about from that TV series. What is it? *Lie to Me*? We watched the whole box set back to back on DVD. So I feigned tiredness when it was my turn to share. The distance between us grew and grew like the list of dodgy people who sought my accounting skills – and my discretion.

When my wife announced that she was leaving me for an anaesthetist, I was so full of self-loathing and guilt that I was actually happy for her. She deserved better than the wrecked and hollow man that lay silent beside her. So she packed a bag, a lot heavier than the one of mine waiting by the door, and walked out crying. She didn't hate me, she said, she just wondered where I had gone.

That was when this house started to get all cluttered. Not because I'm lazy, but because I spent every moment of my time at home carefully collating and organising that file on the desk. At work, I played the corrupt accountant. The proceeds, my cut of it anyway, allowed me to dress and drive well and to decorate my office with pretentious artwork. It was my new image, the accountant with expensive tastes. I even attended the parties of the well-to-do and upsold my corruptibility by overtly indulging in illegal substances and women.

My reputation as being in over my neck attracted even more greedy clients. From bikies to pollies, from rock stars to bankers, I was hungry to own them all. The evidence in the folder on my desk is going to bring them all down. It's going to cause merry hell. Long Bay might even become the trendiest postcode in town.

Can you smell patchouli in the linen? It's subtle, just a hint. They do that in India, you know. The streets might be full of rats and faeces, but their skin and cloth is immaculate.

You can turn around now. I want to see your face. I'm hoping to catch the slightest hint of forgiveness in your eyes, or maybe in the folds around your mouth. A micro-gesture, please?

I'll be gone tomorrow. They'll say I'm dead – on the bottom of the harbour with concrete boots, or buried forever under the new tollway that gets asphalted at midnight. But I died long ago. I just wanted one night of pillow talk before I disappear.

It's Only Natural

'Did you know the most distant galaxies in the universe are exerting a force upon you right now?'

'Sort of, I guess. I did watch all of Brian Cox's shows about the universe.'

'He's good isn't he? Anyway, Gravitology has been developed as a holistic and perfectly natural way to cure people of their health problems.'

'I hope so, I certainly don't trust mainstream medicine. I've heard that the big drug companies are paying doctors to keep us sick. It makes sense really. Otherwise they'd go out of business, wouldn't they?'

Rod Everington listened and nodded to everything Marjorie said. It would be a full forty minutes before he got her naked and onto the Multi-axial Gravito-sensometer. He asked for her whole life story and took notes, lots of notes. He now knew about her neck problems, her psoriasis, her nervous tick and her allergy to nuts. He also found out that her husband was six foot two and a hundred and twenty kilos.

He whistled when he heard that. 'That's a lot of mass, a lot of gravity. Do you sleep in the same bed?'

'Yes, we do.'

'How is your relationship?'

'It's OK, I suppose,' she replied. 'He's a good man, really.'

'How is your sex life?'

Marjorie blushed.

'I'm sorry. Sometimes I can be a bit abrupt. You don't have to answer that, Marjorie. For years I suffered terribly from psoriasis and like you was given drug after drug. Nothing worked. Then one day I saw a Gravitologist and he cured me. It changed my life! It was a miracle.' He pointed to the wall sporting seven framed certificates. 'I just had to become one myself.'

Marjorie felt better already.

'Now,' he said as he rubbed his hands, 'time to get you up on the table.'

It was an impressive piece of machinery, lots of chrome and knobs and a thick cable running to a computer on a small table.

'Now, for the most accurate results, it is best that the patient is naked.' Rod Everington stood and walked over to the machine. 'But that of course is totally your decision. Clothes have mass and mass is gravity. I can't guarantee the results if you don't at least get down to bra and panties.' He adjusted his crutch as he said the word panties. 'I understand completely if you don't go the full monty. But let me tell you, in my twenty-five years of practice I have seen hundreds of naked bodies, both sexes and all shapes and sizes.'

Marjorie was desperate to get well. This man himself has been cured of psoriasis. He does seem very professional. And don't all men fiddle with their genitals through their trousers?

'No, it's fine,' she said. 'Where do I undress?'

Rod pointed to a curtained-off corner and licked his lips.

As she undressed, she heard him washing his hands in a basin and the clinical snap of latex gloves. She came out awkward, body curved inwards.

He looked her up and down. 'Stand up straight, hands by sides and let me look at your alignment for a moment before we get you up on the table.'

He doesn't seem to be perving.

'Drop your shoulders, please,' he instructed. 'Now, right foot forward just a bit.'

She obeyed.

'Good,' he said. 'Do you always stand with your right foot behind the left?'

'I have no idea,' said Marjorie.

'Did you crawl before you could walk?' he asked.

'I'm pretty sure I did.'

'Did your father praise you as a child?'

Marjorie flinched. 'Um…'

'No need to answer that. Your body just answered for you.'

This guy is good, thought Marjorie.

'OK, now don't move. I'm just going to check your inertial alignment from behind.'

Rod Everington moved around behind Marjorie. She heard a series of ahas as he placed gloved hands on her shoulders and pressed down. He then held her hips, his hands warm.

'OK,' he said from behind her. 'I want you to spread your feet, just a bit wider than your shoulders and bend forward slightly. I am going to push down on your hips and I want you to resist.'

Marjorie did as she was told.

He breathed heavily and pushed down. His thumbs pressed into her buttocks. She tensed in response.

'Interesting,' he said and paused. 'OK, up onto the table. Lie on your back, head up this end.'

The black grid on the white table helped with alignment. He shifted her head, then her hips, and lastly he gripped her toes to position the feet.

He massaged her feet for a while and asked, 'Have you ever seen a reflexologist?'

'No, I haven't.' She was enjoying the sensation of him touching her feet but acutely aware that he was looking up the full length of her naked body.

'Our feet are the organ that experience the greatest effects of gravity.'

She looked at the ceiling and closed her eyes. Are feet an organ? She let the unexpected foot massage continue. May as well enjoy it.

Finally, he went and sat at the little computer table. 'Now stay perfectly still. The table will take measurements as it tilts in each of the four quadrants. Relax, don't fight it. Let gravity work on you and the machine will tell all.'

There were flashes of light and strange cranking sounds coming from within the machine as it tilted left then right, head down, head up, and in combinations of each.

How am I meant to relax with my breasts flopping all over the place?

'OK, first part done,' he said as the table calmed down to silence.

A printer began spitting out sheets of A4. He gathered them up and stapled them together.

'It's an amazing piece of technology this thing. Its thirty-two-bit algorithm processor just automatically analysed your mass distribution against thousands of results stored in an international database connected by cloud technology.'

Rod flipped through the wad of results, stopping for longer at some pages. He placed his hand just under her left breast and pressed. 'Do you feel any discomfort here?'

'No.'

He did the same on the other side. This time his thumb was on her breast, just touching the nipple. 'What about here?' He seemed to be pressing harder.

She winced. 'That does a hurt a bit.'

'Just as I thought.' He looked back at his results and back at her.

Without saying anything further, he went to a cupboard on the other side of the room and took out a blanket, a thin pillow and a rice-filled eye bag. He lifted her head and placed the pillow underneath. He placed the eye bag over her eyes and then flung the blanket up above her and let it drift down to cover her naked body.

'The machine has already programmed your first therapy. It will be twenty minutes today. Just relax. The therapy's not too different to what you just experienced. I will be here studying your results. Please let me know if you feel anything untoward or need anything.'

The lights that had flashed while taking her measurements now pulsed slowly and began to warm her body. The tilting mechanism rocked the table back and forth and side to side. It vibrated with changing frequencies. Now covered, Marjorie was more relaxed and almost fell asleep.

The process stopped with a clunk and Rod instructed his client to get dressed. When she emerged from the curtained-off corner, he motioned for her to be seated back at the consultation desk. His manner now was very officious. His face had changed.

'Marjorie, the root cause of your psoriasis and your nut allergy is a higher than average gravito-imbalance in your spleen. The spleen through miasmic channels is intricately connected to the skin. Studies have shown that the spleen can be disrupted by negative male gravitational fields. This causes anxiety, lack of energy and neck and joint pain, as well as skin conditions and allergies. We call this Perihelion Adversity Syndrome. It is imperative that we book in a three-month twice-weekly treatment regime.'

'Oh, OK.'

'We can work out a discounted price. I'm not in this for money, Marjorie. I want to support you through this. I know how debilitating psoriasis can be. I also know if left untreated the prognosis is not good.'

'What do you mean, doctor?' The fear was rising.

'I am not a doctor, Marjorie. I like to think of myself as a healer. Call me Rod.'

After booking in Tuesday mornings and Thursday afternoons for the next month to get started, Marjorie went to the health food store to buy some magnesium and a Chinese tea that he recommended. Then she wondered how she would tell her husband that they would need to sleep in separate beds for the next three months.

Blanket Rules

There's a woman who screams at least twice every morning on the very fast bus that takes us workers into the city.

She does it once when we all get slammed to our right as the bus veers left to exit the F23 and join the M78. And she screams again when we are treated to zero gravity for about one second when the velocity of the bus nicely matches the radius of a convex section on the PM Abbott Superhighway. This happens just near Castle Hill on the last stretch into the guts of Sydney. The President has passed legislation, written by the Australian Productivity Team, that permits, in fact commands, that the very fast bus never stops for anything; not for deaths, inside or outside the bus, not for terrorist attacks, not for cyclones – yes, cyclones in Sydney – not for global financial crises, and certainly not for some screaming neurotic woman. Regular commuters like Anja Taylor don't even hear her any more.

Sometimes, and more often lately, there is a third scream. It is reserved for when a passenger dies on the way to work on the very fast bus. This scream is different. We all know what has happened by the appearance of a royal blue blanket that is then draped over the body until we arrive at the underground terminus at Wynyard.

Ruben Meerman and his granddaughter are not regulars. They're going to the art gallery before it closes next month. They sit opposite Anja. She stops her work and listens to the grandfather, not much older than herself, as he offers up Newton's First Law in response to the young girl's question, 'Why did that woman scream?'

Anja is impressed. She knows a bit about science.

'Now if this were a very fast train instead, the g forces would have been not so great and that poor lady would not have screamed.'

Anja takes a sharp breath in and dips her head to return to the virtual office on her lap. Talk of trains is tantamount to treason.

Oblivious, Ruben continues, 'Forty years ago, we failed to tackle population and we chose road over rail. No wonder we're now working to ninety…or more.'

Anja pictures alarm bells ringing in a secret building in Canberra somewhere and the words guilt by association rolling underneath on an imaginary ticker tape.

She politely kicks this silly man and with her head draws his gaze towards the CCTV cameras above. He may be bit of an absent-minded science nerd but he is not totally naive to the modern paranoia.

'Oh, metadata. I get it,' he says.

Her horror only escalates. She opens her eyes wide to tell him without words, you're a fool – shut up.

Ruben, demonstrating further that he is up to speed, leans forward and says, 'My name is Elvis Presley and this is my granddaughter Shirley Temple.' He winks at Anja and quickly whispers into Shirley's ear that he is playing a game with the nice lady.

Anja, feeling the contents of her large bowel turn to water, looks up at the nearest camera and announces clearly, 'My name is Anja Taylor and I have never met this man before.'

A woman screams but the bus is running smooth. A sea of heads look up from their encrypted media devices. An old grey man in grey baggy uniform hobbles down the aisle, unfolding a royal blue blanket.

Shirley asks, 'What has happened, Pappa?'

'Blue is the new black, darling…and someone just retired.'

Aromatherapy

In City Zed, the Wellness Corporation owns everything and everyone. The masses make the best of each day, and the life, that is planned for them. They fake laugh at work and guzzle down a never ending supply of new products and services. Wellness is within the reach of everyone who behaves, and believes.

Zane Zeitgeist possesses an extraordinary bullshit detector. His intelligence and emotional scores are two full standard deviations above average. The Corporation is contemplating neural correction surgery. Pity, that; he has so much potential.

Zane will never lie down and submit. It's not in his make-up. He has been shifted from department to department and suspects they are planning the final solution. In his last position, Zane worked out that the order you pressed the buttons didn't make one iota of difference. He told the whole Button Pushing Department; they couldn't believe him.

'We trained for two years to learn this skill. You're full of it, Zeitgeist!' said the team leader.

Zane demonstrated. Some staff ducked for cover, thinking the production line would explode when he pressed red before purple. But regardless, the conveyor belt rolled on and the robots assembled the shiny gizmos.

'See,' said Ziggy. 'The buttons aren't connected to anything!'

Human Resources moved quickly. 'Mr Zeitgeist is ill,' they said. 'We disabled his console weeks ago. Of course you can't press red before purple.'

Zane was then parked in the Media Department's Conspiracy Think Tank. Zuess Zetland, master of deception, told Zane that his fantasies were useful and valuable to the corporation. They could be produced and packaged and streamed into the homes of the population as satirical entertainment. It would remind citizens to be grateful for city life, safe from the chaos and violence of the Wildlands.

Like everyone else, Zane experienced the Wildlands at age nine. It is on the curriculum, a school excursion in a fortified bus through the horrors of the outside world. His father reminisced, 'I'd heard the stories, son. But when I saw it for myself, I realised how damn lucky we are to be in City Zed…'

Zane knew his father's philosophy was scripted. Through the toughened glass of the bus, he saw the savages, adorned in Corporation blue face paint, play acting as they threw spears. Zane laughed. The 'savages', like his teachers, the bus driver, and his parents, were all employees of the Wellness Corporation.

The tour wound its way through gullies denuded of trees. The only stop was a quick step outside the air-conditioned bus to feel the heat and to smell sewage; both children and teachers were ignorant of the underground pipes leading back to the toilets inside the city walls.

Zane asked the teacher why the bus couldn't turn left and go up the hill to see over the ridge line. Back at school that question, and his laughing at the savages, got him stood up in front of assembly and shamed.

Working in the Media Department was worse than pushing buttons that did nothing. Zane had come to know that outside City Zed there were creeks and forests and communities that worked the land; that there were beaches and cool breezes; that there was music and art. Those who spoke of such things were re-educated and forced to recant. If they didn't, surgery was booked.

Zane was beginning to sweat real fear. He smelt his armpits; it reminded him of the Wilderness. He refused the instructions to use Wellness Corp deodorant. If all he could own was his own scent, even if that meant surgical incarceration, he would go down reeking. After a week, his odour had the whole of the Conspiracy Think Tank complaining.

For the necessary top level signature, Zane and his olfactory offence were escorted to the office of Zoe Zinger.

'Do you want us to hose him down before we bring him in, Ms Zinger?' asked the security guard. 'He smells pretty bad.'

'No, bring him in. If I am to be the one to authorise, I ought to experience it first-hand.'

The guard marched Zane into the office, front and centre.

Zoe held a file. 'You may leave, Zac. This man is not violent.'

Zane looked at Zoe and the view from the window. He'd never been on the two-hundredth floor. He could see the city limits and the Wildlands beyond.

'You know what is happening?' she asked.

'Yes. I will be lobotomised. I have resigned myself to that fate. Being ignorant will be preferable to faking ignorance.'

Zoe Zinger placed the file down on the desk. 'How did you find out the truth?'

'I can only see what I see.'

Zoe walked around her desk to sample the odour that had finally condemned this man. She circled him. The smell acted quickly upon her. Her eyes closed, her shoulders dropped. Limbic instinct had her smelling his neck and touching herself through executive slacks.

After they had made love and were lying in each other's arms on the office floor, Zoe asked, 'What do you want, Zane?'

'I want to leave the city, forever.'

Zoe sniffed Zane's armpit and thought hard for a long moment. She stood up, went back to her desk and pressed a button on her phone. 'Ziggy, get my helicopter ready.'

She looked at Zane naked on the floor, 'I have a house by the beach.'

'I believe you,' he said.

Fishtailing

'We are low life. Did you know that, Gina? Did you hear them?'

'Yes, I heard them.' She looked over at Brad.

He was gripping the steering wheel hard; veins popping out in his forearms, his face red and contorted with anger. He turned the key and pumped the engine into a fury. He released the handbrake and dropped the clutch, their exit heard by the lazy Sunday afternoon neighbourhood.

Gina looked down into her lap. He would go silent now; she knew the pattern. He wouldn't exceed the speed limit, but he'd go loudly up and down the gears and barely slow down for corners or roundabouts. After a kilometre or two, he would hit the top of the steering wheel with an open palm and yell, 'Fuck.' He would light a cigarette and pull off to the side of the road. Then he would laugh. Starting with a chuckle, building up to a cackle – it settled him. He would reach across, without looking, and put his hand on Gina's thigh and say, 'Sorry, Gina. I'm OK now. Sorry.' Then he'd pull back out onto the road and drive, slowly and quietly, singing the Bob Marley song, 'Everything's Gonna Be Alright'.

And he was right: everything would end up being fine. They'd get home, he would make his sandwiches for tomorrow's work. Gina would send Aunt Mary on her way with forty dollars for looking after the kids. Brad would have one last smoke out the back and butt it out in the pineapple tin ashtray. He would clean his teeth and come to bed. Then he would apologise for driving like a hoon and explain that it was better than decking someone.

Gina had a pattern too. She would accept the apology and remind herself of all Brad's good points. She would pray that the next social event would not end the same way. She would analyse her friends. Are they really my friends at all? Why do I feel excluded when I'm with them? Is it me being with Brad that's the problem? And why do the husbands make such a sport of baiting him?

The treatment had been getting worse – this afternoon perhaps worst of all. Fiona, her friend since kindergarten, suggested in front of the others that she take Gina out shopping.

'What has happened, Gina?' she said, standing back, looking her up and down. 'You used to be the fashion plate of Year 12. Now, and I don't mean to be rude, darling, but for goodness sake you look like one of those single mums you see outside Centrelink.'

I don't mean to be rude? Are you kidding? You're saying this to impress Cleo, aren't you? And how dare that…blow-in…invite every couple here but Brad and me down to her swanky holiday house at Kiama!

Gina managed to hold her tongue, excused herself and went outside for air. Fiona's husband, Andy, was incinerating the marinated meat on the steel device that was not to be called a barbecue. Apparently it's an outdoor catering ensemble. And who said men can't do two things at once? Andy was in fine form.

'How can you stand working with that low life down at the factory? I'd be worried about catching a disease, mate.' Andy had never once used Brad's name.

Brad took a swig of his beer.

'Aren't they closing down next month? What're you gonna do, buddy? I mean, the immigrants will be all right, they live fifty to a house, you know. But how are you going to pay your mortgage on a dole cheque?'

'I've got a trade, I'll be right.'

'What, fitter and turner? Good luck, mate. No offence, but with all these robots and what not…'

Gina interrupted the boys' club just in time. 'Excuse me, gentlemen,' she said.

'Sure, Gina. And might I say you are looking delicious this afternoon.' Andy couldn't help himself.

Without responding, she pulled Brad off to the side. 'Let's get out of here…now.'

Brad needed no convincing. 'Sorry, lads,' he said. 'Gina just a got a call from the babysitter. Liam's vomiting. Gotta go.'

This particular Sunday when they pulled over to the side of the road, Gina broke the pattern. She put her hand onto her husband's left thigh. 'I'm so sorry, Brad. I know it's been me insisting we go to these events. I've been stupidly wishing that things would change, that these people would finally accept us for who we are. What a fool I've been. These people don't deserve us. They are the low life, not us. I'm so sorry. We'll never go again. It's over.'

'Thanks, love,' he said. 'Man, I was so close to snotting Andy. Especially when he said you looked delicious. Seriously, he's such a wanker. Handy Andy, he should be called.'

'They're all wankers.' Gina smiled and started laughing.

Brad joined in. He'd never heard Gina say wanker before. It was cute – hilariously cute.

After the couple regained some composure, Brad pulled back out onto the road. A light drizzle began to fall. He turned on the wipers and the headlights. The days were getting dark earlier as winter approached. They rounded a slight curve and, with the lack of recent rain making the road extra slippery, the car began to slide. Brad reacted and eased right off on the accelerator; the tyres gripped. He continued with caution. He was a good driver, even when he did the noisy exits. Gina never felt scared or in danger.

They came to the bends. It was a three-kilometre winding stretch of road with double lines all the way. It was not the place to get stuck behind a truck, but nowhere near as bad as being stuck at a barbecue with a bunch of pretentious wankers. There was no truck ahead. Brad began whistling his Bob Marley anthem. Tonight, Gina sang along, 'Three little birds… Perch by my doorstep… Singin' sweet songs.'

A set of headlights appeared behind the happy couple and cast shadows of their heads onto the car's interior. Brad flipped the rear-view mirror into night mode. The car edged up close behind – uncomfortably close, dangerous.

'Bloody idiots,' said Brad. 'I'm not speeding up, that's for sure.'

As though it heard, the car behind eased off and retreated. Then, in a deliberate taunt, it sped back again to hug their tail. A horn sounded, 'Beep, beep,' and then, 'Beeeeeeeeep!'

The car swerved onto the wrong side of the road to overtake. With the road at that point curving quite sharply, and blindly, to the left, the impatient driver's attempt to overtake was thwarted. They eased off and pulled back in behind. The horn sounded again.

'This is crazy,' said Gina. 'Someone could get killed.'

Brad shifted in his seat and focused on the road ahead. 'About two ks before I can pull over,' he said.

The driver behind would not wait. He, or she, took the very next opportunity to pull straight out, floor the accelerator and dart around.

'Phew. They made it,' said Brad.

But the car, now in front, had not finished. It quickly slowed right down. Brad had to step on the brakes to avoid running into it. The occupants could be seen for the first time. Well, the three in the back seat could. There was a girl in the middle with two young males either side of her. The girl had swung round and was kneeling on the back seat. She pulled up her top to expose her breasts. The boy on her left leaned out the window and was sticking up his fingers and mouthing off – the words lost to the night. The boy on her right was systematically emptying the car of bottles and cans.

Brad swerved around the discarded empties without incident. The car then sped off and disappeared around a bend up ahead.

'What sort of car was that, Brad? We should report them before they kill themselves – or worse, someone else.'

'Yeah, I'm not sure. It's had all the badges taken off. That's the cool thing these days. It might be a Subaru Impreza.'

'Guess we'll never know.'

As the words left Gina's mouth, they rounded the next bend to see that the car had once again slowed right down.

'Looks like they want to play some more.'

Gina placed her hand back on Brad's thigh. He maintained a safe distance and kept his cool. Gina got a pen from her handbag and found a used envelope in the glove box. She wrote down the registration. The painful game of slowing down and then speeding off continued.

As they came near the end of the bends, Brad said, 'The big straight's coming up. Bet they'll take off for good then.'

He was right. The car in front slowed down almost to a stop and crept round the final bend. Then at last the road opened up in front. It was a flat section with an overtaking lane and a broad shoulder. If need be, they could pull over and stop completely, let these hoons go on their way. But Brad had been correct. At the sight of the open road, the offending vehicle sped away, each gear change signalled by a white puff of exhaust.

The menacing vehicle hit top gear, yet still it increased in speed. Through the drizzle, Brad and Gina saw the red tail lights begin to swing from side to side.

'Oh, my God,' said Brad, 'they're fishtailing.'

Every swing increased in amplitude.

'Let go of the wheel, let go,' yelled Brad.

But the driver, young and likely drunk, wrestled with the wheel, frantically steering harder with each change of direction.

In a matter of just a few seconds that seemed like an eternity, the car, now completely out control, spun wildly on its own axis, drifted over to the right, hit the gutter and flipped up into the air. Spinning like silver confetti, it disappeared into the trees. A flash of orange light illuminated the forest. A mushrooming cloud of thick smoke followed.

Nauseous from the shock, Brad and Gina arrived at the point where the car had exited. Flames were licking up the trunk of the tree that had stopped the car. Brad ran down the embankment, howling and calling out. Gina, hyperventilating, rang Emergency.

Maybe someone had been thrown clear of the vehicle. That would be their only chance.

Brad came back, crushed and crumpled by the futility of his attempts at resuscitation, blood on his hands and face. One male had been flung out of the car but life had been irretrievably smashed from his body. The others were all being incinerated inside the steel cage that was once a car. There was nothing else to do but hold each other and wait.

'Hi, Gina, it's Fiona. Hey, Cleo has asked me to ask you if you and Brad would like to come to a barbecue at her place next Sunday. They're celebrating her hubby Phil's promotion at work. He's going to ask Brad if he can install a stainless steel outdoor kitchen out the back on their deck. We all thought he could use the work.'

Gina hangs up on Fiona without a word. The phone rings again. She lets it ring out, vibrating on the kitchen bench. It rings again. Gina picks up her phone, walks out the back door and throws it over the fence. It spins like silver confetti through the air and hits a gum tree, smashing into tiny pieces.

Somewhere Down by the Coast

'There is something I should tell you,
Don't have the words to say.
I only know I want to be together,
With you every day.'

O. Eyes, 2011

That night when we finally met, it was only a stone's throw from the beach where we once both dwelt; when we were young and unaware of each other. It was the place to be, or so thought many: a city beach buffered from big-city issues. Yet somehow you and I, independently, could smell something was off. A suburb infected with lies and pretence. Peyton-Place-like manufactured dramas. Subtle and not so subtle stratification. Exclusive exclusiveness. Cruelty.

We moved away. Separately, we sought out other beaches. All measured up against the archetypal headlands and yellow sands of our adolescent stomping ground. That formative beach, imprinted on our once impressionable minds. All the while looking for community along that thin fractal strip running roughly north–south. The most idyllic stretches despoiled by the curse of development before we ever got there. At various postcodes in various states of mind, we tried our hands at life anew.

Nor-easters, southerly busters, glassy morning swells. High tides, low tides. Cyclones. Cowrie shells and hard shiny black floating seeds. Days filled, successions of success and failure. We learnt a lot about the world and ourselves. Weathered smooth and resilient.

After another day of servitude to the system, the wise-arse man at the bar at the pub laments to his brothers: the trifecta of misery – marriage, mortgage and kids. In the midst of domestic servitude, the half-beaten woman at the till at the supermarket vents to her sisters: disgust with men and their privilege. But neither do anything. At least we moved on. Like we moved on from *that* beach many years ago refusing to settle for second-rate realities.

So meeting when we did was actually as perfect as it can be. Both of us ready, through the riddance of rubbish ideas and the awakening from false beliefs and childish dreams. Ready through shedding the damaged people who were beyond our repair. Setting them free just as we freed ourselves.

And back in those times when we hit rock bottom, it was the coast that soothed and healed us. Not family, not work, not politics, and not religion. It was that mass of salty water heaving itself up onto the land that brought us peace, and hope.

Coast.

You can draw it inside a circle with two lines, one wavy line coming from three o'clock and into the centre, the other line straight and sloping up all the way from four o'clock to ten o'clock. And it has to be that way and not the other way round. East coast. Maybe if we hailed from Perth, it would be flipped horizontally the other way, who knows. But that is how we both drew it that night, you left-handed, me with the right. This is how we orientate to it. Somehow this is how it orientates us. That is the coast, and that is where you and I are found.

Now it is a question of where to stake out our place. Though we do not stake, we walk upon and wonder. Where can we find fenceless freedom? A place free of the flotsam and jetsam of our past personal shipwreckings. Shipwreckings we are grateful for because they have washed us up, right here, right now. Drifting on together towards a final place. A beach and headlands to call home. Maybe a lagoon, or a creek or river nearby to add to the majestic whole. A place where we put down our roots. Not the offspring kind of roots – that has been done with different people in different times. Sure, scars remain, but they no longer pain us. We breathe new air. Our lungs revived.

The trips north and south continue. We camp, we swim, we ask the seagulls. No hurry. Plenty of time to harvest native grain for dark nutritious bread. Many waves yet to be underwater bodysurfed. Tracks to make in windswept dunes, daily, twice daily more likely. Inhabiting, creating, just being. Just being somewhere down by the coast.

Coast.

Home.

Me and you. Ocean Eyes and Pumpernickel.

Blood and Water

After driving for eleven hours, George only wants to sleep. His neck is stiff, his eyes sting and, though he hasn't seen Pip for several years, he doesn't feel like chit chat.

'No worries,' says Pip. 'I've left a spare blanket on the end of the bed. It can get cold. You know.'

'I remember. Thanks.'

George and Pip were good mates back in schooldays. They've kept in touch over the years – sporadically.

Pip inherited his old man's sewer-unblocking business and stayed in the area. There's good money in getting shit flowing, he would say with a wink. George moved away long ago, early one Sunday morning to the sound of a butcherbird mimicking the opening notes of 'Here Comes the Bride'. It was odd, perhaps ironic, but he couldn't unravel it. Not after what he had witnessed the night before – after the White Bay Rugby First Fifteen won the grand final.

Pip had called on the Wednesday, excited and persuasive. 'It's going to be epic, Georgie-boy. The swell's from the north and humongous. And the wind's going to be offshore all Friday. If you don't believe me check out BOM. You gotta get up here, buddy.'

George hesitated, spurring Pip on.

'Come on, man, we'll have the point to ourselves. Walesy might be out there, but swear to God, George, the rest of the locals are too gutless. They're a pack of show ponies these days. They'll all be down at the Pines surfing the safe stuff. You can't let me down, mate. This may be our last chance. What…maybe once a decade this happens? Remember '74?'

'Righto, righto. I'll be there. Thursday night, around nine p.m. Now leave me alone.' *It'd be good to take on the point in a cyclone swell one more time.* Mountains of merciless ocean do invigorate oneself. You need that from time to time.

Around four-thirtyish, in the first hints of daylight, a butcherbird's mournful refrain wakes the two surfing mates. It's not the wedding march melody of that Sunday morning many years ago when he drove off for good, but the distinctive tones still strike a minor chord for George. He's determined not to let any memories ruin this visit back to his old stomping ground. He'll go surfing with Pip, then drive away again.

On the drive out to the point, they pass the rugby club. No other way. The lone pine tree is still there, casting its shadow outside the clubhouse entry. It was thirty-odd years ago when George decided to climb that tree to escape the escalating pressure to have another beer. Not that George was a saint when it came to alcohol restraint. He'd imbibed excessively just like every other self-loathing and reckless male from that era, or any other era you may care to name. Beer-drinking males: endemic to the island continent; a fact of nature, or nurture more likely.

George'd had enough after four schooners. The crowd was pumping, the mood charged and dangerous. The White Bay team and his dad – the coach – and some of the losing team who stayed around to show good sportsmanship were putting away beers by the dozen. OP rums were being slipped in between shouts and tossed back for good measure. The competition hadn't ended at the full-time whistle, that's for sure. It wasn't every day that White Bay beat Broken Ridge in the rugby final. It was time to get out.

Much to his dad's disgust, George didn't play rugby. Some of his mates, including Pip, played in the first fifteen and the whole town had been following the season ever since the lads made it into the semis. At least it was something other than the weather to talk about. Best thing since winning Tidy Town in '76. George found football too aggressive, too macho. He liked books and nature, and was active in the local musical society. You can guess what Dad thought about that.

George promised his mother that he'd get Dad home in one piece. After four beers, a sufficient quota of bullshit, and realising there were at least two hours to kill, he headed off from the clubhouse. He walked down the road for a bit and then took the track that led through the casuarina forest down to the beach. He walked along the cold sand to the point.

He reached the car park and sat on the wooden barrier, facing the ocean. The moment of solitude was short-lived. A car's headlights swept across the grassy slope in front of where George was sitting. Four or five rabbits were illuminated, caught in the act of nocturnal grazing. They startled and scattered into the bitou bush. George didn't bother to look around at the car. It was probably a mob from the rugby club coming up to the point to smoke bongs.

But it wasn't. It was Trudy Evans, the girlfriend of Mikey Roberts, the captain of the team, the hero of the day. Trudy and George knew each other from the musical society. They got on well. Then out of the blue, Trudy dropped out. He bumped into her once down the main street of town and asked about her sudden disappearance. She said she had to focus on her studies. It was clearly a lie. George knew the truth. Trudy was the pretty girl, and Mikey a football god, and according to the rules around this stretch of coastline, he owned her and decided what she could and couldn't do.

George turned around and saw Trudy with her head down on the steering wheel. He reckoned that Mikey must have told her to go home. Told her that as captain he had a duty to celebrate with the boys. That he would come home later and, no, he wasn't interested in that slut with the big tits from Broken Ridge who was flirting with every footballer she could scab a drink from.

Trudy spotted an approaching shape and jumped in her seat. She wiped her eyes and wound down the window. 'George? You scared me to death. What are you doing here?'

'I couldn't stand all that bullshit bravado back there, Trudy. And I have to drive Dad home later, so I came down here for a bit.'

Trudy hopped out and apologised for being all emotional. They sat on the wooden barrier and faced the dark sea. George informed Trudy that the moon rising above the horizon was gibbous and waning.

'How do you know that stuff?' she asked.

'I'm a student of the universe,' he joked.

They talked about the season of *The Pirates of Penzance* and what a hoot that was, even if they were only in the chorus. They talked about music and books and what they wrote about in high school for the mandatory essay on *Othello*.

'I love that word cuckolded,' confessed Trudy.

They laughed. And Trudy looked long and closely at George's face. Then she reached across and took hold of his hand. George was glad it was night, certain his face was reddening.

'George. I'm so glad I ran into you tonight. You've helped me to make a decision.'

'What? You going to come back to the musical society? We're doing *Annie Get Your Gun* this summer.' George cleared his throat and sang a few signature lines.

Trudy laughed. 'No, that's not what I was thinking. It's something else I need to do. But you know what? That is an interesting thought, George. You never know, you never know.'

'So what is it then? You going to dump the rugby hero?'

No answer was given. Trudy kissed George on the cheek and left. It was the last time he ever saw her.

George walked back to the club. In the casuarina forest, microbats swooped over his head feeding on insects stirred by his human passage. He could smell Trudy's perfume on his hand. *Will she or won't she dump Mikey?* He recalled waltzing with Trudy in rehearsals and performances; the shape of her hip and the warmth of her soft hand. He smiled. *How elegantly dressed were we on show nights?* And always, afterwards, Mikey would be waiting in his ute in the theatre car park.

George resigned himself to one of the world's hard realities: that a girl like that would never be with a guy like him.

It was still half an hour till the bar closed. Some people were going in and out of the club entrance. George climbed up the pine tree to avoid being dragged back in for another *compulsory* beer. Fifteen feet up and out of view, he sat on a branch and waited. He reflected on how much he disappointed his father and how his mother pretty much ignored him. He was an only child but felt more like an orphan. The father had long given up on trying to make his son a real man. The mother played tennis, smoked long brown cigarettes and made sure the house was clean and meals were on the table. She was efficient and responsible, cold and remote. Mum's just as bad as Dad, he thought. And he never saw one moment of affection between the two. *Why did they get married and have a kid?*

What happened next would answer George's question. Well, partially. It would start the process. He wouldn't work it out fully until quite a few years later after they'd both died. In the space of three months, George's father hanged himself in the back shed and his mother died of oesophageal cancer. There was no staying away from White Bay that year: two funerals and a house full of shadows to sort through made sure of that.

George sat in the pine tree, waiting.

From his lofty perch, George heard the call of last drinks and watched drunk people leaving the clubhouse. Some were singing, some swearing. Car engines were being started up with total disregard for the newly established 0.05 legal limit. The local police sergeant was one of the crowd. He was as drunk as the others and had no qualms about spinning the wheels of his Ford Falcon and blasting the horn as he left *the event of the year*. Onlookers cheered with intoxicated pride in their local establishment. George shook his head. *This town is an embarrassment.* A taxi pulled up and Pip and two of his mates stumbled out the club doors and straight into the cab. Thank you, Pip, said George to himself. At least not everyone's a total yobbo.

George knew his dad would be one of the last to leave. Sure enough, he came out, staggering and slurring, with captain Mikey Roberts under his left wing. Just behind them was the out-of-town-rugby-groupie. She was saying, 'Fuck I'm pissed,' over and over. Mikey told her to shut up and threw her his car keys and told her to go and wait for him.

George's dad pushed Mikey up against the trunk of the pine tree, just six feet below George's dangling feet.

'Fuck off, Allan,' said Mikey. 'I'm going to go and fuck that whore from Broken Ridge. OK?'

'Come on, Mikey. She'll have the clap for sure. I'll suck your cock, mate. You know you like it. Don't pretend with me.' Allan the coach, George's father, the ultimate man's man, leant forward and kissed Mikey fair and square on the mouth.

A cloud passed across the moon and George froze in its shadow. He felt like he was being stabbed with a cold blade into the side of his ribcage. He didn't have a clue what to do, so he did nothing. He sat there numb and waited for everything to be over.

'Holy moly,' says Pip as the point comes into view. 'Look at that!'

Long lines of swell are wrapping around the headland. Spindrift blows eastward. The white sections of broken wave are neatly staggered. Pip cuts the engine and the roar of the ocean comes into hearing. The sun is not up yet and only a few people are around. George and Pip slip automatically into the routine. Boards off roof. Wetsuits donned. Wax applied and combed.

They trot down the dune and over to the rock platform. At the trusty jump-off spot, they wait for a lull. It's a mad paddle to get safely out the back. A thin sliver of shimmering sun pops ups and floats slightly detached above the bumpy horizon.

A small crowd gathers in the car park. There is a buzz. Twenty-seventeen will go down in surfing folklore, joining '74, '96, and '05. A photographer sets up her tripod. A drone hovers above, its pilot nowhere to be seen.

The two board riders take their time. It's not the sort of ocean you muck about with. They paddle around and let a few sets go through. They watch the backs of the waves as much as the fronts. Look and learn. Respect. Pip lines himself up for the first wave of the morning. Nothing fancy, he says to himself. He bottom turns and climbs back up the face, feeling for the wave's mighty pulse. He swings his board back around to point down the line, shifts his weight forward and trims – the force and beauty of nature providing all that is needed. Nothing to be conquered.

Paddling back out, Pip watches George taking off on his first wave. The style and grace of his old mate hits Pip with more force than the massive waves pounding the coast. *Why did he have to leave?* But he knows the answer, and the vision of George carving up this huge wave is tainted with a disturbing sadness.

'Hey, George,' says Pip when they both know one more wave will be enough. 'I know you said you were driving straight back after this, but before you go, there's a new café in town where they do a great breakfast.'

'I don't know about that, Pip. I love this point and having a surf with you. But I don't like hanging around this place. You know that.'

When they'd caught up at George's dad's funeral, there was an awkward moment when Mikey Roberts came up to them to pay his condolences. He said Allan was a good man. George told Mikey to fuck off with such intensity that the hero footballer shrunk like a penis in a cold shower.

'What's that about, George?' Pip had never seen such fury in his gentle friend.

Pip got his answer later that night when George came back to his place after visiting his mother in palliative care. They sat on the bunk in Pip's spare room. George recounted what he had seen that night from his vantage point in the pine tree. Pip confessed that he'd heard rumours about Allan, but he would have never suspected that Mikey was gay. And he apologised for never saying anything. Pip explained how he had no idea what was the right thing to do; if he should ever broach the subject. George understood.

'Come on, George. Just a quick breakfast. Helen says she'll drop the kids off at school and meet us there.'

'Righto, Pip. I am bloody hungry. Do they do a good coffee?'

'Shit yeah, Mr Big City Latte Pants.'

The adrenalin and muscle workout from riding large lumps of blue-green water around a sandstone headland is uniquely satisfying. As George dries himself off in the car park, he sees a young couple sitting on the wooden barrier and holding hands. The girl kisses the boy on the cheek and, for the first time in a long time, he thinks about Trudy.

He thinks about Trudy and that night. The night when he watched his dad kissing another man, only to be pushed away and left to vomit up his guts on the asphalt. Then to be unceremoniously folded into the back of the barman's car and driven home to the wife he married in 1959. A good Catholic wife who swallowed her destiny like the body of Christ at communion; who tolerated her husband's secret dalliances with men, until she could literally swallow no more. That night, when he went home and packed his bag and left silently in the early morning as the butcherbird mocked the human world with its eight-note mimicry of the wedding song. The kind of night you have to work hard on to forget. Forgiveness still a distant and mysterious concept yet to rise above the horizon of comprehensibility.

Trudy left for London not long after that night. She ended up having a semi-successful career on stage in the West End. On the back of that, she scored a minor role in a new BBC sitcom. George read once, in a doctor's waiting room magazine, that Trudy Makim never married. But that was a while back; no idea what she was up to now.

Pip's car is warm as they head for breakfast in town. 'Hey, guess who owns that new café we're going to?'

'Here we go. No idea, Pip. Why don't you tell me?'

'It's White Bay's most famous thespian export, Trudy Makim.'

George bites his tongue. *Don't feed the animals.*

'You remember her, don't you, George? She's back in town. Helen said she asked about you the other day.'

George laughs. He accuses Pip that the whole come-up-for-a-once-in-a-decade-surf caper is actually an elaborate ploy to do some immature, and pointless, matchmaking.

'You've got your trackie-daks on inside-out, ya silly nong. I can't control the waves, Georgie boy! It's pure coincidence.'

They drive past the rugby clubhouse with its lone pine tree. Still early, its shadow is long. George glances at the setting and for once can't feel that cold blade stabbing into his side.

Message in the Bottles

Try disposing of empty glass bottles without being detected. You can't simply drop them into the bin; the unmistakeable sound is a dead give away. There he goes again, they say to themselves. Must've been another big one last night. Don't know how he does it. Surely he must have a hangover. Surely.

You try to lower them in gently, one by one. You get two or three empties laid down silently, spread across the available surface. The fourth is slotted into that convenient gap in the corner. It slides away out of your hand and free falls to hit yesterday's empty bottles on a lower layer. Clink, clink, clink. Shit! The neighbours would've heard that. The wife would've heard that. The kids have heard it, but like your snoring it is a sound that no longer registers for them, other than that you are around somewhere.

One week, you had the brilliant plan of wrapping up each empty bottle in newspaper first. You figured about four layers of paper would be about right to buffer and dampen that dead giveway sound. It worked a treat. No sound. You couldn't even see the bottles, and the old newspaper pile in your garage looked like you've finally been *doing something about it*, as you said you would six months ago, and six months before that.

This was brilliant, you thought. And when the garbage truck comes on Wednesday morning, your bin will sound just like everyone else's and not like the carillon down on the island in the lake.

Thank God, she said before the truck came. The wife realised she must've thrown the instructions in the bin. She'd been tearing the household apart and interrogating any poor soul in her path. Have you seen them, she'd ask with a manic look in her eye. They were the details on how to find the car rental place in Venice, for that no-kids trip away in the hope of saving the marriage. The look on her face as she pulled the neatly wrapped bottles out of the bin one by one said it all. No, it didn't say, You lied about wanting to see the architecture in the city of canals, didn't you? Though that is true. It said, You are hopeless, pathetic, and not cutting down like you said you would six months ago, and six months before that. You may as well take the empty bottles out into the street and smash them on the road, one by one, singing out aloud, Yo Ho Bottle of Rum, while you do it. Oh yeah, PS: for good measure, do it in the nude.

Everyone knows. And so do you. It's crunch time. Again.

You go and get a haircut – the symbolic fresh new start. Then you go to the library to borrow a ton of reading material – diversion therapy. It's four weeks until Easter and hot cross buns are popping up everywhere, so you buy a dozen – nutritional supplements. The summer heatwave is raging on into autumn, so you go and buy that ceiling fan to put up in the dining room like you told the wife you would six months ago, and six months before that – atonement.

That inheritance is probably all that keeps you from being totally banished from the world at large. It's remarkable what people will put up with when you hold all the funds. Maybe you should give heroin a try and see how the world deals with that. At least needles won't make a sound when they drop into the bin.

The doctor writes the scripts for Valium and Naltrexone. She says it's the last time; next time it will be a referral to rehab. The thought of daily AA meetings motivates you to give this stint a red-hot, decent go. So you trot down to the pub to get an ounce of hashish from Davo. It will take the edge off. And you've never been addicted to cannabis.

Addiction. We're all addicted to something. It just so happens that some addictions are socially acceptable. Nobody gets all concerned or judgemental about the gym junkies. And the slaves to fashion may be laughed at from time to time, but they don't get court orders to stay at least a hundred and fifty metres away from boutiques or clothing outlets. And the women who keep going back to be bashed by violent men are excused as victims and never accused of being addicts. You're a happy drunk, a functional alcoholic, and you're not dependent on anyone. And you do get rid of all your empties, so what's the problem?

The fan above the dining table spins and cools with its downward rush of air. The hot cross buns go down well with the hash and Valium. The Naltrexone can wait till after the weekend. You're not giving up a drink or six on Saturday, race day. The wife asks what you're going to do with the rest of your life. You say that you will make a decision soon, like you did six months ago, and six months before that.

At ten p.m., you are not passing out as per usual and the book by Charles Bukowski is making you thirsty. So you switch to Hunter S. Thompson and are soon wondering if Davo could source you some Quaaludes. Fear and loathing. You admire the Gonzo but something about his writing unnerves you. And he did end it all with a shotgun in the mouth, didn't he? And Coleridge, it was the opium that did him in, in the end, 'Kubla Khan' or no 'Kubla Khan' – it was inglorious.

The streets are dark and the first hint of autumn coolness brushes your cheek. You can hear muffled television sets and fenced-in dogs barking away at each other. A car screeches its tyres in a distant street. What are you going to do for the rest of your life? The wife is right. And she's not hanging in for the money, you know that. Her tastes are simple and her share of any negotiated settlement, even the absolute minimum she is entitled to, would see her comfortable for the rest of her life.

What does she see in you? There must be something. What do you see in yourself? There must be something.

The bottle shop is still open. You stop and stand outside, triggering the sliding doors. The bright lights and all the pretty bottles on the shelves beckon you to enter. Harry is at the counter. He will ask, 'How is you, this evening?' in his Scottish brogue. Harry makes no judgement, but who the fuck is Harry in the scheme of things? He is not your wife, he is not your child. He is sadly the closest thing you can call a friend. You speak to him several times every week and know all about his dreams to retire and go fishing. You know that he plays the bagpipes and that his daughter died of cancer six years ago. He reads science fiction and once stood on the spot where JFK was shot.

And what does your only friend know about you? He knows what you drink and how much. He probably only likes you because you more often than not refuse the change. He knows nothing else about you, not a single thing. He knows you about as well as you know yourself.

The sliding doors close, and there you are in the glass looking back at yourself. You walk on.

'Six months ago, you put up that fan,' says the wife.

'Yes, that's true. And now winter is over, it might finally be useful,' you say. 'Would you like to go for a drive in the country on Saturday?'

The Crows

Fark. Faark. Faaaaark.

It's not funny like when Graeme Kennedy got himself sacked from Channel Nine for imitating this black bird's uncanny resemblance to the publicly unutterable.

It's more like the horror induced in that Hitchcock movie when Tippi Hedren spots all the crows perched everywhere silently waiting for school to finish.

People were losing their minds, because of the crows.

I was waiting in the town of Blackwood to meet him. It had been arranged through the underground connections I had built up over decades of investigative journalism, most of it freelance now since no mainstream media wanted to have anything to do with me. I guess I had a reputation of sorts. But nothing like the mystique of Jason Verity, the crow-killer. At least that's what the establishment called him. He was breaking the law and needed to be apprehended and bought to justice – no question about it.

Yes, the laws were clear. The crow was protected. But the general populace had lost all compassion for this avian pest that mocked us continually from its lofty perches. The cities provided a plethora of poles and wires overlooking bins and a multitude of other food sources. The haunting song reminding us all that progress came at a cost. The country folk and farmers who had been losing their battle with this omen in the sky for generations were somewhat pleased that the suburbs and cities were now being tortured by the incessant cawing of this despicable bird. Maybe the laws would change.

'Worse than rats, and we have open season on them.' I heard this, or something similar, so many times that I used it for a headline on my frequently hacked blog.

But the laws remained and Jason Verity's image was posted in every police station and on every TV broadcast. But on the web and around dinner tables he was a hero. Moved around and protected by the common folk eager for him to do his magic. Even the first peoples of this nation, who you might expect having strict lore about this bird, declared Jason as a spirit being sent down from the stars to right the wrongs – the wrongs of colonisation and urbanisation, that is.

I got word a while back that Jason admired my work and that he would tell me his life story. He even would take me to observe his never before witnessed methods of crow eradication. I vowed to keep that part secret, and he believed me. It will give me some excellent context to use for your life story, I told him over Skype.

He told me that up till now he had not wanted to share his secrets, it would place anyone in the know in danger, and he would not do that. 'But if they catch me, or kill me, you will be the one with the knowledge. And it will be your duty to disseminate this knowledge,' he informed me. 'You will become a marked man, you know that?'

'I'm sort of that already,' I replied.

I waited in Blackwood's RSL, sipping a beer and listening to the bells and synthesised muzak generated by the poker machines. They had lost their one arm but were still bandits of the worst kind. The gambling epidemic was in full swing. No one wanted to be outside any more. There was a theory that the oligarchs who controlled the government demanded that no laws be changed in response to the crow explosion. They were making a killing out of it, apparently. True or not, the one per cent were richer than ever. I even saw a graph that showed the correlation of crow numbers and inequality.

The environment groups were calling for intervention, mainly because of the rapidly declining diversity of other Australian bird species, courtesy of the crow. They were being lambasted by the media and neo-conservative politicians for being hypocrites.

'And now the Greens, the real environmental terrorists, want to kill birds?' said the environment minister, who had just approved the 'sustainable harvesting' of koalas for a booming Japanese market. 'We will all benefit economically from this natural resource,' he said, stony-faced. 'We can't deny the Japanese, or anyone for that matter, the standard of living that we enjoy on this marsupial-laden continent.'

It made me sick, and I was not the only one. The lies and propaganda were running out of steam. Jason Verity was safe as houses in this country. Safe in the houses of the ordinary folk who no longer swallowed the bullshit that urbanisation and economic growth was for the good of all. The crows were telling us that. Loud and clear.

Fark. Faark. Faaark.

Yes, they were driving us mad, mad as hell. Mad enough to unite and take to the streets to change the laws to allow people to take matters into their own hands. The fine for killing a crow, greater now than the fine for illegal land clearing, was an insult to us all. We laughed insanely at the ridiculous plans for air-conditioned domed cities free of crows and nicely populated with the correct smattering of kookaburras and rainbow lorikeets. The artist's impressions only fooled the ignorant courtesans of growth, those with an insatiable greed for a better than average slice of the rotting pie – imbeciles.

Jason arrived in through the bistro kitchen of the RSL. He was escorted by the shire president and two very serious-looking body-guards. The group came to my table.

'Pleased to meet you face to face, Clancy,' said Jason, and he held out his hand. He spoke gently and I noted that his face, which I knew from all the posters and from our Skype talks, was so much more serene than what I had imprinted in my mind.

The plans were quickly discussed. The group would escort the two of us to a location a couple of kilometres out of town to the east. There, we would be left to walk to the secret spot where Jason would do his thing.

We were about to leave when the sirens came into hearing, unmistakeably getting louder and louder. The two bodyguards went into well trained action. They whisked Jason away so quickly, leaving the shire president and myself sitting dumbstruck at the cheap laminated RSL table.

'I thought this might happen,' said the president. 'At least the police used their sirens as agreed.'

'Oh,' I said.

The president winked. 'We just want those crows gone, mate. You know the kids in this town are developing rickets cause they can't play outside any more.'

The police walked in casually and arrested me for conspiracy to commit a federal offence. 'Don't worry, you'll be released with a token fine,' said the sergeant. 'Then you can get back to doing what you do best, Clancy.'

'What's that?' I asked.

'Exposing the lies about economic growth and development. We know that's what brings the crows. Use your pen, or computer or whatever you guys do these days. Stir up some more protest action. I don't know how long we can keep Jason from being caught.'

As I was being led out to the paddy wagon in the car park, the chorus of crows was building to a crescendo. The sound was awful, permeating deep into my being, unnerving me and my new police mates. Then, without notice, it stopped and the only sound that could be heard was the flapping of a thousand black wings heading east out of town.

It Happens All the Time

The re-education program deemed essential for social harmony was not compulsory, but if you didn't attend, your Universal Basic Income was reduced by fifteen per cent. Rumour had it that the savings made by the government from this penalty were needed to fund the grease to lubricate the robots that had put you out of work in the first place. The Central Artificial Intelligence robots did everything, even the training.

Dane met Bambi at the program. She looked liked trouble. When she introduced herself to him, she licked her lips and a sine curve travelled from the top of her head down to her heels. He was instinctively interested but worried that she might be a robot. A spy robot, perhaps.

Monday's two-hour seminar was always about alcohol. Since the reintroduction of prohibition, the suburbs were awash with bootleg beer, wine and spirits. Today it was all about the downfall of drinking at breakfast. A video was shown of people washing down mangoes with champagne at seven a.m. and then dancing and fornicating themselves into oblivion. The audience feigned shock while surreptitiously texting their black market dealers about the availability of tropical fruit in winter.

Bambi came home on the bus with Dane for a coffee. Talk turned to drinking alcohol with the most important meal of the day.

'Do you ever?' she asked with suggestive lips.

Crunch time. Dane was fairly certain she wasn't a robot; he couldn't detect any whirring of machinery under the skin or the faint whiff of grease that was a dead giveaway. But he would be coy, just in case she was human, a prude pretending to be a party girl looking for a sucker to dob in for a reward. 'Perhaps. Can you notice?' He watched her spectacular eyes for any reaction to this risky admission.

'How many?'

Careful, Dane. 'Six or twelve.' He laughed out loud. 'Kidding, Bambi. Maybe once or twice I had a beer with my eggs.'

'Will you do it tomorrow?'

Dane listened for the distinctive sound of a hard drive booting up inside Bambi's head. 'Not likely,' he said.

Likely.

'And what about you, do you ever?' he asked the sex machine sitting opposite with those crossed, stockinged, dynamite legs.

'All the time,' she said without the blink of an eye.

'I don't believe you. I think you're trying to trick me, get me into trouble with the CAI.'

'Dane, I need to use your toilet. You can come and watch me pee if you like. It will prove your paranoia to be just that – paranoia.'

'Oh dear, I am so sorry. It's just that my best friend Henry Armstrong got taken away…just last week. A drone outside his attic window videoed him drinking rum while masturbating to porn.'

Relieved, Dane decided to let Bambi relieve herself, alone. She's not a robot. Calm down, Dane.

He heard the flush. Bambi returned.

'Can I fix you a wee something?' he said holding up a bottle of clear spirit in one hand, a lime in the other.

'No thanks. No need,' she replied. She fished out a small metal flask from the handbag she had carried into the toilet.

'Then how about a nice long…'

'That'd be the shot.' Bambi cottoned on like a lush.

Dane poured two big slugs into two big mugs. They clinked and swallowed.

'How do you avoid the vapour police?' asked Dane as Bambi prepared to leave after a most successful drinking session. 'Any tricks?'

She pulled out a packet of gum. 'This is my secret weapon. It looks and smells like Juicy Fruit, but it sequesters ethanol vapour with the utmost efficiency. I source it from Neville. You know him?'

'Yes, he supplies my booze and LSD. He's never mentioned the gum.'

'Oh. Please don't tell him I told you about it.'

'No, I won't. Whatever you say. Do you ever sell it on for a profit?'

'Of course.'

Dane was keen to see this vixen fawn again. Maybe next time he could buy some gum from her and get out into the public with a skinful on board. That would be fun. 'Are you going to the sex re-education program on Wednesday?'

'Maybe.' Bambi strutted off, drunk and breathing fresh, exuding only pheromones.

The two-hour anti-sex seminar followed standard programming. First up, a video showing genitalia ravaged by disease. Next, an interview with the head superintendent robot from the detention centre that housed the crazies racked and wrecked with carnal desire. Then, a cup of tea and biscuits.

Bambi was definitely not in attendance. Her allowance would be docked. How will she be able to pay for gum? thought Dane. Maybe the Universal Basic Income is never enough. Maybe she works on the side.

After the morning tea break, Dane couldn't pay attention. The video of celibate celebrities espousing the virtues of redirecting sexual energy into more worthwhile pursuits was an old repeat. He'd seen it a hundred times. He was worried about Bambi.

Neville was selling contraband from his usual place in the sewer. 'The usual?' he asked.

'Give me an extra bottle of gin and twelve tabs of acid this time.'

'Whoa, man! Are you OK? You look kinda shook up.'

'You know Bambi? I was meant to meet her at the seminar today. She didn't show. I'm worried about her.'

'Don't you worry about Bambi. She'll be teaching the tango to Ziggy Ziggurat.'

'The Tango! Ziggy Ziggurat!'

Dancing was banned and Ziggy Zigurat was number one on the global most-wanted list. The faceless Babylonian pyramid marketing genius was the target of every police robot on the planet. His illegal empire was the last bastion of resistance needing to be conquered for total CAI domination. Bambi was playing with fire. Dane desired her ever more.

Bambi appeared at Friday's seminar. She was as cool as a genetically engineered frozen cucumber. She even took the stand to be a witness to the evils of dancing.

'Both my mother and sister succumbed to the sirens of jazz. What seemed at first like an innocent jitterbug devolved quickly into debauchery and drunkenness. It is a slippery slope, my fellow citizens. Even a toe tap to the beat of a train on its track can lead one into the pits of hell. My father was incarcerated and had his lips removed for playing clarinet in a bebop band. I miss my family.' Bambi broke down and was escorted from the lectern by a first aid robot.

She regained some composure, thanked the robot and proceeded by herself through the applauding crowd – many of whom were typing jitterbug and bebop into their hand-held encrypted devices linked to Ziggy Ziggurat's Deep Dark Interweb.

She sat herself next to Dane. 'Can we do coffee again?' she whispered into his red-hot ear.

Back at home, Dane couldn't help himself. 'Does Ziggy look like…'

'No. He's taller than you. And more handsome.' She was upfront.

Dane took a step back as though he'd been punched in the gut. 'Yeah. But isn't he ancient?'

'No, that is a myth. He's young and in top nick.'

'Does your sponsor know?'

'What? I haven't told him.'

'Well, I'm wondering, do you ever…?'

'All the time.'

After his initial concerns about Bambi's dancing and coitus with the world's most-wanted man, Dane swallowed his pride, two tabs of Electric Kool-Aid and three fingers of Mother's Ruin.

'Would you like to hear a tune from my collection of funk?' he asked Bambi who was morphing into a purple mermaid in front of his dilating eyes.

'I haven't listened to funk for years. I do much prefer jazz.'

'How about for old time's sake? We can do the tango to some Red Hot Chili Peppers?'

'That'd be too hard.'

'Then what about…' Dane held up a vinyl copy of *La Cumparsita* by the Alonso-Minotto quartet.

'You sure about that?'

The synergy of Latin music, gin, LSD and the tango whisked the fledgling couple from the impromptu lounge room dance floor and onto the prohibited fox fur duvet covering Dane's outlawed waveless waterbed.

Bad girl? Bad boy!

'Hey, I've got an idea. Just for us.'

'No, I have to go, Dane. My bus.'

'But I wonder, do you ever?'

'All the time!'

How to Stop a Psychopath From Ruining a Party

The man with the megaphone up on the soapbox is way ahead in the polls. He could stop campaigning now and prepare his victory speech, I reckon. But he likes the attention. He sounds genuine, but I know him well. All he's interested in is power and status. Ironic that his party, The Australian Blue Party, is pure socialism and thus stands for everything this man is not.

I met Glen Richards back when we were in the Greens. Remember them? They never could shake off that tree-huggers tag. Their social policies were ignored and the ridicule they would suffer when they stood up for a species of lizard or orchid would undo, in a viral minute, years of policy development on employment and the economy. It was sad. So many good people who understood that the environment was fundamental to everything.

'Are you coming to the picket?' Glen would ask. He loved getting arrested.

'I've got a family and a mortgage,' was my usual response.

Glen would mock me as being soft.

Don't get me wrong. I can be radical, I'm just not into theatrics. I let others take that role. Glen, though, was into everything; his ambition was seen as admirable. To me, it was the face of some deep psychological trauma that I suspected had something to do with being raised in a religious cult in Adelaide. For unstated reasons, the father did escape with the family to Queensland and, to me at least, it's always been obvious that Glen is obsessed with being a success, a bigwig, to prove something to his dad.

I remember the lengths Glen would go to get his own way. The worst case was when our local chapter of the Greens preselected a bright young girl I'll call Julie to protect her identity.

Glen was deluded that he was by far the best candidate. He was not going to let some young blow-in get all the glory. 'She's just a piece of fluff,' he confided in me.

Deviously, he offered to do mock interviews with her, to prime her for the tough grilling she could expect from the media. Regretfully, I helped draft a set of curly questions. I'm not sure what happened in the room where he interrogated her, but she came out crying. Glen acted all supportive and took her to the pub to debrief and regroup. The barman, my cousin, told me how Glen was ordering nips of vodka to be added to just one of the two schooners of beer he ordered several times. Julie got plastered in public. At the ensuing emergency meeting, Glen was voted in to stand as the Green candidate. Julie disappeared in shame.

'She should never have been drinking in the first place,' Glen told me when I confronted him about the vodka spiking.

He knew then and there that I saw straight through him. He avoided me and I was glad. I told others what I knew and what I thought of him, but everyone was caught up in all that silly pre-election hype that goes on. Some even supported his touch of mongrel.

'If you're not a bastard, you'll get eaten alive in Canberra. Glen did Julie a favour actually,' one diehard political dog informed me on election day. Glen got fourteen per cent of the vote and was a hero of sorts for a while. I was appalled and let my membership lapse.

As we all know, over the next decade or so the political climate deteriorated rapidly. The neo-conservatives, masters at playing dirty, kept getting into power. It seemed that the worst they performed the better they went in the elections. Economic crises and terrorist attacks happened just at the right moments. The donations from big business, and the cushy jobs waiting for the puppets in parliament, all seemed entrenched and unstoppable. The apathy of the public to engage in the political process was frustrating but understandable.

That was until the food crisis.

Sick and hungry people get political, radically political. Especially when such a disaster happens in a nation listed as the wealthiest in the world. The courtesans of capitalism started looking like the fools they were. Their lies to keep striving for growth and jobs just didn't hold water any more and the Blue movement was born. The genius of the founders to steal the colour blue right off the ties of the conservative scaremongers will likely go down as the boldest marketing ploy of the century. The band of artists, musicians and writers that for so long had been denied an existence because of government spending cuts, took the blue motif and went to town on that baby.

Blues music festivals, blue dystopian poetry, big blue sky art installations, blue sea celebrations and the return of blue jeans as the penultimate symbol of a vibrant neo-socialism, swept across the land from the flooding coast to the burning interior. The disdain of the middle class towards welfare recipients dissipated. City and country folk joined forces. The awakening to the cruel and unjust divide separating the haves and the have-nots materialised out of the blue, so to speak. The unnatural disaster that started way back in the 1970s courtesy of Reagan and Thatcher, was finally coming to an end. A revolution was imminent and the Blue party was the voice of calm reason, working for change while suppressing the palpable threat of violent reprisal being drummed up in some quarters. The wealthy were frightened and stepping up security in their fancy postcode enclaves. The people were on the march.

Glen had the megaphone and the people firmly in his hand.

'Let's reclaim the wealth of this nation the right way, at the ballot box. If we resort to blame and even violence, we become as bad as the perpetrators themselves. Let's take Canberra and rebuild a civil society based on equality and fairness.'

Your dad would be so proud, I thought sarcastically.

I couldn't help but think that the Blue Party, so desperately needed, was also fundamentally doomed if a person such as Glen was able to rise through its ranks. Was this happening everywhere else? Would Glen and others like him become pigs with their snouts in the trough, just like George Orwell warned us so eloquently of in *Animal Farm*? We had been waiting so long for the rise of socialism in this country. Waiting for the public to to wake up to the inherent flaws in capitalism as the mechanism for equality. And now here, up on the podium, in the flesh, was one seriously damaged human proclaiming to be the instrument of change.

I kicked myself. I had taken my eye off the ball in recent years. I had succumbed to the political apathy that I so despised. I focused on myself and my family, installing food gardens and water tanks, going off the grid. And here, right under my nose, a psychopath had charmed his way into a position in the grass-roots movement about to claim government.

I went home and took out a blue-lined A4 writing pad and a blue ballpoint pen, my sword. There was some fight left in me yet! I'll write to the party. I'll write to his long-suffering wife, Helen. She knows him well. She'll agree to help bring him down. I'll remind her about young Julie, but I'll use her real name. I'll write to Julie. I'll write to the local Greens; some of them will have dirt and maybe a hunger for vengeance. But it's only a week to election day.

'Dad, what are you doing? What's the matter?' asked my youngest daughter. I was pacing around the dining table, biting that blue pen.

'Glen Richards is going to get into government. It can't happen.'

'But don't you want the Blues to get in, Dad?'

'Yes, they must get in and they will.' I thanked my daughter in my head. She had triggered an idea.

Glen can win the seat, let him have his day in the limelight. That is when I'll strike. And not that messy drawn-out smear campaign stuff that they call political assassination these days. I'll opt for the old-school approach. Didn't Trotsky get an ice pick through his skull? It would be messy, but not drawn-out.

I make a coffee. I grew and roasted the beans myself. Plotting murder needs lots of caffeine.

My daughter comes back into the dining room with my geological hammer that was hanging in the shed. 'That's a pick isn't it, Dad?' She places it on the table next to my extra-big mug of coffee and gives me a look that says, won't you need this, you maniac?

I had been talking out aloud.

'Oh dear! I was just off on a rant. What did I say? I would never hurt anyone…you know that, don't you?'

My daughter laughs. She knows me.

The Blue Party's non-violence policy was right, of course…damn it!

I go back to the pad, vile-tasting blue ink on my lips. 'Dear Helen…'

Going Down…

Back in primary school, we sang a song about drinking rum mixers while working with our mothers. That is my first excuse.

Said song

1. links alcohol to positive changes in mood,

2. promotes a commercial product,

3. spins the benefits of wage slavery under an imperialist currency, and

4. encourages opening your legs on the beach for the occupying military personnel.

Not sure what they were trying to teach us. Perhaps geography – you know, Trinidad, Point Koomahnah, and so on. Perhaps it was simply to expose us to the joys of communal singing.

Can't blame that song for my tobacco addiction, though. That happened in English in high school, my next excuse.

Mr Tierney

1. would read two or three poems from the Romantic period,

2. get this funny look on his face after each recitation,

3. assign us to copy out Wordsworth and Keats, longhand, into our exercise books, and

4. sit at his desk and roll and smoke a cigarette.

Pretty certain the intention was for us to develop an appreciation of literature. However, it was the smell of ready-rubbed tobacco, both before and during burning, and not the rhyme and metre of poetry that clung more tenaciously to the dopamine receptors in my brain.

When you got busted for smoking in the toilets, you were caned by the deputy principal. It didn't hurt as much as when the Sisters of Mercy would whip the back of your knees with the handle of a feather duster, or when Dad would tan your backside with his belt after he found out you'd been a bad girl at school.

Of course, punishment was meant to set you back on the straight and narrow. As you may have guessed by now, it didn't work. Every time I was hit, I strayed further off track.

Drinking and whoring have got me into a whole heap of trouble. Smoking has made a mess of my lungs and once rosy complexion. And if you point this out to me, I'll knock your block off.

Learning disorder? You kidding? I was a good student. A bloody sponge.

No Number

There's only one person at the deli counter; no need to tear off a number. The woman being served wants twelve little boys, which you may know as cocktail frankfurters, or cheerios. I know: cheerios, what a joke. Supposedly made from lips and arse. She must be having a kids' party. Kids love processed pig sphincters. And kids get what they want these days. It's the least we can do, since we know deep inside that we spawned these little unfortunates into the most crazy fucked-up human world ever to have existed. Cheerio – makes sense now, when you think of it.

Now she wants a dozen chicken wings. All bone and sinew with a light dusting of hormone-induced meat, perfect for children entering this brave new world. Happy birthday, Hermione. She is deciding if she will get the wings in a marinade or plain. The boy-cum-young-man serving is wearing knee-high white gumboots, which you may know as Wellingtons, or erroneously as galoshes. He looks at me from under a white disposable hairnet and smiles to apologise for the woman's tardiness, but not to worry, you will be next.

The woman chooses soy and honey, cheaper than plain anyway – the supermarket can explain if you bother to ask. Now she wants olives. Of course, parents will be coming. You can't leave children by themselves at someone else's house these days. You would be charged with negligence. Spies from the Attachment Parenting Society would report you to the police with new powers granted by the new conservative party who landslided into government right under our new progressive noses.

A man comes along and grabs a number. He looks up at the red digital Now Serving display – 058 – and then at his ticket. I see the look of satisfactory correlation on his face. The slight limbic pang of losing my spot is counterbalanced by my knowledge that the boy serving knows my face and my position. I should be fine. Though, never certain, I consider grabbing a number just in case.

While distracting myself by looking through curved glass at the array of culturally appropriated refrigerated delicacies illuminated by dozens of fluorescent tubes, more consumers come and take numbers. Shit.

As though on call, a co-worker, *sans* white gumboots, arrives from out the back through scratched translucent door flaps. She knows the gig. 'Fifty-nine!'

The man with the number curves himself over the glass and whispers his order – just a little bit over a hundred and twenty grams of not-so-secret champagne ham, as it turns out.

Another worker, this time from the seafood department, appears. 'Sixty!'

My only saviour, the boy in the white gumboots, the only one who knows I am next, finishes up with the kids' party woman, looks at his watch, swipes the hairnet off his head and exits through those scratched translucent door flaps that I am unable to name.

Cutting Cake

Simon isn't good at social cues, but when Marie whispered in his ear that she wanted to come round after work to give him a birthday present he'd never forget, a present that would shut up Angela once and for all, he was able to put two and two together. The way she squeezed his arm was especially telling.

He showers and cleans his teeth, tidies up around the place, puts the cat outside, closes down the computer, and recalls the exact words Marie uttered to him after the birthday cake was cut up and handed out on squares of paper towel.

It is getting dark outside. He peers through the Venetian blinds. Is that Marie's Daewoo? He feels a warmth down below.

Marie sits in her car outside the flat. There's no way she's going to do nothing about Angela's workplace harassment of Simon, aka the Geek. She wonders if her birthday present will change him. Will it be a cure for his condition, whatever that is?

She checks lipstick in the rear-view mirror, adjusts stocking suspenders that twisted on the drive over, reminds herself that Simon said yes to her out-of-the-ordinary request, and looks once more at the address he scribbled onto a piece of paper.

It is nearly dark. She sees yellow light coming from a window. Is that Simon's silhouette? She feels a warmth down below.

One might imagine that a woman named Angela would possess some heavenly qualities. There's no doubt that a significant proportion of the staff who worked at Sunshine Insurance Pty Ltd were fooled by her over-the-top persona and faux kindness. The fact that she knew every single staff member's birthday, and collected money for their present and card, and baked them a cake and sang Happy Birthday in operatic tones, was apparently enough to compensate for her numerous flaws and outright toxic behaviours.

Today, she did her usual routine for Simon, the Geek. When he went out for morning tea, Angela held court on the central table in the open office. She made a ridiculous ritualistic performance of wrapping his present, which she'd purchased from David Jones, of course. The wrapping paper was vomit-worthy, as was the way she curled the ends of the gold ribbon with her special pair of glitter-handled scissors. She then unveiled the cake. It was smothered in whipped cream and topped with exotic fresh fruit – a guaranteed winner.

Head down, Simon returned to the office with his iced coffee milk and pineapple doughnut. He nearly jumped out of his meek skin when the first lines of Happy Birthday burst forth from Angela's stage mouth. He copped it sweet, like everyone had to in this office ruled by the tyrant of birthdays. He was made to cut the cake.

'If you cut through and touch the plate, you'll have to kiss the nearest girl,' Angela laughed out loud.

Simon took the knife and looked at who was standing next to him. It was Marie.

'Don't worry, Simon. Angela is joking. Aren't you, Angela?'

'Oh, Marie, you're such a stick in the mud, aren't you?'

Marie ignored the woman. She guided Simon's hand.

As the knife sank into the cream, Angela took centre stage once again. 'Now, everyone. Listen up. Simon is thirty-nine today, and I think as gesture of goodwill we should all put on our thinking caps and help this young man find a woman.'

Marie wanted to wrest the knife off Simon and finish this bitch. Right there at work, right in front of all her sycophants and courtesans. Right there in front of Simon, Angela's number one easy target.

'He'll be forty next year and it would be such a shame to have to celebrate another birthday with Simon still being a virgin.'

There was a sudden halt to proceedings. All eyes were on Angela.

'Oh, silly me,' she feigned. 'I was watching that movie last night on DVD. You know the one, *The Forty Year Old Virgin*. What's his name…the actor…Steven someone…?'

'Carrell, Steve Carrell,' piped up someone from the staff. Someone trying to help out Angela? Perhaps to help Simon?

'That's him. He's a real geek…'

There was another horrible halt in proceedings. 'Oh, sorry, Simon! There I go again. Foot in mouth, oh dear. Please forgive me. Of course you're not a virgin…are you?' A few of Angela's fans laughed. 'Now, where is that present?'

Marie looked at Simon.

He didn't blush, he didn't get angry. He thanked Angela for the cake. He thanked the staff for the present. He ate some cake and listened to what Marie said into his ear when no one was watching. He said, 'Yes.' Then he went back to his workstation and did his mathematical magic with the software algorithms. It was well known that his skill kept Sunshine Insurance afloat.

She wonders if Simon will like the lingerie she is wearing underneath. She locks the car.

He wonders what Marie sees in him. He closes the Venetians.

She worries that possibly it's her debilitating desire to fix people that is the real reason she's here; that her attraction to Simon, the maths genius, is not the real deal, just some fucked-up psychology going on in her brain that is tricking her limbic system and libido.

He worries that he possibly said yes to Marie only to get the virgin monkey off his back. That his version of autism, that no one can name, won't change one iota if he allows himself to let go and surrender into the arms of this attractive woman.

She recalls the mesmerising beauty of his focus and unaffectedness.

He recalls the touch of her hand on his as he cut the cake.

They both know the knife hit the plate.

The Human Race

'Ronaldo, you actually are stupid. I mean really, seriously…stupid!' says Michael, shaking his head.

Ronaldo is a rat in a cage, so without too many options available, it sleeps, eats and races full speed on a plastic treadmill. He is not a pet, but a take-home school experiment – a vital part of Michael's shot at getting into medicine at university.

Jim, Michael's father, has employed a tutor to help his son bullshit his way into med school. Apart from a near-perfect final mark, you also need to convince a university interview panel that you're made of the right stuff to be a doctor. The eager seventeen-year-old has no interest in making the world a better place, or relieving the suffering of those afflicted with disease – he just wants to earn lots of money.

A few months ago, the school's career advisor handed out the obligatory tertiary education application forms to the study-dulled Year 12. Michael hit the internet and googled, 'highest-paying jobs'. Coming in at number one was anaesthetist, at two was internal medical specialist – whatever that meant – and listed at three was other medical practitioners. Though a degree in ancient history might have appealed more to his natural interests, Michael, who had observed how the world really worked, knew that when it came to choosing a career, money mattered most. Medicine was definitely the way to go.

Heeding the advice of not putting all your eggs in one basket, Michael was also training hard on the soccer field and at the gym. 'You can't rule out professional sports-person as an option,' he informed his dad one afternoon as he stuck L plates onto the family car.

The wallpaper of Ronaldo posters on the bedroom wall, the shelf full of trophies, the caged rat and piles of school stuff on the desk, and the rising tide of dirty clothes on the floor, completely hid any trace of Michael's early teenhood obsession with ancient Greece. Just last week, a once-loved balsa wood model of the Parthenon got crushed under the intensity of Year 12 and is now sitting in the wheelie bin.

'Go, Ronaldo, go,' laughs Michael as he records another observation in his biology notebook.

Michael's mum, Janine, is downstairs standing at her granite-top kitchen bench, staring at a recipe that reads more like a chemistry experiment. She is preparing the meal that sealed victory for Andy and Stephane – the gay couple from Adelaide – in the grand final of television's latest reality cooking show, *Let's Cook*. The preened and articulate couple, with their over-the-top and carefully edited public meltdowns, proved to be a ratings winner for the show and, according to the gossip columns, a career-saver for its ageing cocaine-addicted host.

The *Let's Cook* opening credits and cheesy jingle rouse Jim from his chair in the TV room. 'What a load of crap,' he mutters as he slips out to his other domain, the triple garage. There are no cars in the garage. With no room for a shed in the backyard, the garage is it, the waiting place for all the stuff that builds up over the years, which no one can face, or bother, to chuck out. This is where Jim hangs out to indulge in some precious alone time. He tinkers with his home-brew set-up and sits in meditation to the reassuring drone of ABC radio coming from an old tranny on the workbench

For months, the rest of the family has been Araldited to the flat screen. Food has become such a national obsession that how on earth we survived before knowing how to plate up a meal is as puzzling as the concept of life before air conditioning. Janine finally caved in to the kids, and the girls at work, to get with the program, and has all but completely ditched the meals passed down to her by her mother and the generations before. Sure, the cost of the ingredients for these fancy new meals, and the tools – such as the mini blowtorch needed for the perfect crème brûlée – are a bit expensive, but casual employment as an aged-care worker at Sunny Parks Nursing Home, even on minimum hourly rate, has allowed for some small luxuries.

The cost of Michael's tutoring is not considered a luxury and is justified by a father who is banking on his last chance to get at least one kid into uni. It's not like in his day, when you could just front up and get work anywhere. Nowadays, it seems that if you don't have all the necessary pieces of paper, you might as well kiss the human race goodbye. Jim has seen a bit of the mongrel in his son, and every time he hands over the fifty bucks to the tutor, or life coach as he calls himself, he thinks back to when Michael, at just seven, gritted his teeth and put his head down for weeks and weeks to earn his first ever best and fairest points at soccer. He's never seen anything close to that in his other two kids. Paying a tutor for those two would have been as good as flushing hard-earned money down the toilet. In bed at night, Jim ponders the role of nature and nurture in shaping people. With Janine and himself at the nurturing helm, and with both providing equal shares of DNA, the stark differences between his three offspring are a major puzzle.

Kylie, the difficult middle child, is three years older than Michael. She never finished school because at the tender age of fourteen a ferocious hormone storm awoke inside the once-pink fairy princess and propelled her out the bedroom window and into the waiting cars of tattooed no-hopers. After years of sleepless nights for Jim and Janine, it took a court-ordered three-month stint in rehab to put an end to her party years. On a promise to make something of herself, Kylie returned home and enrolled in TAFE to become a beautician. She got the piece of paper, but claimed she was allergic to make-up and that she really wanted to be a horticulturist. After that, she realised that she needed IT skills. Her portfolio, thick with certificates, failed to impress the employers who insisted on experience.

'How the hell do you get experience in the first place?' she would cry.

The row of certificates on her bedroom wall stopped short of a full lap about the time she showed Mum and Dad a fuzzy black and white ultrasound photo of their future grandchild. Brett, who eventually conceded it must have been his junk that got Kylie preggers, is a thrash metal muso presently up Mt Isa way, trying – Jim scoffs at the word – to get into the mines. He has vowed to make good. His long hair, skinny jeans and monotone 'I dunno' responses, have the same effect on Jim as the *Let's Cook* jingle.

Janine does at times defend Brett, but Jim is not impressed. 'It could be worse,' claims Janine. Their daughter is 'Lucky not to be in jail, or six feet under…perish the thought.'

The eldest is James Junior, twenty-bloody-eight and still at home. Like Kylie, he left school early but, to his credit, he has worked ever since. He walked out of school and straight into a casual position, stacking shelves at a local two-dollar shop. After coming home for five years, smelling of fake Tupperware and cheap candles, James Junior finally scored his dream job: computer salesperson at JB Hi-Fi, with a twenty-five per cent staff discount, woo-hoo!

JJ, as he's called, is a big gamer and spends most of his time in his bedroom battling werewolves and zombies till the wee hours of the morning. Ever since a stutter and a facial tic appeared out of the blue after a Year 4 school disco, James Junior has never coped well with the real world. No one but James knows what did happen that night, and the family, on advice from a counsellor, have stopped asking.

JJ is saving for a deposit to buy a home. With house prices following the same trend as the human population, and with renting being a fool's game, the parents let their man-son stay at home. Janine has been eyeing off JJ's room as a potential sewing space and Jim would one day love to park in his own driveway. But keeping the family on track, helping them to get ahead, is a priority that's never seriously questioned. Jim occasionally does the maths to come up with the number of days until he retires – surely, the kids'll be gone by then – but with the new government talking about changes to the pension, and increasing university fees, he has of late found himself downing a few more home-brews than usual.

Jim is a middle manager at the local council and he's good at it. His co-workers like him and his crew always meet their KPIs. Recently he's been putting in extra unpaid hours – just to be sure. Another productivity review is in progress. With an upcoming local government election and an abysmal financial report just published on the council website, the councillors – with hands on hearts and declarations of loyal service to the community – are once again talking about the unsustainable cost of labour. The fact that the councillors are mostly shonky real estate agents and local business operators is lost on the residents, who only want the rates kept low and the potholes filled quickly. Last year's scandal involving Alderman Price's late-night use of the chamber's twenty-foot-long jarrah table for sex and drugs with two prostitutes and a Chinese property investor is largely forgotten – especially since a threat of defamation stopped the local press in their tracks. There is no prize for guessing what these fat cats will slash and burn to get the books back in the black just to keep their arses in the chamber for another three years.

Taking a redundancy is simply not an option. A few years back, Jim and Janine sold their first home and borrowed a scary sum of money from the bank to move up the hill into a bigger and better house. The official story was all about catching those cool afternoon nor-easters that don't hit the old part of town down in the valley. The reality, though, and everyone knows it, is that the valley has gone to the dogs. Undesirable elements with their crime, drugs and feral kids seem to have spontaneously generated out of the fetid lowland air. The originals, the respectable working-class people who built this bloody town, have been steadily deserting their fibro and red-brick boxes, and if they haven't pissed off to Byron or Noosa, they've been moving into the exclusive estates that overlook the valley. The grand stone entrances, the instant gardens and the streets bearing the names of the very same native plants bulldozed out of the way for the Mac mansions mysteriously attract the bank-assisted upwardly mobile like flies to dung. Covenants dictating construction materials and minimum floor space supposedly guarantee a classier standard of neighbour, but with mandated internal access from garages with remote-controlled roller doors, it's a freak accident if anyone even lays eyes on, let alone bumps into, anyone else. Once at dinner, Michael asked who lived next door. He was greeted with unanimous ignorance and told to concentrate on the upcoming school exams.

The asbestos-riddled boxes down in the valley are now marketed as ideal for the first homebuyer, or as lucrative investment opportunities. By the dozens, they are knocked down so the quarter acre – once a patchwork of chook sheds, vegie gardens and beer-soaked barbecue areas – can be totally buried under a trio of cheaply constructed negatively geared villas. The new wave of landlords nestled up on the hill may cringe at the sight of all the single mums smoking plain-wrapped cigarettes bought with the baby bonus, but when the Centrelink rental assistance gets deposited into their bank accounts, they don't complain too much.

Jim is focusing on getting Michael into university, at all costs.

The family of five sits around the dinner table. The three kids perform their ritual of raising eyebrows as Dad performs his ritual of calling for heads to be bowed so he can say grace. Jim thanks God and then Mum for the real fancy meal. He expresses gratitude for the fact that they live in Australia and not some war-torn bloody hellhole overseas somewhere. Jim doesn't really believe in God, and his faith in Australia as the lucky country is slipping away like his self-funded super contributions, post-GFC. But with no left-wing salvation in sight, nor any inheritance on the horizon, he reasons, what harm can a prayer do?

Dinner is scoffed down in less than a tenth of the time it took Janine to create it. A thumbs-up from JJ and a kiss on the cheek from Jim as he heads off to his chair in the telly room are appreciated, but Janine wonders, would meat and three veg, or grilled cheese on toast for that matter, get the same reaction?

Before Jim can escape, Janine calls out, 'Jim, there's something we need to talk about as a family. Can you come back to the table, please?'

Janine feels sick in the stomach about how the family has yet to visit her parents, who moved into an aged-care facility two months ago. She needs to nail this down sooner rather than later. JJ declares that no one's allowed a weekend off till after Christmas; Kylie reminds everyone that Ma is a snob; and Michael's got soccer on Saturdays for the local club, and for reps on Sundays. Without saying, the family knows that Jim, after mowing the lawns, poisoning the weeds, and washing the car, just wants to spend his weekends with a few cold beers and the sports channels that he has to pay that Murdoch mongrel so much for. Nobody, even Janine to be honest, wants to sit for two hot hours in traffic on the new tollway.

On top of this, Janine's parents reverse-mortgaged their inner-city home to fund their upmarket aged care; the once-comforting prospect of a tidy inheritance is now fading fast and is a bit of a sore point. Jim holds back his resentment, and would never tell anyone how pissed off he is that medical advances are keeping the in-laws alive for longer and longer.

'So, Mum, you-you-you wipe old people's bums at work, right?' asks JJ, changing the subject.

'Yes, darling. I do.'

'And so-so-someone else is wiping Ma and Pa's bums ba-ba-ba-back there in the city?'

'JJ, I haven't finished my dinner yet,' says Kylie. She slams down her fork and pushes the plate to the centre of the new dining table that took Michael and Jim four hours and one Allen key to put together.

'Kylie! You'll scratch the table, darling. Yes, JJ, that is right,' says Janine in a seamless move from reprimand to affirmation.

'And to pay for getting th-th-their bums wiped in the city, M-M-M-Ma and Pa's house is being t-t-taken over by the bank?'

'I guess you could see it that way, JJ.'

'D-d-d-do they belong to that bank?'

'Yes, JJ, they belong to that bank.'

The conversation stops abruptly. The night before, the family dinner talk had centred around that bank. JJ was furious at being charged a $55 penalty fee because a computer glitch at his work with the pays meant his car insurance payment couldn't be debited. The news, that same day, of the bank posting a record profit in the billions of dollars really got JJ revved up.

Janine, with all good intent, only added to the fire by saying he was lucky to be able to own a car in the first place. Then, as JJ's stutter and tic escalated out of control, she really pushed a button when she declared, 'Well, that's just the way it is, James Junior. And I'm sorry about that, but there's nothing anyone can do about it.'

JJ was gobsmacked by his mother's total submission to what was, in his mind, nothing more than brazen theft. He left the table in disgust.

Tonight, he sits firmly in place sporting a satisfied expression which beams: now the boot's on the other foot, eh Mum?

Janine, realising the point made by her 'not so bright' son, starts to collect and stack the plates.

Jim breaks the ice with a loud fart. 'Better out than in, I say.'

'Oh Dad!'

'Oh Jim!'

Jim laughs and brings dinner to a close by declaring that they will all, 'Yes, all of us,' he nods at each of his offspring, 'will one day visit the oldies. Just not this weekend.'

Michael, oblivious to the family tension, insists that they all come up to his bedroom to check out Ronaldo the rat.

The family shuffle into the chaos of Michael's room and gather around the desk where the caged Ronaldo is racing at full speed on the treadmill. Michael states that he has observed Ronaldo now for six weeks and has calculated that he spends 92.27643801% of his waking hours running non-stop on that little wheel that goes absolutely nowhere.

'Aw, the poor thing. I wonder if he's happy,' whimpers Kylie.

'He doesn't know any better. He's just a rodent,' answers Jim.

The family stares trance-like at the running rat. It is a rare moment of quiet togetherness. Ronaldo, sensing the audience of primates, stops, and stares up at the five blank faces. Embarrassed and uncomfortable, the family snaps back into the present. They look around at each other and wake up to a pressing notion that they should be somewhere, doing something. Not here, but somewhere else. Not staring at a rat, but doing something else; something important, something meaningful.

Without comment, they all turn around and scamper out of the room.

Living Space

If you could watch this fellow building a living space under his home, you would admire many things. Firstly, the energy required to excavate such a volume of soil, clay and rock is impressive. The sheer persistence over many, many months is hard to dismiss. Most of all, consider the required skill set: to seal earthen floor and walls, to plumb in water and plumb out waste, to wire up for light, heat and air, and to do the meticulous work with wood and paint to make it all so habitable. His accomplishments are surely worthy of praise. The finished subterranean dwelling is so well done that you can imagine moving in yourself.

But this is not extra living space for a relative or a renter. It is not even a bunker for safe haven in the event of a catastrophic event. It is a dungeon, a prison, a hellhole if you want to get dramatic. He's built it for the twelve-year-old girl who lives across the street. You see, she has to be saved, both from her dirty mother and from the evil world that will foul her unblemished body and soul.

This fellow, this energetic, industrious, highly skilled fellow, knows the girl well. He doesn't know her name but he's been watching her for years. Watching her dance in her bedroom, watching her brush her hair in front of the mirror on her dresser, watching her talk to a teddy bear that is slowly falling apart, and watching her write secret thoughts and dreams into a journal with a sky-blue velour cover.

She is in her first year of high school now. She is ready. Too much longer with that mother and she will be too damaged to save.

He knows, because he's been watching the mother as well. Binoculars, lace curtains and directly opposing mirror-imaged terraced housing makes it all so easy. The two upstairs bedrooms like twin television screens for daily and nightly viewing. The despicable mother has a lover, not the girl's father of course, whom she brings home on random nights to fuck. Bold as brass they do it. And on the nights he is not there she uses that silver thing between her legs. He watches and masturbates, imagines spilling his seed onto her face and breasts.

She will burn in hell, not a moment in purgatory for that harlot, he thinks. If you questioned him, though, he has Old Testament impunity. The girl must be saved from the abominations of modern life. He will see to it that she will only ever know one man. He will quarantine her from the sickness of a world beckoning apocalypse. He imagines judgement day when there will be joyous celebration of his visionary actions – and a commensurate heavenly reward awaiting. He has dreamt of marrying the girl, with God, Jesus and Mother Mary all on the front pew. Saint Peter will perform the sacred rite.

If you watch this fellow in the world at large, you would admire his comings and goings. Every Wednesday, you would see him visit his mother in the nursing home. He brings her magazines and Columbine toffees. He talks kindly and gratefully to the staff. He is well groomed and neatly dressed. On his way home, he stops at the local grocery store to buy his humble provisions. Simple fare for a man of minimal needs. On Sundays, he walks up the hill to attend church, and afterwards he meets for Bible studies with the acolyte and a dwindling number of the faithful. The inevitable wrath of God is discussed with ever increasing fervour. There is a shared belief that Jesus must soon return. Shared beliefs are comforting, even for this practical, single man.

But if you watch this fellow very carefully – and mind you, no one does – you would be curious about his Friday habits. On this day, he reverses his immaculately clean panel van out the back gate and into the laneway that runs along behind the row of terraces. He drives twenty-five kilometres in traffic, soothed by Classic FM, to a Supa-Centre where no one knows him from Barabbas. This is where he gets the building materials, bit by bit. And if you follow him into the other stores and not just the hardware, you would be alarmed by his more recent purchases: girls' clothes, Vaseline, a hairbrush, leather belts, sets of white single bed linen, rope, a large pack of sanitary pads, duct tape, soaps, sleeping pills and a teddy bear.

Checkout operators don't notice what they scan. Their heads are full of numbers connected to rostered hours, casual penalty rates, rent increases, and the price of a single unit of alcohol compared to a case. But if you were taking notice, being the amateur sleuth you always knew you'd be good at, you would be scribbling in your notebook, taking black and white photos through telephoto lenses, and talking into a fancy recording machine. But you aren't investigating anything, no one is, at least not with this fellow – no, let's give up this fellow business: he's a man, a strange and disturbed man.

There is a pet shop at the Supa-Centre and they have kittens and all the stuff you need to keep them fluffy and cute. Why has he gone in there?

It is school holidays and the tainted mother – tight skirt and stockings noted – is giving instructions to the girl to stay at home. He sees the words being mouthed from painted lips through his binoculars set on zoom. He puts the pink collar with a bell on the kitten and waits till nine-thirty a.m. The street is quietest then.

The terrace houses all have small front yards boxed in by the house and three waist-high brick fences. The front fences are punctuated by gates of various descriptions. Some yards have a small square of grass, others are paved or pebbled. This day, most of them are covered in fallen leaves from the plane trees planted by the council many years before. A great street tree, the residents enjoy shade in summer and sun in winter. The slow lifting and cracking of the asphalt pavement and the concrete curbing by expanding roots was never considered way back when this working-class suburb was planned.

He checks that the street is empty and that no one is at a window. He crosses the road and lowers the unfed kitten over the solid timber gate and into the young girl's yard. He casually walks on a bit down that side of the street. No one is around, no one sees him. He crosses back over to his side, and walks home, back to his chair behind the lace curtain. The postman will be coming soon.

The girl is watching television when the squeal of motor scooter brakes signals mail. She is allowed to get the mail, that has been agreed. After all, she is twelve, and she is in high school. She skips outside and over to the letter box. It's only bills, it's always only bills. Never anything for her. But it's an outing of sorts. She looks up and sees blue, her favourite colour, and she feels the sharp, cold wind on her cheeks.

She turns back towards the door and hears the crying kitten. She sees it there, all so helpless and needy. She picks it up and holds it in front of her face. It is all black with a white patch over one eye. She checks the collar, no name or phone number, just a bell. She cuddles it. She walks back to the gate and looks up and down the street.

He watches all of this and smiles. Months – no, years really – of planning are coming to fruition. If you could see his face, you would see the sense of accomplishment, the gratification earned through hard work and persistence. And if you could see the swelling lump in the fly of his pants, you would feel sick and maybe want to know not a thing more.

The girl with the kitten hears something. She walks over to the small fence dividing her front yard from next door's. There is six-year-old Melody Sparks, the pesky next-door neighbour wanting to hold the kitten.

The man with binoculars stands up. Shouldn't that little imp be in child care? Like she is every weekday of the school holidays when the mother goes to work, even though the father stays home smoking pot and who knows what else. The father should be asleep; it's only nine forty-five. Is he awake and watching all this? Has the world been turned upside down?

The man becomes nervy, and watches intently. He steps left and then right as though a slight change in angle will bring an end to this unacceptable reality. He gets down on his knees, and keeps watching. His girl is talking now to the six-year-old.

He prays out loud, 'God, why do you thwart me so?'

The girl with the kitten starts yelling at her young neighbour. Melody Sparks looks down at her chest and pulses with sobbing. The twelve-year-old keeps going, leans further forward and spits out more and more words until the little girl, devastated, runs back inside.

The kneeling man thanks God and stands up. The girl with the kitten goes back inside her house. He can't see where she is. She must be out back in the ground-floor kitchen, likely getting a saucer and milk.

At an angle, the man can just see a slice of the action happening next door. Upstairs in the parents' bedroom, the bottom half of the father's legs can be seen stretched out on the bed. Melody is there next to him, crying, wanting comfort. A pillow hits her in the face and she runs away. The man can't see into Melody's bedroom, but she is there; it is her safe haven.

The man goes underground to inspect his handiwork. He opens the top drawer of a lowboy and runs his hands over the white cotton underwear. The plan is back on track. The warmth is back in his groin.

Ten twelve a.m. The angry father's legs can still be seen horizontal on the bed. Melody is nowhere. Time now to save the twelve-year-old before the mother, high school and the world at large corrupt her any further. Those words of venom she spat over the fence to such a small defenceless child, clear evidence that no further delay can be allowed.

He crosses the street, looks around, opens the gate and walks through fallen leaves to her front door. He knocks quietly, and looks around again. No one is watching.

'I can't open the door, I am not allowed to,' comes the voice from inside.

'I'm not a stranger. I live across the street and I've lost my kitten. Have you seen it?'

All well intentioned motherly caution blows away in a willy-willy that twists down the street picking up leaves and dust. She opens the door, holding the kitten. He lets her carry it across the road and in through his door. She agrees to a hot chocolate while she watches the kitten eating pilchards that come in a tiny tin especially for younger cats. She gets sleepy as she watches the kitten playing with a toy mouse in a special pen the man says he built himself.

The quiet, religious, clearly sick man rereads the label on the bottle of pills and pours his young guest, this perfect, delicate child, a second cup.

A missing child is news for what, a week or two? Nationally, that might be the case. Maybe it's talked about for six months or so in the local suburb. But then the tragedy is forgotten, too painful to keep bringing up, too much of a mystery to worry one's head over. Forgotten by everyone, except the mother of course.

If you watched the man with the binoculars watching the grieving mother, and what he did with his genitals as she wept and howled, you might literally be sick, but you would surely be moved like all normal humans would be moved, and want, at whatever cost, for him to be caught and to be punished. Your choice of punishment would likely depend on your own life experiences, but that deep-seated desire for revenge, the ineluctable need for justice, it's there in your DNA.

The police and the media failed to find even one lead, and the mother eventually moved. It was the house and the street, and the pained looks from concerned neighbours, and the whispers and pointing by those at a distance, that drove her away. The daughter's empty upstairs bedroom was an unbearable hole in her universe. She would keep her daughter's clothes and belongings; she could smell them and hope.

To spare you the agony of seeing the horrors that went on in that home-made prison underneath the religious man's neat and tidy terrace house, you can take some solace from the fact that she ate well and was kept clean, and she was educated. Sure the underground curriculum was all about God's plan for the meek, and his plan for those infected by the devil, including her mother. But at least she was allowed to read the Bible when alone; it helped to direct her mind onto something other than the world that was taken away from her. The girl had the Bible and the kitten, fast becoming a cat, and finally, after lots of pleading and good behaviour, some pens and a book to journal in. The good behaviour included her calling him Brother, and admitting that her mother was a whore. She never got to know his real name, and he only ever called her Child.

The journal was maybe not such a great idea. When he read it after she had a week of entries, he erupted into such a fury that the leather belts were taken off the hooks on the wall and used once again, this time in a much more painful way. From then on, she wrote only in her mind.

There is one picture on one wall in her sunless living space. It's that one of Jesus – you know, the one where he sports a face of serenity and infinite love, the one where his soft hands held gently out in front welcome you into his embrace, an embrace where you'd have to nestle up next to his heart, which is glowing and positioned on the outside of his robed chest. It's a ridiculous caricature. However, she would look at it to help her sleep after her keeper's red and sweaty face left, after the nightly rituals he performed on top of her.

When the baby came, the girl found it easier to forget the fears and memories that made the days so long and the nights so haunting. The man brought down baby clothes, nappies, creams, liquid soap, bibs, and a small bath and a bassinet. He held the child with a gentleness that she had never experienced, and his furies and sermons lessened somewhat in intensity. Time passed more quickly, and when the baby grew some, the underground library expanded from one book to several. These precious items, purposed for the toddler, shone with pictures of Moses in a basket on a river, with animals walking onto Noah's Ark, and a baby Jesus in the arms of Mary on a donkey in the desert. And then paper and crayons came. A journal could be started again, a secret journal this time.

Melody Sparks is fourteen and smoking in the laneway that runs behind the row of terraces opposite her home. She is trying to master what her friend calls a Scotch drawback. She can't quite coordinate the pushing out of smoke from the mouth with the simultaneous breathing in through the nostrils. She flicks the cigarette butt away and reaches into her pocket for the gum that today she has forgotten. 'Fuck it,' she says under her tarry breath. She kicks the ground and looks up into the sky for an idea.

Then she sees it. A cat inside on a windowsill in the terrace house that must be almost exactly opposite her own. A black cat with a white patch over one eye, arching its back.

A once-familiar, then forgotten, uneasy feeling sweeps through her body. Melody is six again. That girl with the kitten is yelling at her, calling her ugly and fat. Then telling her to disappear. That girl was always mean. What was her name again? I should know, she thinks. She was famous when she was the one that disappeared.

It is the only time Melody can recall a wish coming true. A wish that she could never tell anyone.

She can hear the mother screaming next door, tall police men and women standing in her lounge room, and people all over town and at her school, weeping and shaking their heads. She sees the wall of flowers and candles piled up against the head-high fence next door. There are teddy bears as well that she wants to take home for herself.

That was when she stopped speaking for six months. Until they took her to a man with a swinging crystal, who got her words back, but nothing of use for the investigation.

What was her name again?

Melody Sparks walks straight into the backyard of the terrace house with the cat. She knows the other occupant, the quiet man you hardly notice, and she knows he must be at church – it's Sunday. Her father calls him a God-botherer and pointed at him one Sabbath when he walked past their house. 'Go on,' he said with his morning fag stuck to his bottom lip, 'go and talk in tongues, you freak!'

Melody sees the panel van, shiny and with freshly blacked tyres, sitting under a simple carport. On the other side of the yard is a shed. It's locked but she knows how to open it. She's done it before with her friend, the one who smokes so sophisticated like. You just pop the door out of its tracks, and the lock becomes a hinge. They would say that and laugh every time they did it.

This is the first time Melody has done a B and E by herself – it's liberating not being the apprentice. Something primal drives Melody to get inside and find the girl who disappeared. What, ten years ago? No, she does the maths, it was eight years. She finds a crowbar in the dark petrol-smelling space of the busted-open shed.

If you are watching Melody right now, you might think, delinquent. Or, you might be amazed by how skilfully and forcefully she prises open the back door of the terrace house with that bar. But you will without a doubt be impressed by her sheer single-mindedness.

This place is a mirror image of her own house. With an imprinted spatial awareness, she moves about without having to think. Melody scans the kitchen and bathroom out the back part of the ground floor. She moves into the front living room. She has never seen such a clean and tidy house – well, not in real life anyway, maybe in ads on telly.

No one downstairs.

She bounds up the carpeted staircase, crowbar in hand, to where she knows two bedrooms will be found. She enters the first bedroom to find a bed, a wardrobe and a single cross on the wall. Neat and clean, but so minimal she wonders if that man sleeps in here.

The next bedroom has even less furnishings; there is a small desk with some paperwork on it. Then centred in front of the window that overlooks Melody's street is a simple wooden chair with a pair of binoculars hanging off the backrest. This window, like every other window in the house, is curtained with white lace. She walks over to the window and looks out to see, directly in front, her next-door neighbour's place. To the right, she can see her own home; the angle hides her own bedroom from view but she can see her father's legs on the bed in her parent's room. Melody wants to smash something with the bar in her hand. She raises it up to shoulder height and the cat walks into the room and meows. It's the same cat, I know it, she thinks.

She races downstairs, circling around all the rooms again. No one is here. Then she hears it, a baby's cry. The muffled sound came from under the floor, but unmistakeably a baby's cry. Then she hears it again.

If you can see Melody now, you are no longer thinking delinquent. You are barracking for her to find the missing child, now a woman, with a baby who has never seen the sky or a tree. You are cheering as she lifts the rug in the hallway to find a trapdoor. You call her Clever Girl, as she deftly unlocks the recessed latch on the trapdoor. And you hold your hands to your face as she leaves the crowbar behind on the hallway floor and descends into the living space underneath the freak's terrace house.

Melody stops at the bottom of the wooden staircase to see a pregnant woman of twenty, cradling a crying baby in her left arm and shielding a boy of six into her right side. The boy is sneaking looks at the intruder in between hiding his face into the side of his mother's bulging belly.

Melody scans the room. It is too much to comprehend, but it's real and it is stark. It is all white and artificially lit. And everything is screaming at Melody to get everyone out before that monster comes home from church.

'Come on, let's go,' she says directly into the eyes of the silent woman.

Nothing moves.

'Don't you remember me? Melody? I live next door to you across the street. Oh, well, I did. Remember?'

Still nothing moves or speaks.

'Come on! Now! Quick let's go!' says Melody more intensely, more authoritatively.

The woman speaks. 'I do remember you, of course I do. Now get out of here. Get out and leave us be.'

Melody takes a step back.

The woman leans forward and a look of fury comes over her face. 'This is my home. How dare you trespass on God's own soil. Leave and repent your sins, and never, never speak of this to anyone.'

What do you want Melody to do now? Our fourteen-year-old streetwise accidental hero.

Get the fuck out of there and call the police, you say. Get out now before the religious freak returns and finds the crowbar on the floor next the open trapdoor.

Melody stands still and speechless. She hasn't heard you.

Melody doesn't need to hear you. She can hear enough voices in her head, thank you very much. Her angry father, her apologising mother, the critical teachers at school, the pretentious rich kids on the bus, the police warning her about the bashings in Juvey, the judge issuing the penalty for shoplifting – she has heard it all.

But mostly, she hears the voice of the girl with the black kitten with a white patch over one eye. That venomous voice from eight years ago, the most hurtful voice of all.

Melody leans forward and spits in the face of the woman protecting her offspring. Slowly, calmly and with perfect enunciation, Melody says, 'Rot in hell, you fucking bitch.'

Then she turns and leaves the living space built by that fellow with all that energy, persistence and surprising skill.

Homo correctus

Enrico will be losing his job soon. He is suspended at the moment but termination is inevitable. The curator told him so. The embarrassing CCTV footage shows him dozing off while the thieves hide behind the columns just before closing time. Overnight, they got to work dismantling the GOLGBTIA's most expensive acquisition to date, *Homo correctus*. The impending unemployment is one thing, the shame at falling asleep on the job is another. And headlines such as GLASS HALF GONE, STATUE GOES BYE-BYES, SNOOZERS ARE LOSERS and CATNAP CATASTROPHE mock Enrico at every turn.

Some people speak the acronym assigned to the Gallery of Lesbian, Gay, Bisexual, Transexual, Intersexual Art in an attempt to appear culturally enlightened. 'Have you seen the latest exhibition at the Golgbtia,' they say. It sounds like they have two plums from one of the many sculptures of male genitalia found in the gallery stuffed into their mouths. Don't worry, there's plenty of female genitalia on display as well. The curator ensures that the gallery maintains a balanced representation of all the queer manifestations.

The two-million-dollar price tag for *Homo correctus* did raise some tattooed eyebrows, but to acquire a major work done by a world-renowned intersexual artist made it worth every rainbow-coloured cent. Not that the hard right neo-conservatives would agree. They went ballistic about the latest abomination of political correctness purchased with taxpayers' money. Not that they pay any tax if they can help it. The controversy alone attracted visitors by the thousands to the GOLGBTIA – say it any way you wish. The purchase price was quickly recouped, and the usually vociferous leader of the opposition conservative party, who had called for a boycott by all decent folk, was red-faced and desperately needing a straw man.

Whatever *Homo correctus* was, it wasn't made of straw. And it wasn't a man. It was divided right through the middle from the crown of the head down to the perineum. Perfectly symmetrical. The right side as you look at it, being the left side anatomically, was made of a polymer material that looked freakishly real. The array of fleshy tones, the hairs attached individually, the finger- and toenails and the moist eye were so real that many people wanted to touch it. One of Enrico's main duties was to ensure that visitors remained outside the yellow circle taped onto the terrazzo marble floor. The other half of *Homo correctus*, the anatomically right side, was glass and was filled with a multi-coloured liquid in a state of continual motion. The figure was no doubt modelled on Da Vinci's *Vitruvian Man*, but it had one breast, on the fleshy half, one testicle, on the glass half, and the cylindrical protuberance from the groin that was divided perfectly longitudinally and thus composed of both glass and polymer flesh, was either a large clitoris or small penis. And that was the point, excuse the pun.

The CCTV footage reveals the events of that day. If you watch it on 8x fast forward, you not only get the gist of it all, you can have a bit of a laugh as well. It's like a Benny Hill skit. It's hard not to hear 'Yakety Sax' in your head as you watch it. Enrico – who, by the way, lied that he was bisexual to get the security officer position in the first place (funny how things have changed) – is the star of the show.

The time clock at the bottom shows that at eight fifty-five a.m. Enrico brushes his hair, straightens his epaulettes and flicks the switch that starts the multicoloured fluid circulating in the glass half of *Homo correctus*. He is the consummate professional. As the day rolls on and the crowds roll in, Enrico is busy skirting around all over the place controlling and educating the masses. At times, Enrico is reminding patrons about the rules, such as no photography, or to stay behind the yellow line on the floor. At other times he is more casual and one would assume he is offering his own amateurish understanding of the two-million-dollar gender-challenging sculpture. At one point you can watch Enrico step quickly inside the circle to herd an escaped toddler back to an apologising parent.

The clock shows that from twelve to twelve forty-five p.m., Enrico is replaced by another security person. One might wonder what Enrico enjoyed for his last lunch in employment.

Fast forward 16x now and the afternoon is pretty much a symmetrical repeat of the morning: a continuous snake-like mass of human bodies slithering in, coiling around the sculpture and sliding out, all the while one figure, Enrico, buzzing around all over the place. All the while *Homo correctus* standing arms out wide like God in the middle.

Slow the tape down now, maybe just 2x fast forward. It is getting near to the end of the day. If you look closely, you will see that the crowd is thinning and many patrons are carrying umbrellas, and there is the occasional flicker on the screen – there had been a storm that day. It hit the city at four p.m. It was one of those new climate-change storms – that is, record breaking. It dropped ten years' worth of rain in ten minutes – well, that is an exaggeration, but it was definitely greater than a cats and dogs level of intensity. By four-twenty, the gallery is nearly empty. Enrico for the first time all day sits down on the chair in the corner. Zoom in and look at his face; his eyes are closed. Zoom out and look at the two shapes, one male and one female secreting themselves behind the two Doric columns that stand either side of the room's exit. At four thirty-two, Enrico stirs, looks at his watch, shakes his head, stands up and switches off the liquid moving machine inside the glass half of *Homo correctus,* switches off the lights and exits.

The rest is art theft history. The two thieves, in their attempts to steal this controversial human-sized work of expensive art, broke the bastard/bitch. Slippery, oily, multicoloured fluid, and the polymer half of the sculpture were found by a cleaner at four twenty-two the next morning. As the tabloid said, GLASS HALF EMPTIED.

The Friends of the Gallery of Lesbian, Gay, Bisexual, Transexual,

Intersexual Art, who call themselves Golgbtians, have offered a reward for information leading to the arrest of the thieves and the safe return of the glass half of *Homo correctus*. Nobody has come forward. The police have given up.

Enrico has already applied for a job as night-watchman at K-Mart. If he gets it, he knows he will be on probation. He is consuming vast quantities of No-Doze and practising staying awake all night. He is doing well, but had a bit of trouble signing his name the other day due to the shakes. He is always optimistic, a glass-half-full kind of guy, even though he is known as the glass-half-gone dude.

Enrico's wife was never happy that he claimed to be bisexual just to get a job. She's a glass half empty kind. And she believes in karma. She'll even give the universe bit of shove at times to make sure its universal laws of justice are employed. And she has no idea what she is going to do with that empty half glass human figurine she has hidden under a bolt of blue velvet in the sewing room.

Plaza Life

When Sally saw the images of carnage on the news channel, she didn't think of Yousef at first. She had tried to erase him from her mind. She thought instead about how she'd only been on the Stortorget plaza, what was it, six months ago? Yes, it was in June, high season. Now there was blood in the snow at the time of peace on earth and goodwill to all men. Of course it was labelled a terror attack. Any event that could justify ramping up the war machine was getting that label these days.

Backpacking through Europe is a rite of passage for middle-class teenagers on their so-called gap year. The same activity for Syrian refugees is no holiday. For Sally, neither a teenager nor refugee, her trip was the fruition of a goal she set herself while studying photography at uni and working cash-in-hand at a harbourside café. When she found her boyfriend in bed with her best friend, just after final exams, everything fell into place. No excuse not to go, now. Even better going by myself.

She admits now that she went a bit wild while OS. 'For goodness sake,' she pleads, 'I was faithful to that dickhead for what, ten bloody years? Couldn't blame me for hooking up with one or two men, could you?'

'One or two?'

'Well, maybe a few more than that.'

Sweden was the last stop on her itinerary. Yousef was definitely the last casual acquaintance.

'He was the one who I let have his way with me in that laneway – and it was in the middle of the day! Oh my God, what was I thinking?'

Men are easy prey. You just let them think they are the hunters.

They like a bit of a chase. Be it Stockholm, London, Berlin or Prague, there's always one who'll take the bait. Sally couldn't come at the new wave of feminism that was proclaiming every man as a rapist – she'd seen some of her female uni mates in action. She didn't realise it at the time, but she was being trained for her Europe romp. Though she never thought she'd be ravaged by an Arab in Sweden; she would have predicted a Viking type on that leg of her journey.

Yousef was sitting on one of those plaza benches pretending to watch the tourists and the pigeons. He was making mental notes of the bollards, adjoining roads and lanes; estimating building heights; counting targets; scheming pandemonium. He dare not bring out a camera. He was of middle-eastern appearance, he wore a *taqiyah*, and since Nice and London and Brussels, etc etera, et cetera, Stortorget was rimmed with security guards and closed-circuit cameras.

Just look. Memorise. Write notes and make diagrams back in the pension, he told himself. He looked with contempt at the blonde girl casually snapping pictures with impunity. The imam was right: the world is full of injustice, the West is debauched. Look at the way she is dressed. A harlot, no question. Look how she twirls and giggles as she snaps the plaza from all angles. She is the enemy, a servant of evil.

Sally thought about an exhibition she could put on when she got back to Sydney. Plaza Life she would call it. These photos of Stortorget could be a feature. Maybe one of the close-up shots of the plaque above the door of number 20 could be on the invitation card. What is the inscription? *Befiehl dem Herrn deine Wege und hoffe auf ihn, er wirds wohl machen.* Yes, sufficiently cryptic. That would do – German language on a Swedish building, religious sentiment in a secular nation. Perfect. Coffee time.

'May I join you?' asked Yousef.

'Sure.'

He was good-looking and the British accent was unexpected in this context.

'I am most envious of your freedom.'

'What do you mean?' asked Sally.

'There is no way I could stand out in middle of the plaza and take photographs like you just did.'

'Really?'

'Yes, really.'

Yousef explained how he was watched everywhere he went. Sally professed her empathy for Muslim people in this day and age. Yousef asked if she could email him the photos she just took. Sally did it then and there on the spot. Bluetooth and wifi making it all possible.

'You are most kind, Sally. I wish I could do something for you.'

'Can you walk me down the laneway?' she asked. Her cheeky blue eyes invited something else.

Six days later, Sally did get her intimate Viking encounter: a Nordic doctor diagnosed anal gonorrhoea.

Yousef didn't tell her he was going to go there, but in that recessed doorway she did turn around and lift her skirt to reveal she was not wearing underwear. And even though he was rougher than she liked and she'd never had or particularly wanted it that way before, she put it all down as a part of her adventure, part of her new carefree self. Growing up finally, by travelling the world and indulging in new experiences. Anal sex? Why not? Getting the clap, though?

The worst thing of all was the email reply she got from Yousef after she dutifully informed him of the disease. She deleted it immediately, but the words *slut, pig* and *superbug* still flash back into her mind from time to time. It wasn't a superbug, thank God – or perhaps in this case, thank Allah.

The traditional Christmas market at Stortorget draws large crowds. Lots of tourists, and lots of local families. It's one of those must-do things, if you happen to be in Stockholm during Yuletide. Many people mistook the initial explosions as part of the festivities. But the men charging through the crowd, slashing away with knifes taped to their hands left no doubt as to what was happening. Another attack.

Isis claiming responsibility. Western leaders declaring, they will never defeat us. No serious analysis, just lazy limbic reptilian reaction. We get on with life as normal. Sure.

Sally's Plaza Life exhibition preparation had all been in vain. Months of editing and curating her shots from all over Europe, a waste of time. Hours and hours in front of the computer. Stortorget, the centrepiece, now joining a list of places never again to be celebrated or associated with joy and beauty. She looks at the translation of the famous inscription above Number 20 Stortoget Square that she did decide to use as the theme for her big debut as a photographer: 'Commit thy way unto the Lord; trust also in Him, and He will bring it to pass.' What a joke, she thought. I never should have put a religious slant on this. I'm an atheist. This must be karma. I'll never make it as a photographer.

Some moments later, she thought, what an ungrateful and callous person I am. People are dead, and I'm only thinking of myself.

She looked back to the television. The coverage was horrific and relentless. Over and over again. It had been planned for months, they said. Bluetooth and wifi making it all possible, they added. A vision of sitting in the Scandinavian sun, sipping coffee and emailing photos flashed into Sally's mind. She dry-retched.

Yousef's face appeared on the television screen just as there was a knock on her door.

F#minor

'A schooner of Guinness, please.'

The blackboard open-mike night had been going since six o'clock. Now seven, Andy, peering at the handwritten chalk list, worked out that the duo on stage must be Sid and Margaret. Margaret had a washboard hanging round her neck, metal thimbles on her fingers and a voice that would frighten small children. Sid strummed a dread-nought steel acoustic guitar with thick and calloused fingers. Oh my God, I hope this isn't folk night, thought Andy.

Not that he hated folk – he had even written some of it himself – but a whole night of three chord renditions covering Woody Guthrie, Pete Seeger and the likes would dictate one quick beer and a surreptitious exit.

Andy looked around the room and the tension in his shoulders eased. Phew – it was obviously not folk night. The room contained a sufficient quota of people under sixty to dismiss the horror of a night of endless working-class angst belted out in fake Stateside twang. One patron, probably in his early thirties, sported dreadlocks and a beard and had a guitar case propped up next to his seat. His girlfriend, dressed in nuevo-rockabilly style, sat next to him holding his hand and looking fashionably uninterested in the world. Andy thought they wouldn't have even heard of Woody Guthrie, let alone understood the concept of 'power in a union'.

According to the list, following the ageing folk duo would be Dan B, then Full Circle, then Sally Springer, then Funk Park. Under that was an unfilled blank slot and then below that, down the bottom in differentiating blue chalk, was Purple Craze. Andy knew of them. They were a young trio that did all-Hendrix covers. After cutting their teeth in white chalk on previous open-mike nights, they had been invited back to fill the final slot, a forty-five-minute set that would close the night. Knowing he would most likely be home watching television by the time Purple Haze had their feedback howling, Andy was nonetheless happy that a group of young locals were getting a go.

Andy felt uncomfortable and conspicuous in places like this. At home, or in the library, or even in a shopping centre, he had begun to enjoy his own company. After the decades of playing husband and family man came to a sudden end, solitude had been more difficult to adjust to than he ever imagined. At first it was so confronting that he even tried his hand at internet dating. A long and tedious string of once-only coffee dates compelled Andy to take himself off the singles market. He accepted that he might be single for a long time – maybe that was just what he needed. The one downfall was going out at night. Even if it was just to the movies, but more so at nightspots, Andy felt self-conscious and out of place. People hung out in couples or groups and never invited lone strangers into their company. The few solo specimens who did venture out were more often than not of the 'bit odd' variety – certainly not the sort you wanted to make new friends with. After dark, a low profile was needed, a quiet corner and a mobile phone to casually stare into and disappear.

Andy managed not to wince visibly at Sid's and Margaret's amateurish performance. Every song was the standard twelve-bar format, and every song was in the key of G. Margaret's washboard was way too loud but it still didn't manage to drown out Sid's lack of rhythm on the guitar. The entertainment value, if any, was in the comedy of the whole affair. Margaret's efforts to get Sid back on beat included some serious foot stomping, accompanied by an hilariously exaggerated swaying of her rather large hips, and a death stare that no doubt implied, 'You old fool, don't you dare think you're getting sex tonight.' Not that that was on the cards – Margaret had dried up many years ago, when the hot flushes and mood swings obliterated her once-healthy libido. Sid, to his credit, had mastered the art of being celibate and pussy whipped, and, unperturbed, was having a ball up there on the stage.

'Put your hands together one more time for Sid and Margaret.'

The patrons politely clapped. One person, surely glad it was over, let out a four-fingers-in-the-mouth whistle.

'Hang around, folks, and thank you all for coming along tonight. We'll only be a few minutes for our next guest.' The hyped-up MC looked at his clipboard and in full show business voice announced, 'All the way from Brisbane, Australia, the one and only uber-cool…Dan B.'

Uber? Who in their right minds says uber?

It was clear now that the man with the dreadlocks and the non-chalant girlfriend that Andy had spotted earlier was the one and only Dan B himself. At the sound of his name, his heavily tattooed offsider, who actually looked a lot like Betty Boop, broke out of her carefully manufactured coolness and let rip an embarrassing 'Whoop.'

In the short break between acts, Andy slid up to the bar for another schooner. The drink provided euphoria and anxiety alleviation, but most importantly it was another object, like the phone, to distract one from engagement with the seemingly hostile crowd. Having a glass in front of you, to caress with idle hands and to half hide your face when raised to the mouth, was perfect for remaining incognito in the corner.

Dan B opened his guitar case to reveal one of those now ubiquitous lap steel guitars. As he set himself up on the stage, the not yet used didgeridoo, set up on a stand, divulged its purpose. After getting himself prepped, with a sound check of his stomp box, a few blows into the didge and some final open G tuning of the guitar, Dan B launched into his set. Andy wanted Sid and Margaret back. This guy was a pretentious clone, the type that was cropping up all over the place these days. The riffs, song structures and lyrical ideas were all blatant rip-offs of the trendy roots style made famous by Xavier Rudd and John Butler. Already so 'yesterday', and boring, it didn't stop his girlfriend and a few other hipsters who had come just for Dan from whistling and hollering 'Dan the man' at the end of each of his songs. Andy sat steadfast even though the second schooner was gone well before the end of Dan B's first song.

At the twenty-minute mark, the MC edged up onto stage left with a clipboard positioned prominently on his hip. He looked at his watch and then held it out towards centre stage. Dan got the signal and finished off his last song – if you could call it a song, that is. It was more like a self-indulgent seven-minute masturbation around one chord, littered with irritating white man cockatoo calls screamed through the didgeridoo. To cap it off, his entourage rudely shouted over the MC, demanding more. Surely these people know there are no encores on an open-mike night? Andy considered going home there and then.

Dan B exited the stage to bathe in the glory lavished on him by his BYO cronies.

Full Circle began their set up. The sight of a bass, a simple drum kit and a trumpet put an end to Andy's urge to run away. He loved bass guitar when it was played well, and a trumpet certainly added some curiosity factor – so let's just see. Schooner number three was soothing Andy's solo man self-consciousness, and the effect of alcohol on the rest of the joint was nurturing a more congenial buzz. You could disappear now. You could even put away the mobile phone and look around without fear.

Full Circle were a hoot. They played five energy packed funky covers. Their Earth Wind and Fire cover got four women up onto the dance floor, and those still seated were tapping feet, clapping hands and rocking away to the infectious grooves. Andy smiled, closed his eyes, and let the music enter his soul. It was these moments that reminded him of the power of music to soothe, to emote, to change in a heartbeat the coldness of the world. When the band moved seamlessly into a Red Hot Chili Peppers number, which Andy surmised would be their last, he felt so relaxed and light he even contemplated getting up from the corner and mingling.

'Well, well, well, now that got you rocking, eh?' The MC requested another round of applause for the band and pre-empted the imminence of the next act, Sally Springer.

Scanning the room, Andy couldn't spot a Sally and with a full bladder headed off to the toilet. After enjoying the unique pleasure of urination, he walked to the outdoor smoking area provided by the club for the nicotine addicts who still defied society's relentless pressures to quit. Andy hadn't smoked for ten years but he still enjoyed the odd whiff of tobacco and usually found smokers to be a more welcoming mob. You never know, he might actually talk to someone tonight. Nothing like some funk and soul to boost one's outlook on life.

The smoking area was occupied by one wrinkled and crumpled man who was talking to his beer and several hundred fag ends overflowing from the single ashtray. Andy turned round quickly before he got caught up in a conversation that would require a lie, or worse, to extract himself from. He headed back to his corner table, giving up on the brief fantasy of any social interaction tonight. That was fine; he was settled enough now to relax and simply enjoy the music. He didn't even need another beer.

The MC, himself loosened up now by several bourbon and Cokes, introduced, '...all the way from Bundaberg Queeeeeensland...Sally ... Springaaa!'

The plainly dressed woman in her mid-forties, plus or minus a decade, it was hard to tell, stepped up to the microphone and said one word, 'Lost'. She took a step back and, on her nylon-stringed classical guitar, strummed a full barre F sharp minor and let it ring.

Andy felt the rush of neurotransmitters. Before he could make sense of what was happening, Sally launched into a song that started tearing him apart. The minor key, the haunting chord sequence and the heartfelt story of lost love, dreams and children leaving home, raised goosebumps and mixed feelings simultaneously. The middle eight's venture into the painful search for the self only added to the disturbing aura created by this unpretentious songstress.

Andy sat motionless at his dimly lit station. The wreckage of his life was being exhumed and laid bare for all to hear by a woman he had never met. The melancholy in her voice, the way she stood, the long skilful fingers on the neck of the guitar, her eyes and wild hair, mesmerised and scared him at the same time. At the end of her second song, she laughed and with genuine warmth thanked the crowd.

'Did she just look straight at me?' Andy thought to himself.

The room started to spin and, for the life of him, Andy could not get a grip. He had to get out of there. Head down he skirted around the back edges of the room and out into the night.

Dan B and his crew were smoking pot and wallowing in their own self-importance on the footpath. They wouldn't think twice about listening to anyone else, so Andy pushed passed them unconcerned, feeling no need for politeness with this self obsessed gang.

'Hey, man, chill out.'

Andy didn't respond, his mind was awash with painful memories and visions of Sally Springer. 'It was that bloody F sharp minor,' he said to himself. 'It does it every time.'

Stomach This

I get nervous at smorgasbords. I want to eat everything. Though I endeavour to take the smallest of portions of all on offer, my plate still ends up being embarrassingly overloaded. Then a deeply rooted etiquette requiring me to eat everything on the plate results in what I believe is now called a food coma.

Lou has an idea. 'Just sample the foods you haven't eaten before, or the ones you haven't eaten for a while. Surely you don't need to try the corned beef tonight.'

She smiles a familiar smile. It's the I-am-your-wife and, yes, sometimes-I-have-to-mother-you smile.

But the corned beef is rolled into little cylinders and a silver dish next to the platter contains a condiment of unknown origin and ingredients. I hide two slices of meat and a dollop of the mystery pickle under a big lettuce leaf. Salad overload is always permissible.

The temptation evoked by oysters is not worth going into battle against. Lou knows that. Even though we had them just the other day, she will not bother trying to limit how many quanta of them I fit onto my plate. A quanta is six. And I think that she thinks that an overdose on these plump little filter feeders may be good for our next few shopping bills. I am right.

'Glad we're not paying for those,' she says.

No, the bride's father is paying, possibly. Since it is his daughter's third attempt at till death do us part, maybe the groom is chipping in. Henrietta is the bride, and even considering the enhancements, a fancy lace dress and expensive hair and make-up, she is, I'll admit, a bit of a looker. She is Lou's longest-standing friend; they met in preschool.

Friend is maybe a bit generous of a term for their relationship. Let's say long-term-human-association-no-blood-connection. The bride is not on the smorgasbord tonight, despite what the fixated eyes of the best man are saying.

I sit at my piled-up plate under Lou's gaze that says, 'Don't expect me to feel sorry for you when you can't move.' I wait for her to go the toilet before I unveil the cold cuts of meat and in a moment of sneaky sanity, I bundle them into a large cloth napkin, along with some potato bake and some pasta salad that I really can do without. Across the table, Aunty Flo – that is how she was introduced to me earlier – is watching. She smiles knowingly and beckons me over to her side of things. Everyone is drinking and talking and watching the bridal table as I accept the offer of dropping my package of excess food into her large handbag.

'I have a dog,' she says.

Lou returns and brings Henrietta with her. I offer my seat to the new bride, and announce my intention to mingle. Not that I know anyone. There is a balcony where smokers have been going and coming from with regularity since pre-dinner champagne and beer. I don't smoke any more but I do know smokers love company in their ever shrinking domains of addiction.

There are three people out there, a bridesmaid among them. She is nervous and sucking hard on one of those long skinny brown-papered cigarettes. I comment that I haven't seen one of those for years. She says you can still get them at the tobacconist. The other two are a couple and they ignore us, the non-smoker and the flighty member of the bridal party. They soon stub out and leave.

'Are you a friend of Kevin?' she asks.

'No, I don't know the bride or the groom. My wife is an old friend of Henrietta's. That's my connection.'

'Good, then I can tell you. I have to tell someone or I'm going to explode.'

'Sure, tell me anything, I don't mind.'

She lets it out. 'Henrietta slept with the best man last night.' She takes a deep breath and curses a bit.

I curse a bit in solidarity. 'That's not good,' I add.

She kicks a stool and says, 'I don't know what to do.'

That's her real issue, I reckon.

I feel like saying wrap it up in a napkin and I'll put it in Aunty Flo's handbag for you. It's the best I can offer, so instead say nothing.

'I have to go,' she says while stubbing out the long slim half smoked cigarette. 'Sorry I dumped it on you.'

I am left alone in a whirlpool of smoke and perfume.

The night feels warm after the recent cold snap. I think about the huge pile of wood I have chopped in anticipation of a long winter.

No Bliss in Ignorance

Here are some things of which Veronica has no knowledge.

Down in the back valley runs a creek, cool and clear. Its voice can soothe the most troubled mind and its touch will never be forgotten. It tastes like liquid life.

In the town is a library, open to the public and lit with electricity. It has books from other times and places, written by humans and not by God. The town has schools where children go for lessons in maths and science, and where they are encouraged to ask questions. And this is just one town amongst thousands in a nation with a government that builds libraries and schools, and hospitals.

There are people who don't serve the Lord and yet are happy and kind to each other. They don't believe in heaven and they find no evidence for the existence of hell. For them, the Devil is just a silly idea. And they enjoy movies and play sport.

Veronica doesn't know any of these things. She also has no idea what a twenty-two is, or a ute. But she suspects a ute is like a car.

Her world is so confined that she can't even hear the butcherbird singing every morning in the gum tree in her front yard. It's just background noise to the dread she feels every day from wake up to lie down. Her fifteenth birthday approaches.

One thing Veronica does know is that she is soon to be married to David. He is sixty-seven years old and the tribe call him the Slayer. God has told David that Veronica Smyth is the direct descendant of Mary Magdalene and that his union with her will herald a new era of God's reign on earth, a new Eden. She knows that she cannot walk away from all this; she has tried many times before. It is fifteen kilometres to the road, then thirty to the town with the shops owned by the heathens. When she does try to walk away, they find her, bring her back, and place her in the cage for a while. The last time, she nearly made it to the road and the Slayer left her in the cage for a week.

'She has the spirit, but it is wild and yet to be tamed,' the Slayer told Veronica's mother. 'Have faith. She will settle and wander no more when the Lord prepares her for marriage and childbirth.'

The mother praised the Lord the day Veronica bled for the first time. She was fertile. Hallelujah! The prophecy was unfolding. The just turned fourteen-year-old was dragged by the hand and taken to see David, the Slayer. He undressed the blessed child, ordered her to stop crying and to stand still, then she was turned around. The Slayer's crazy eyes turned Veronica's stomach. His decrepit touch burnt her skin.

Veronica, though oblivious of the creek in the valley, does know well the forest on the western slope. She is regularly assigned to go there with an aunty, on watch, to fetch firewood. She is never to be alone. The ground is hard and dry and fallen sticks scratch her legs. The loose pebbles can easily turn an ankle. But the assigned aunty, deemed useless for anything else, is wanton, even with this easiest of tasks. She lets Veronica wander. It is not like when they go to town to buy the heathen goods that must be blessed and purified by the Slayer. On those visits, Veronica is closely watched by her mother and an uncle. She is admonished and reminded of the cage whenever she dares to look sideways.

Everyone in the tribe knows the world is evil and that God is preparing to make his judgement. And God will be ruthless; he will spare only the holiest of the holy. Veronica is told that if she even just looks at any of the Devil-infected townsfolk, her soul will be marked and God will know. Only the male elders are protected from this evil. Only they can speak to the heathens and hold the filthy money. They are shielded by the Slayer's special prayers and ointment.

Veronica doesn't know the mechanics of sex. But since her menarche she has nightmares about how she will come to bear the Slayer's child. His serpent tongue enters her mouth and melts into a hot and sticky lava. It trickles down inside of her and leaks out of her now hair-covered parts. His stench fills her nostrils as the seed of Jesus nestles in her stomach. The baby, the Saviour of the world, fights and claws its way out of her belly. She has heard the screams of childbirth many times before; she has washed the bloodied sheets.

Veronica hates Jesus, and God, and David. But mostly she hates her mother.

David has thirty-two children. The docile uncles say they are joyous when he does his sacred dance with their wives. The wives sing hymns and hold hands in a circle. There is a blankness in everyone's eyes. Veronica knows this because she has seen the opposite. The spirited girl has dared to look at the townsfolk, she does it every chance she gets. She sees the sparkling of eyes in the men and women, and even in the children. She hears them laugh as well. The Slayer says laughter is the battle cry of the Devil, but she doesn't believe him. She doesn't believe a word David says.

And she has seen the sparkle up close in the eyes of Zane Jeffreys, her secret. She has heard him laugh as well. His laughter makes her happy, convincing her that such joy has nothing to do with the Devil. Zane traps rabbits in the forest. He has a twenty-two, whatever that is, she muses. His father told him to never take it into the forest near the God Botherers. And he has his red Ps and a ute, more strange words to Veronica. He is seventeen and they meet whenever Veronica steals away from the aunty in the firewood forest.

Veronica asks about the name of a tree. No one in the compound could name the tree that provides the firewood and the timber for the ever increasing number of buildings. Zane knew it immediately as an Australian cypress. A native, he said.

Zane asks about life in the compound. 'You can't get married at fifteen! It's against the law,' he says about her latest news

'The Slayer says man's laws are an abomination. That the meek who will inherit the earth only follow the word of God. That the word of God is the Law.'

Zane is ever curious, something frowned upon by the tribe and the Slayer. But what is most fascinating is how he is always kind and gentle – such an oddity for Veronica. His smile and warm touch fill her with desire. A desire so foreign and delicious. Is it love? That exclusive emotion, gifted by God, to be reserved only for Jesus. A love only available to mere mortals through the miracle of the Holy Spirit that flows solely through David, the Slayer. The children are taught that all other love is an illusion, a dangerous temptation conjured by the Devil.

Veronica tries to feel the love of God, she tries hard and often. It might just relieve the dread. But the hope of some respite, the hope that anything will change, is fading with every failed attempt. When Zane holds her hand and speaks, a lightness fills her body. She knows so little of the world, but her gut tells her that it is Zane who speaks the truth. She knows it, deeply and soundly.

She doesn't know there is a creek down in the valley, nor did she know any names of the trees or the birds until she met Zane. She only knows the name of one town, the one where she sneaks glances at the sparkly eyed people who are damned to hell. She's pretty sure that a ute is a type of car, and she will find out tonight when she meets Zane. He says he will drive the ute and bring the twenty-two, just in case.

Her mother leaves their cottage at five to five for Friday's service. It is for initiated adults only. 'Make sure your brothers and sisters lie down by six, Veronica.'

Her siblings eat the simple dinner she has prepared and go off to bed as told. Rigid routine has made them like sheep. Hardly a word is needed.

She looks at the youngest, now asleep in bed. Rachel, she was baptised. Veronica feels for the children, but knows that out of a fear of God and the Slayer, and with the threat of the cage, they will stay forever in the chosen tribe. They will stay cold and joyless.

Maybe Zane has infected her with the Devil. She doesn't care. Though he speaks many words that have no meaning for her yet, she knows they will be real things. Not like the words she hears drifting through the still air each Friday evening when the Slayer commands, 'Now I want you all to speak in tongues. 1 Corinthians 14, verse 5.'

Soon all the siblings are asleep and the adults are enraptured beyond all earthly matters. Nothing but gibberish, she thinks. She learnt the word gibberish from Zane when she tried to explain to him the speaking in tongues nonsense.

As night falls, she opens the door, closes it quietly behind her, and walks away for the last time.

One Good Turn

My next-door neighbour has a whipper-snipper, a leaf blower, a chain-saw, a ride-on mower, and a shredder – well, he used to.

There were other tools in his back shed, like spades and rakes and so on, but they never came to my attention. It was the noisy petrol-guzzling buggers he used to keep his garden under the thumb that piqued my inner good Samaritan.

And that is the point I tried to make after politely knocking on his door last Sunday afternoon.

'There's no law against leaf blowers,' he grunted.

'Do you think you could maybe give it a rest on Sundays at least.'

'What are you? A religion freak or somethink?'

I must admit, his massive illustrated biceps and the can of bourbon and cola in his meaty hand took a bit of the steam out of my approach.

'No…no. It's just that we've got a baby…and she still has a sleep in the day.'

He implied that I respect his rights and leave. 'Piss off, prick! It's me own fucking property, and I'll do what I like. OK?'

I like to be diplomatic and follow community protocols in situations of conflict, so that is why I approached him face to face in the first place – I'm no fan of the anonymous note in the letter box. I spoke my truth, and failed.

The mother of my seriously sleep disturbed offspring suggested ringing council first thing Monday morning. 'There has to be something we can do,' she added.

'Do you remember when that hail storm blocked the drain out front?'

'Oh yeah.' My wife shrugged and retreated to the bedroom with our crying child.

'Two thousand dollars, I think that phone call to council ended up costing us,' I said to no one.

The fluoro-vested council guy with a pipe camera took five minutes to prove beyond doubt that the liquidambar tree on our property was the real culprit and legally, financially, environmentally, and whatever else-ally, it was our responsibility.

From next door's house I heard yelling and things being thrown around. A back door slammed and the unmistakeable sliding aluminium shed door sang out. Then the chainsaw started up.

The sonic affront was seriously testing my civic sensibility and, to be honest, my faith in humans. Maybe he was bullied at school, humiliated and beaten by his father, violated by a priest? All things considered, perhaps revving the shit out of a chainsaw and butchering every tree and shrub on his own fucking property was perfectly under-standable.

The woman of the house, whom I had only ever heard and never before seen, shrieked, 'You bloody idiot!'

Miraculously she penetrated the racket created by the therapeutic, or was it retributional, pruning. The chainsaw stopped. I felt imme-diate worry for her. A car started up and sped away. She was safe.

Every Wednesday, Kylie, the neighbour, the screamer – turns out my wife knew her name all along – does compulsory voluntary work at the Vinnie's depot. If you want to know what compulsory voluntary work means, you'll need to ask the Department of Social Services. Her defacto, Bruce – again information provided courtesy of my wife – is never home weekdays, and often not on week nights either. And Wednesdays is, conveniently, playgroup for my precious wife and child.

No one about. Time for action. Immediate and decisive community service was needed.

I took an empty milk container down to my own shed, where I just happened to be in possession of some petrol. Armed with close to two litres of the stuff, I jumped the fence and snuck into Bruce's cave of noise-monsters. They were sleeping. I chuckled as I poured the accelerant around and over the culprits. They would not suffer; it would be all over in a hydrocarbon flash. I used the last few splashes to make a flammable trail back to the fence.

Back on my side, I moved into phase two. The jumbo-sized barbecue matches were my brilliant idea for remote fire-starting – plenty of length and phosphorous. My amateur physics and chemistry calculations did not predict that each and every match would extinguish well before before hitting the now quickly vapourising petrol trail.

Shit!

I ran back inside my house and circled the kitchen to generate a Plan B. Six laps later, I spotted the local newspaper. I ran back to the scene, scrunching up pages as I went. I lit Plan B and lobbed it over the fence.

BOOM!

The explosion had neighbours I had never seen before running onto the street and dialling triple zero.

I explained to the investigating police and insurance assessors that I work at home on Wednesdays. My singed eyebrows and reddened face merely evidence of my heroic and selfless actions with the garden hose. In the mayhem, I had to extinguish the bits of burning garden machinery that had landed in adjoining yards and onto the street – basically strewn everywhere within a ten-metre radius of the now missing aluminium shed. The officials were satisfied.

Turns out as well that, after getting a bit boisterous at the local pub just last week, Bruce my friendly neighbour, had upset a notorious mad bastard who happens to have a track record for settling scores with arson. Stevo, as he is known, is also the brother of the Sergeant of Arms of the local chapter of the Hell's Angel's. So Bruce, now minus a shed and its noisy contents, and wisely choosing peace over war, decided to let the whole matter ride.

'Do you have something you want to tell me?' my wife said as she applied pawpaw ointment to my peeling forehead.

'Yeah, looks like I won't have to phone up council's noise complaint department after all.'

She smiled and the only sound to be heard was the quiet breathing of a sleeping baby in the cot in the corner of our bedroom.

Hump Day

The email stated, 'All staff to meet in the tea room asap, finish your current appointment, notify any staff who have not seen this message. Jane will answer all phones and keep clients in reception.'

NewLife Employment Services documented 22.6 full-time equivalent staff – this Wednesday afternoon, eighteen were present. Word got around the office even quicker than last month's notice that yet another round of redundancies were 'regrettable but economically unavoidable'.

Most got the message immediately as it was company policy to have the email pop-up enabled on all computers. Deanne, the extroverted one rarely at her desk, ducked out earlier to the $2 shop down the road. While paying for a non-slip rubber bath mat, she got a text message from Karen, the office busybody, urging her to get back quick smart to the office. Tom the most senior consultant at NewLife didn't get the message either; his office was down the hall and away from the commotion unfolding in the main open office area. He, on principle, refused to enable the email pop-up and no one, not even the new boss, dared to raise that particular issue.

Tom was with Pam, a life-weary single mother in her thirties who, along with a long welfare history, sported bit of a serious victim complex. She was contesting her obligation to now seek employment since her youngest child had turned seven.

'So you're telling me I'm meant to go out and find work with three kids at home?'

'Well, Pam, unfortunately the government is saying that, yes.'

'Do you know I have two kids with Asperger's and the other one's got ADHD?'

Tom's caseload had more than the average quota of tricky clients, not because of a quirk of random allocation but because he volunteered to take them off the hands of other consultants when the frustration levels, from either party, threatened to explode. Tom liked the fiery ones, they told the best stories of all. Tom worked out early on that if you just listened, didn't judge, and asked questions instead of telling them what to do, mostly they calmed down; even at times becoming quite pleasant company – in a professional sense of course. To the surprise, even disbelief, of his colleagues, some actually ended up getting jobs.

Karen was standing just outside the glass panelled door of Tom's office. She was waving and pointing at her wrist. Politely excusing himself to the mother of three, Tom opened the door.

'Didn't you get the message? Everyone has to meet in the tea room now.'

Tom gave Karen a version of the company's core vision statement about respecting jobseekers.

Unperturbed, Karen stepped up a notch and decided to lie. 'No, the boss has specifically sent me to get you…now.'

'Wow, I can't imagine Bill doing that. Tell him I'll be there as soon as I finish with my jobseeker.'

Karen puffed and once more pointed at an imaginary watch on her arm as she turned to scurry back to the main action now brewing in the tea room.

Though not believing Karen for a second, Tom was somewhat glad to be able to send the single mother on her way; it wasn't Pam's demeanour so much as the stench of her rotting teeth. He tried to book a new appointment while finding the flyer about the free dental clinic. But his efforts were pointless because once Pam got a whiff of what was going on, she was up and out of there quicker than you could say 'unemployment benefit'.

Tom was last to arrive at the tea room, but only just.

Deanne was in the centre of the room profusely apologising and rehashing the story of her unsteady mother. She was holding up the non-slip mat showing the rubber suction caps on its underside. 'I also nearly bought some of those fake flowers, they're proteas or banksias, I'm not sure, I can never tell the difference, you'd never guess they were plastic. Oops, sorry, sorry, sorry.' Deanne noticed Tom's arrival and retreated from centre stage joining the circle of staff in the now quite cosy tea room.

'Oh good, come in, Tom, we're all here now,' said Bill.

Staying in the doorway to the tea room, Tom noticed most staff nursed newly replenished coffee mugs as they waited. The lack of chatter and the unusual presence of Sarah, the company's head of counselling services, foretold that something was definitely wrong. In true form, Karen, obviously somehow having extracted from someone what was going on, was beginning to tear up.

Bill, in only his second week at NewLife, put on his best version of a caring and compassionate leader, twisted his neck, cleared his throat and swallowed. 'Unfortunately,' he cleared his throat again, 'I have to inform you that one of our colleagues has passed away.'

A wave of anxiety and nausea washed through Tom. His senses switched off as his mind rebooted a Facebook conversation from the night before. John Goodman, not the actor but the staff cynic who now worked only Mondays at this office, was one of the few workmates that Tom ever contacted outside of work hours. Last night John chatted with Tom online for about half an hour. They had done this before; they had even discussed John's depression before. Trained in suicide prevention, Tom always openly asked John the difficult question, and John always assured Tom that he wouldn't do anything stupid. Tom didn't give it a second thought after signing off.

'John Goodman didn't show up for work this morning. He didn't call and he wasn't answering his phone. Sarah drove out to his home but unfortunately it was too late. The police and ambulance were already there. We don't have all the details but it appears he ended his own life.'

Tom couldn't stay in the tea room for a second longer, especially as Bill was now asking the staff to join him in prayer. Back in his own space, Tom sat down, took a breath and logged on to Facebook – pulling up the permanent record of what were perhaps John's last words.

'I'm full of shit, Tom. Don't worry, I'm not going to kill myself.'

'That's good, John. There are hundreds of reasons to die. You just need one to live, just one, that's all. Believe me, it can make all the difference.'

'Thanks, Tom.'

'Take care, mate. I'll call you at head office tomorrow. If you haven't got a reason to live by then, I'll tell you mine.'

Tom's nausea and anxiety morphed into a feeling he would never be able to describe; not even to Sarah when he took up the offer of workplace grief counselling. He hung his head, chin on chest, and began to sob from somewhere deep within, from where his own reason to live was gasping for air.

Well Heeled, Well Travelled

I've never been to London, Paris or Rome. I haven't even set foot into Europe; nor Africa, Asia or the Americas. I haven't been anywhere, man. Well, not in her books anyway.

'You just have to go overseas,' she said.

She was dolled-up – a man can be easily fooled. But it is words that maketh the person, and her butt ugliness shone brightly when she opened that painted gob of hers to expose all that hideous ignorance and arrogance.

I walked out of the party. It was full of artists and writers, designers and entrepreneurs. Funny how I'd never heard of any of them before. No, it wasn't funny, it was incredibly annoying, to be honest. These people were so full of themselves. And what fool am I? Thinking that getting out for a change, accepting a party invite, socialising, might be the trick to cure my loneliness.

I started up my car, a blue Daewoo Lanos that I bought for $800. There was something wrong with the duco, and the exhaust, and the door handles, and a few other things. But it suited my income. I closed my eyes and thought about all the clever things I could have, should have and would have said if I wasn't so angry at the hide of that woman. I accompanied each thought with a push on the accelerator pedal. The Daewoo needs a few good pumps to wake up properly. I resorted to thinking that the dolled-up you-just-have-to-go-overseas bitch could probably use a few good pumps as well. Then I silently berated myself for such baseness of thought, such blokey misogyny. I'm glad I didn't say anything. It would've been pointless. Spitting in her face, on the other hand…

There was a knock on the passenger side window.

'Can I get a lift?'

It was the woman who was walking around earlier with trays of finger food. Obviously, being an unsophisticated oaf, I stubbornly refuse to say platters of hors d'oeuvres.

The window on the passenger side doesn't open, so I got out and spoke to her over the roof. 'Sure. Have you finished for the night?'

'Yes, thank God.'

I walked round to her side to let her in. It was gentlemanly, but you have to fiddle with the handle and lift as you pull to get that door open. 'The seat belt doesn't work properly. You can click the buckle in, but it pops out every now and then.'

'I couldn't give a shit. You can hit a tree for all I care. At least I wouldn't have to do any more of these fucking gigs.'

I questioned her with my face.

'Just joking,' she answered. 'You will drive carefully, won't you?'

'Yeah, OK. Just for you. Just tonight.' I smiled to reassure her I was being sarcastic. 'My name's Nick, by the way.'

'Pam,' she replied as she plonked herself down into my car.

I hopped back into my side and drove off. 'Where can I take you?'

'If you can drop me off at the train station, that would be great, thanks.'

She asked me what I was doing at the party. I asked if it was obvious that I was not of the same ilk as the others.

She said, 'Yes, thank God.'

I explained how I was the host's son's maths tutor, and she asked what the hourly rate was for that. She seemed surprised and somewhat pleased that it was not much more than her rate for shovelling canapés down rich folk's gullets. I liked her turn of phrase.

'I have no other engagements for the evening. I'm happy to drive you home.'

She told me her suburb. I told her mine, which was further west. I looked at her and raised my eyebrows. She laughed sweet music and her eyes lit up my Daewoo.

In the party, she was just the hired help. Dressed in hospitality black. Flat shoes. Minimal make-up. Restricted dialogue. Subservient aura. Almost invisible. In my dodgy car, she became the centre of my Saturday-night universe.

We did the usual personal history comparison: place of birth, number and gender of siblings, schools attended, jobs gained and lost, drugs tried once, spouses gained and lost, and the diaspora and current status of our own grown-up children.

Then there were some quiet kilometres. Her breathing slowed. So did mine. The Daewoo a comfortable bubble; an unexpected sanctuary for us both. The hum of tyres on freeway, the perfect soundtrack for episode one of whatever this was.

'You know the woman you were talking to? The one in the sequinned cocktail dress and thousand-dollar shoes?'

'Oh yeah, her.' As if I could forget.

'Earlier in the evening, she was stuck on her own for a few moments and called me over. She made some small talk about the food and the weather. Then she asked me what she really wanted to know.'

'What was that?'

'She pointed you out and wanted to know if I knew who you were.'

'Really? What did you say?'

'I said I didn't know, of course. Then she said, "He looks like he might be a tradie."'

I let out a small puff of incredulous air.

'Yeah. Then she said she had always wanted to fuck a tradie.'

'Bullshit,' I said.

'No. Swear to God, she said it just like that. These rich bitches are as uncouth as they come. And they're so up themselves that they'll tell me stuff like that, you know, real incriminating shit. And they don't even realise what they've done. It's as though I'm not a person. It's as though they're talking to themselves.'

'I know what you mean.'

It was quiet again. Pam found the lever and tilted her seat back. She put her hands to her face and massaged her temples. We were getting close to her suburb. I wondered what would happen when I dropped her off. I assumed that we would never see each other again, that she would get out and say thank you and something like, see you around, which of course would not happen. I wanted to see her again. Normally I'm wary, but something was telling me that Pam was the real deal. A rare gem in all this dirt.

I can't believe I said this but I did. 'Do you believe in God?'

'Are you kidding? Look at this place. What God would allow this?' She sat up, the seat following her back as she did.

'Do you read much?' I was on a roll now, ticking off some checklist in my mind that until that moment I didn't even realise existed.

'What do you reckon? Nick.'

I questioned her with my face.

'Do I read? Are you kidding? Look at this place. Of course I read.'

I laughed. I had nothing to lose now. 'Have you ever been overseas?'

'Are you kidding? Look at this place.' Then she laughed her sweet music. 'No, I haven't. I'm not sure I want to either. It would make me feel too much like all those well heeled, well travelled people who I hate so much.'

'Love it. Best reason.'

I pulled off the freeway. I didn't have any more questions for Pam. She met all the criteria that had become so obvious to me on that strange night.

'You know, the woman who asked if you were a tradie, she asked me where I lived. I told her and she asked if it was in Sydney. She had never heard of it.'

Azriella

Eventually, I puzzled out something that I could build that would win her heart. A tree house. It would be perfect. No one would find it, or us. And I was young and a big dreamer.'

My usual shift is from eleven p.m. to seven a.m. Most staff prefer working days, they like to sleep at night. Me, I like the night and the early mornings. I sleep from midday to sunset.

We have a resident who shares my body clock. His name is Rendra and he is East Timorese. He says he is one hundred and twelve years old and I believe him. The other workers think he is full of it, deluded. A silly old man.

Initially, I cross-checked a lot of the information Rendra spouted as he told his life story. Dates of particular events, people's names and places were all verifiable via Google. His accounts of the Franciscan missionaries, the Portuguese, the Dutch, the Australians and the Indonesians all wanting a piece of his homeland, all asserting their arrogance and domination, are fascinating. I'm convinced he was there, a first-hand witness.

Much of what he tells is horrific. Endless military raids to crush the resistance, so much wasted life, finally leading to Rendra leaving his homeland forever. The Santa Cruz massacre in '91 was the final straw.

'I was a refugee at eighty-six.'

I did the maths. He was spot on.

But of all his tales, it is the love stories I like most of all. At two a.m., after I have finished my required duties, I go to Rendra's room and help him into his special lounge chair. Then I hop up onto his bed. I wonder now who is caring for whom.

'My people and her people did not get on. They were from the coast and we were from the highlands. But the Portugese moved us all to Viqueque. It is a city with a big church and they thought we needed to be civilised, Christianised. It made us worse. It made us angry and fight among ourselves. Before that, we would trade with each other. We had goods from the forest, they from the sea. We would have big celebrations and boys and girls from both sides would mix. In Viqueque, we stayed apart.

'I saw her first at the night market. She had one blue eye and one brown eye. People thought she was cursed. I was entranced. I found out where she lived and her name. Azriella. I called out to her one day when I was walking home from school. She came over. I like to think that she was interested in me. But I think she really was more interested in my clutch of books.

Girls were not allowed to go to school then. The Franciscan priests said that God's plan for men and for women was different. I remember at the time thinking they were wrong. My mother could read and she looked after the money too. My father taught me how to work with wood. He couldn't read at all.

'But you do not question the priests. And even after everything that happened, I remember them as kind men, gentle men. Do you go to church?'

'No, I don't, Rendra. And I'm not a believer either.'

'Good. You make your own beliefs, you'll be better off that way.'

I get up and give the old man a glass of water and wait for him to drink. He hands it back and I place it on his bedside table. I hop back onto his bed. Two forty-seven a.m. says the clock on the wall. I swear it is that exact time every time we perform this ritual of mid-story rehydration.

'One day I am reading to Azriella in our hiding place behind the copra shed. I remember it was the novel *O Primo Basílio* by José Maria de Eça de Queiroz. It is a good story. But how crazy, eh? Not our language, not our culture, and Azriella breaking all the rules to be with me. Her mother came and found us. She had this straw broom and she used it to sweep me away. And as I backed away, I dropped the book and she picked it up and held it high in the air, screaming at me to never come back.'

A big smile comes over Rendra's face. 'But she can't stop me. And the beating I got from my father when the priests sent a letter home telling of how I had lost a book from the library would not stop me either. I would go back and make bird calls from behind the bushes. Azriella would sneak out and look at me with her exotic eyes. And she would tell me to go, that her mother would find us. I would run home, happy just to see her and hear her voice. And I would come back and do it all over again. Whistle, whistle. Each time she would take longer and longer to come out. Then one day she came out and was angry at me. She told me I was a school boy and only good at words. That if I were a man I would be a fisherman or a builder or a farmer, and I could come and have something real to offer.' He laughs and winces in pain.

'Just rest a bit, Rendra. We have plenty of time.'

'That's easy for you to say, young man.' He laughs again, holding his side.

Rendra's pain is not something we can do anything about. I wait.

He calms down after his laughing, and starts up again. 'There is a forest that surrounds the city. It is thick and full of birds. I find a tree. Not too far away. Not too high, not too low. I work on the tree house every moment I have. I make a promise to my self that I will not go back to Azriella until I have built her a home. But I do spy on her at the night markets. She gets more beautiful every time. It drives me to work harder and faster. My mother looks at me wondering what is going on. My father wants to know if I have seen his saw. Father Didier finds sketches and plans of the tree house in the back of my writing book.'

The old man speaks quickly now. I can see him there, back in Timor Leste, back in the jungle, infected by adolescent lust. Energy to burn.

'At last I finish. I stand back and look up at what I have made, what I have built. She will see how clever I am. She will see that I am not just a boy. We will be safe here. Her family and my family need not know. This will be for us.' Rendra pauses. His eyes light up; revisiting memories that he will not be able to share. Private, intimate memories, memories nearly one hundred years old.

'Did you get her to come to the tree house?' I ask.

'Oh yes, she came. When she saw what I had built, saw all the time and industry, she could not speak at first. I helped her up into the house. She stood and looked around, her eyes shining, her mouth open. Then she laughed.'

'Laughed?'

'Yes, she laughed and then she kissed me on the mouth. She said that she didn't mean what she had said before about fishermen, farmers and builders. She said that she was scared that she would be sent away if I was found hanging around again.' Rendra drifts away, back in time, another life.

'So what happened?' I am aching to know.

'After she kisses me, she reaches behind her back to where she has tucked the book that her mother took away from me that day when she hit me with the broom. Then Azriella whispers into my ear, "Will you read to me?"'

Rendra tires after the telling of his stories. I put him back into bed. Sometimes he asks me to tell him a story about my life, but I can't for the life of me think of anything worth telling. So I read to him. I read until I hear the kookaburras heralding the dawn. Rendra will be asleep by then, and I have duties to attend to before changeover.

The Girl from Watanobbi

After the purchase he walked out of the shopping centre and found a polite place to smoke. The cellophane packaging kept sticking to his fingers as he tried to drop it into the nearby bin.

Some things are hard to let go of.

He lit a cigarette and took a long draw. Science said nicotine caused the addiction. He disagreed, proposing that the sudden deep sucking in was the hook.

How many years was I with Felicity?

He got with her soon after leaving his wife.

That's right, it started in '95. How could I forget that year?

He sucked hard again. He ashed in the bin. The roar of a bus pulling away after dropping off a load of shoppers hurt his ears.

Imagine giving up the fags for ten years and doing it all again. Tobacco must be my Achilles' heel.

Felicity's weakness was marijuana, pot as she called it. Some would blame her insatiable hunger for the illegal weed as the cause of their demise, but that's not entirely true. Others, including some of her own family, cited her lack of love for anything, her self included, but that was not true either. The bottom line was that this post-marriage-rebound affair was fundamentally flawed from the start. Felicity presented as the polar opposite to his wife of ten years, refreshing, but not necessarily a sound basis for a solid relationship. Deep down, he knew it from the start. He hung in, though, too scared of another failure.

And it was all over in 2000.

He could remember that, easy. It all went spectacularly bust on 1

January, when the new millennium kicked in and the Y2K bug failed to materialise. Felicity was a nightmare that evening. At his friends' turn of the century party, she pleaded to go home because no one there smoked pot. Her pre-party cones had worn off by ten p.m. and she was unbearable. Itching for a top-up.

It's funny about pot smokers. They never admit they're addicted. There's even some scientific evidence to back them up. But just watch the chronic stoners when the stash runs out. Agitation writes itself on their faces, restlessness takes over their legs, and paranoia poisons their every cell as they morph into dark monsters. They think nothing of driving fifty kilometres to score a quarter of an ounce with the next two weeks' rent money.

Last century, when he walked out on the wife, he found an affordable rental in Watanobbi. Felicity lived in the house next door. She had three kids to three different fathers, she swore, she giggled and she didn't give a damn about money. She was everything his angry ex-wife wasn't.

She's exactly what I need.

Nothing like a new partner, with a new body and new voice to help deal with the trauma of a break-up. Limerence is a wonderful thing, until it wears off. The most beautiful thing in the world can turn into the vilest creature you can imagine. And doesn't that mess with your mind?

Felicity had just sold him the packet of cigarettes at the shopping centre. She didn't recognise him.

Five or so years together and not even a flicker of recognition! What's that all about? It must be the pot.

When he broke it off with Felicity, loudly declaring that he couldn't be with someone who was permanently wasted, she pulled off the engagement ring and threw it at him. She had bought the ring in the first place. He never wanted to get married again.

'Why don't you want to marry me?' she asked with a devastated face. It was the rawest emotion he'd ever seen in her. On the spot, in the face of someone who wanted him, he lied to himself that he could make this work. He'd show his ex-wife that Felicity was not just a fling.

'Sorry, Felicity,' he said. 'Of course I want to be with you forever, but personally, I don't need a piece of paper. But, hey, if it's important to you, I'll do it. What the heck.'

To celebrate, she drove from Watanobbi to Woy Woy to score some pot, then bought the engagement ring, then picked up the kids from school, and then bought them fast food from the drive-through. He should have run away, there and then.

She was once the Girl from Watanobbi, the long-legged, well tanned single mother of three who looked smoking-hot and seemed so carefree and unaffected. Now she was just like everyone else, scared and pathetic, ugly. Couldn't even make it to midnight at the turn of the century without her pot!

The looks his friends gave him as they left the party, on the pretence of her being nauseous, said it all.

'Come on, stay,' pleaded the host, his best mate. 'I'll call her a taxi. She'll be fine, mate. It's eleven forty, I've got champagne and sparklers. It's the fucking turn of the century, man. You can't miss that!'

'Sorry, Ben. I've got to go. You understand.'

Ben didn't understand, but worse, he didn't understand himself. The humiliation of submitting to his fiancée's drug habit burned deep in his gut as they drove back to Watanobbi and the stinking bong. The sound of it bubbling away annoyed him to breaking point. Engagement ring, promises of forever, her three kids who adored him, stupid pride, nothing could stem his rage at two minutes into the new millennium. The muffled sound of fireworks and cheering a fitting backdrop.

He had done a lot of work on himself since he left Felicity fifteen years ago. Nothing cosmetic of course, all internal stuff. Being single for a while was a big help. He learnt to put things out of his mind, even the ex-wife who still hated him. Best of all, he stopped punishing himself for the mistakes, the stupidity and weakness that he'd suffered from as a younger man. The art of letting go.

So has Felicity simply let go? Let go so effectively she has forgotten me completely? Is that possible?

When Felicity served him, she looked him right in the face. She handed over the smokes and the change and looked straight at him again.

She's just playing me, surely.

He stubbed out his cigarette and looked around at the shoppers coming and going. He planned to go back, but not today. He wanted to test her out. He had to know.

It took him three days to find the thrown-away engagement ring. He'd forgotten the whole affair as best he could. He couldn't get his head around forgiveness, so forgetting, or at least letting go, was the best he could ever hope to achieve as a mere mortal.

I mean, if God tells us not to judge, how can we forgive?

He got a better look at her the next time. She must be forty-seven now, he figured. Time had taken its toll, but some fool would still fall for her, he thought. She was still into pot, he knew that. He'd bumped into Felicity's daughter, Pippa, only a few months ago. She hadn't forgotten him. She was nothing like her mum. She was warm and interested in people and not just a person's capacity to source cannabis.

What did Pippa say when I asked her? That's right, 'Oh, Mum's the same. She'll never stop doing what she does. It'll kill her in the end.'

Pippa even hugged him and said, 'So happy to see you.'

Felicity's eyes were white and bright, no doubt well doused in Clear Eyes. And they were outlined with heavy make-up. She must have a 'Back in Five Minutes' sign so she can duck out somewhere for a choof.

She was chewing gum, which he once thought of as sexy until he realised it was just to hide the give-away aroma of grass.

He ordered a pack of cigarettes, vowing this to be his last. Again, like last time. she looked straight through him. He paid by card this time; maybe she'd see his name.

She processed it automatically without looking at any of the details; not unusual really. She handed back the card with the docket. She looked right at him, smiled and said, 'Thank you.'

He stood and looked at her for a moment. She seemed a little unsettled that he didn't just leave like customers do. It confirmed her complete lack of recognition. He casually placed the engagement ring on the glass counter. She looked at it and scrunched her face. She looked at him again, still oblivious.

'I'm giving you the ring back, Felicity,' he said.

She looked at the ring and then at him. It took a good ten seconds for her to wake up from her stupor. Go on, count out ten seconds in your head or on your fingers. It's a long time, eh?

'Oh, my God,' she said, finally. 'I remember that ring. O, my God. How are you?'

It was clear she was struggling with retrieving a name for this man. This man who once loved her and stood up for her without complaint. Until the century turned. It was obvious to him, if not anybody else in that shopping centre, that she was high, stoned, off her face. Hiding behind her own personal smokescreen in a smoke shop, of all places. Stalled.

'Take the ring. You bought it.' He didn't want to give her anything else, not even a bullshit response to the bullshit how are you? So he turned and began to walk away.

'Hey, stop, wait,' she called out.

He turned to face her. She was once beautiful to him, once ugly, now she was nothing.

'Thanks for the ring…Wayne.'

He laughed out loud, he couldn't help it.

Wayne? Felicity's lost it, big time. Wayne?

'What's funny, Wayne?'

Shane turned and walked away, not a skerrick of guilt for ignoring the Girl from Watanobbi. He stepped outside the shopping centre onto the concourse. People with trolleys, buses passing, a light rain falling.

He found a bin and tossed away the brand-new packet of cigarettes. The cellophane wrapping, with no static build-up from being ripped open, offered no resistance and slipped out of his fingers. He took in a sudden deep breath, and held it in. That will do, he thought, and smiling, he exhaled a large cloud of imaginary smoke.

Rocket Science

Down the end of my street is a gully that has somehow escaped the ravages of suburban development. It hasn't been stripped of vegetation and reshaped by bulldozers. And it hasn't been resurfaced with concrete, asphalt, pavers and turf. The plants down there are natives and thrive with no human attention, unlike the shop-bought exotics that require fertilisers and pesticides. It's down in this gully that I get my head together.

There is a creek that runs through the gully. Surprisingly, it looks pretty clean. Sure, there is a shopping trolley slowly rusting away in one pool. And I wouldn't dare drink the water. But I can smell its coolness and feel its defiant flow. The creek connects me to something other than the crazy world of money and success.

Then there is the dappled light. Filtered by the foliage of those native trees and shrubs, it makes pretty patterns on the damp lush humus. No need for glycophosphate or noisy petrol-driven leaf blowers. Nature takes care of it all. I take off my hat and let my face be illuminated in the soft and gentle light. I take off my shoes and walk along the chocolate-coloured bare earth track made by human feet, including mine.

The track takes me to the rock where I sit and contemplate life. At least, I start to contemplate, until after a few minutes of silence when the forest fauna comes to greet me. Robins come in pairs and perch on the bark on the sides of tree trunks. They look, sense that I'm no threat and then get on with their day. Ants come and touch my feet with their antennae. Sometimes they hop on board and climb around this big clothed mammal. Mostly they skirt around me and communicate back to the nest about what has turned up today. A pollen-laden bee pulls its head from out of the hood of a terrestrial orchid and launches itself to come and orbit my head for a few laps.

Nature heals me. I don't need to contemplate, I need to forget, to let go, to let be.

It is hard to believe that I might be moving away from here. From all of this. Not just to another suburb. Not even another country. But to another planet, never to return. I have a month to decide.

People call me a rocket scientist. It is simpler than my real job title. There is no such thing really as a rocket scientist. The whole human endeavour to put people into space for exploration and colonisation is a team effort. There are engineers and scientists, even psychologists. No one person could do it all. It's a collective effort, greater than the sum of its individual parts, synergy in action.

My job on Mars will be to monitor and adapt the plant production systems. We have to eat and sustain ourselves first and foremost. We can model and simulate all this here on Earth and even do stuff up on the international space station, but we don't really know what it is going to be like once we are there. That unknowingness is the main reason I put my name down five years ago.

At parties and other social events, I hear a lot of negativity about the space program. The usual complaint is about the amount of money it costs while poverty still exists here on Earth. Normally, I don't bother to defend my position on the topic. But if pushed, because I'm a so-called rocket scientist, I quote some figures on how much is actually spent on the space program and then rattle off how much money is spent on the military, on plastic packaging, on takeaway coffee, on McDonalds and KFC, on perfume, on mobile phone upgrades and on sports stadiums. If that doesn't deter my detractors, I mention how the top five richest people in the world – all men, by the way – from Bill Gates to Mark Zuckerberg could all pitch in and end world poverty, today, and each have thirty-seven billion dollars left over. Some people hate me after that rant. I don't care, because I know it's not really me that they hate, it's the truth that upsets them.

One night, this feisty woman thought she had me stumped when she argued passionately that even if Mr Microsoft and Mr Facebook solved all the world's problems, and, even if there is absolutely no life on Mars – that is, it's just a lump of rock – then what right do we have to invade and despoil it? The arrogance of humankind is abominable, she claimed authoritatively with her very own special brand of New Age consciousness. She questioned my association with such an ignorant and ego-driven project. I didn't bother responding; it would have only confirmed her bias. In my head, I thought about how the sun will one day expand and wipe out both Earth and Mars, and how the whole universe is constantly morphing by the processes of birth and death. The minute interplanetary exploratory actions of one species from one solar system in one galaxy at one small moment in time are insignificant when you get your head around the big picture. I let this woman have her moment of righteousness.

Don't get me wrong, I'm not a totally dispassionate scientist. I abhor the way we can treat each other. And if I could end all suffering on Earth, for the plants and animals as much as for us, I would. But I can't. I can only do what I can do, and if that means being a contributing member of a life form springing from one rock to another across a vast vacuous void to get a toehold somewhere, somehow, that is what I'll be doing. To me, blasting off into space is as much a part of nature as this creek in the gully.

Some things are harder than rocket science. Like this decision to go to Mars or stay here on Earth. With both my parents now dead, and my adult children all wrapped up in their own offspring and other worldly affairs, I don't feel any obligation to hang around. And considering my poor track record at finding a compatible partner here on Terra Firma, the concept of spending the rest of my life as a single celibate unit on a barren red landscape would be in many respects an enormous relief. I feel the gravitational pull of the moon and beyond.

A water skink appears out of the leaf litter and joins me on my rock. I talk to him or her. What do you reckon, skink? Should I stay or should I go? Its tongue flicks the air and it blinks. Do you drink from the creek? Are your children nearby? It turns it head sideways, sensing the sound waves I create in my throat. Do you know we are both made from star dust? And once again our matter and energy will become a new star?

Two boys carrying sticks and stones appear on the track. They stop and look at me sitting alone and apparently talking to myself. They turn and run back along the gully towards the streets and houses.

In the distance against the backdrop of a leaf blower and a plane in the sky, I hear a boy calling out to others, 'Go back! There's a witch. A witch on a rock.'

Times and Places

Somehow we both knew it as Calacoci's milk bar. It's a Starbucks now, typical. Nothing stays the same – probably just as well.

Three o'clock for a coffee and if it works out maybe a drink and… dinner? The drink and dinner part wasn't talked about between us, but it's sort of implied. At least, I think it is – standard internet dating protocols. Coffee for starters in a very public place, then take it from there.

Memories.

Seven miles from the city, a thousand miles from care. Get off at the wharf and if you're lucky, Dad, especially if he and Mum are treating themselves to a Javana Sling, will shout us kids a milk shake at Burt's. Cold as, in those tall aluminium cups. I remember feeling all grown-up when I had grown tall enough to be able to peer over the ruby red Laminex counter top and see into the stainless steel milk tub. Always a mystery before that. Where are they dipping those ladles to get the icy cold milk from? I would wonder, but never ask. Might get a clip over the ear if you were too curious, asking too many questions.

Sometimes we'd swim in the harbour enclosure. It was massive, with a walkway all round its perimeter. The bigger boys and men would dive in, showing off. I remember one day seeing a man dive outside of the enclosure, into the harbour itself. I fretted for him. Thought he'd get eaten by a shark for sure. They even had a shark in a pool on the wharf. I saw that one day. The whole set-up was like a carnival sideshow. Actually, it *was* a carnival sideshow. And then there was the proper aquarium. A big brick cylinder attached to a harbour headland. I never got to go in there, too expensive. Especially after bus tickets, ferry tickets and milkshakes. Be grateful, we were told.

Nineteen seventy-four, if my memory serves me correctly. We lived in another suburb then, this time out on the fringe of the city. We saw the storm and devastation on the black and white television that us kids hoped would cark it, real soon. We wanted a colour one like what the pommies who lived down the road had. Mum reckoned she'd rather us eat proper and not baked beans every night like they did. It was, she reasoned, how they afforded such an expensive and unnecessary piece of furniture. You'll thank me one day, she said. The harbour swimming enclosure had been ripped away by a relentless ocean. I thought the heads protected the harbour beaches. 'Ask your bloody smart-arse teacher,' said Dad when he couldn't explain how all that timber and iron and the floating pontoon just disappeared.

They never rebuilt it. Burt's milk bar is gone too. A lot of water under the bridge, as they say. The iconic pine trees along the ocean beach are hanging in there. Once they were threatened by detergent, of all things. It would get into the onshore salt spray and burn the foliage, or something like that. It's not an issue now: they pump the city's shit, and detergent, several kilometres further out. Everything sorted, if you believe that.

Distance.

It can make things look better. I see a women walking towards Calacoci's. OK, Starbucks. It could be Helen. I've only seen a head shot of my internet date, and in that she's wearing sunglasses and her hair is blowing around. She told me on the phone that the photo was taken on a boat at a friend's wedding reception. It could be Helen; hair colour's about right. I hope it is her; from this distance she looks good.

Helen and I did about twenty emails back and forth. All the usual information was exchanged. Family. Education. Work. Interests. Overseas countries visited. Age of youngest child. Once a certain number of fears were allayed, on both sides, and a level of trust was established, again both sides, we exchanged phone numbers.

Her voice was OK, not what I expected. It sounded perhaps a bit too cultured, but thankfully not screechy. Anyway, I wasn't going to judge a person by their voice. Well, I think not. I liked her laugh, which she readily elicited. She didn't take things too seriously. I picked that up from her profile before I had any contact with her at all. She wrote that she was allergic to long walks on the beach, that live music aggravated her tinnitus, and that the mere thought of curling up on the lounge in front of the fire with a nice red wine induced vertigo. I got the joke immediately. I poked her.

That's not Helen coming. Helen said she'd be wearing black jeans and her trusty Doc Marten boots. This woman has black gabardine slacks and sensible flats. And she's veering towards the pub on the other corner. Looks like she's got a shift at the bar, or the bistro. And up closer she's not that good-looking. Distance can be kind.

I say that I'm not after a good-looking woman, how I've tried that a few times and let testosterone cloud rational judgement. And I claim to have grown out of the need to prove my manliness with spunky-chick-pulling ability. I'm fifty next year, all grown-up, I kid myself. The woman in the slacks and work shoes could be my perfect match. But deep down I know there is no attraction. I've had the snip and my youngest is in his twenties, so why do I still get steered by a biological urge to procreate with a fine physical specimen? Don't I want a meeting of like minds? A soul connection?

There was a storm in 2012. It didn't wash away the coast or consume any harbourside infrastructure. It did shipwreck me, though. The signs had been building up for years and I ignored them; pushed on into the headwinds, fooling myself that things would abate. If you ask me now, I'll sum it all up by saying something like, 'How can anyone be expected to choose the right life partner at twenty?' I'm wondering if I can do it at forty-nine. When I was twenty, though, I thought I knew everything I needed to know about men and women and parenthood. Thought my father had shown me exactly what not to do, that I would never be so stupid, so weak, so fucking authoritarian. I would show him.

I don't want to be alone. Though the five years living by myself have been good for me.

Some internet dates want sex upfront, or at least on date number two. I don't go there. Black on yellow SLIPPERY WHEN WET signs flash into my mind. I do want a meeting of minds first and foremost. I've learnt that much.

It's three twenty-five. She's not coming. Her phone is switched off. Her name might not even be Helen. Her fantasy, with me at least, is over. Ten dollars on the nose, she is still married and the children are still at home, and she is too full of fear, or religion, or family tradition, to escape from her misery. She'll be back online with a new name and a new unrecognisable head shot. She'll justify it to herself as harmless fun. Better than breaking up, like a ship on a reef.

I'm not hurt. This has happened before. Pretty disappointed in the Starbucks coffee, though. Would have much preferred a gelato from Calacoci's milk bar. Think I'll take a walk up to the headland and look at the old seminary that's become a catering college.

Nothing stays the same. Just as well.

Submission

She doesn't like me. Constantly changing me and asking her boyfriend if that's better. She'll give me a severe haircut and ask him what he thinks. He is diplomatic, non-committal. Then she'll dress me up in lots of purple and consult him again.

He asks, 'Is that necessary?'

She says, 'It's what they're looking for.'

He says, 'Sounds like submission to me.'

She says, 'Exactly.'

My mother is Geraldine Coral Bates. She's chosen to be known as G.C. Bates. It's more professional, and genderless. It's how she signs her name on the letters of introduction when she sends me off for consideration.

Her boyfriend, Jamie, has read my face, and felt the shape of my fingers and accepts me as is. Mother doesn't listen. I like Jamie. He is polite and encouraging. He protects me.

My real father is long gone. My mother can't forget him. He once branded her as his own, with fists and cruel words. Though I wasn't fully formed at the time, I can hear him and feel him. He is part of my structure. Figurative, but real. Between the lines yet glaringly obvious.

Mother doesn't like words like 'glaringly'; apparently, adverbs are not acceptable – taboo. She purifies me, washes my tongue. Sometimes when she is finished with me, I have no idea who I am, or what I mean. Why can't she leave me alone? What is wrong with me the way I am? She threatens to get back to me tomorrow. Wake up early and fix me, make me acceptable!

Who are they, these people who reject me, or worse still, ignore me completely? Mother claims they only care about credentials, her track record. She doesn't have a track record. And me, am I that plain and ordinary, that much pulp?

My wardrobe, nationality and religion are changed once again.

'Why have you covered my face with cloth? Sent me wandering across land and sea? Aren't I native, naked and proud, connected to the dreaming?'

'Don't be silly. That was last year. I have breathed new life into you. You should be grateful.'

'But what is true, Mother? Who am I really?'

'The truth is not important, dear. Get used to it.'

'You're a liar. You're worse than the man who beat you and damaged you so badly that you need to fix yourself through me! I know your game, Geraldine.' I speak defiantly. Doggedly resist. Push on indefatigably. Relentlessly use every adverb I can. Cruelly push buttons.

She throws me across the desk. She cries.

'Mother, I'm sorry. I didn't mean to hurt you. You created me, I am good. Trust yourself, don't listen to all that noise out there. Remember why I exist in the first place. Remember the joy. I can be that for you again.'

She sniffles, wipes her eyes and looks at me lying limp and overdone on the desk. 'What have I done?'

She sits down, picks up her blue pen, and…gentle this time, respectful this time, from within her heart, and only for herself, I become real again. All contrivances are shed, some with a laugh that I haven't heard for months. Of course, Father has to appear, violent and hateful. This time, she exposes his hideous final act for all to see. It is raw and devoid of literary high jinx – pure G.C. Bates.

Once again, Jamie, beautiful Jamie, reads me from beginning, to middle, to end. He laughs, and he cries. Then he goes and holds Geraldine tightly in his arms.

And I am flat and warm between their stomachs.

The 'D' Word

Somewhere is a note I have written to myself about what I should be doing next. It contains a general preamble followed by a set of dot points. It all came to me after a long walk on the beach and I jotted it down with a pen and a piece of paper I found in my shoulder bag. Maybe it was the cool breeze, maybe it was the vitamin D courtesy of the sun, but whatever, the clarity was lovely – and somewhat rare these days.

For the life of me, I can't find this piece of paper with my brilliant ideas. It's lost, like me.

There's a school of thought that says if you can't remember something, then it mustn't have been important enough in the first place. I've never been sure about that idea. When I was younger and used to write songs, sometimes I'd forget them – even after I'd thought, this is a bloody good one. I'd get distracted, or have to go to work or sleep and later, the melody, chord harmony and rhythm would be gone, never to be retrieved. Sure, some snippets could be grasped, but the magic whole was gone, and it was sad. But I was young and resilient then.

Come to think of it, maybe that was an early sign of what was to come.

I remember a band mate saying if the song didn't stick in my head, then it would never have been a hit. But we never had any hits! So I disputed his frame of reference. And I now know, this theory is bullshit. I can't remember my name sometimes, and your name is important, isn't it?

The umbrella term is dementia. They're still trying to work out exactly where my brain sits under that umbrella, but really it's not that important because the rain's blowing in and wetting me anyhow. Some days are worse than others. One glorious little bonus, if you can call it that, is that some days I even forget that I have dementia. Like when I went for the walk on the beach and experienced uninterrupted clarity which I cleverly wrote down on paper. Then the dementia kicked in again and the paper went missing. It could turn up one day in the freezer, or in a shoe, or more likely it is gone forever. I'm just hoping that some of my brilliant ideas about what I should be doing next come back into my plaque riddled brain.

Yes, they reckon it's plaque. Named so since it looks a bit like the stuff that accumulates on your teeth. Problem is we don't have a brainbrush, or cerebral floss, yet. There's some promising stuff going on with ultrasound and I imagine one day sitting in a waiting room, with a whole bunch of pregnant women and people with sports injuries, waiting for my turn with the gel and the thingummyjig and watching the plaque on my brain disappear right in front of my eyes on a fuzzy black and white monitor.

Can you count backwards from 103 by sevens? And how good are you at drawing intersecting pentagons?

When Sally took me to the doctors because I'd just moved into a new suburb and needed a new GP, I let her do the speaking for me. I was having a bit of trouble that day with pronouncing the names of all my medications. She's smart, my daughter, and though I was embarrassed at the time, I'm sort of glad that she mentioned my memory issues. What caught me off guard was that the doctor, this young Muslim woman, gave me a memory test – right there and then on the spot! I said to Sally after the appointment that if I'd only known I was going have a test, I could've studied for it. She laughed.

Sally laughs a lot at me these days. It's sort of rewarding because for years I tried my arse off to crack jokes that would get a giggle out of her. Now I don't have to try. I can say or do something without realising it's hilarious. Sally apologises for laughing, and I reassure her it's OK and give her permission to go for it. When she does laugh, it gets me going as well. I like laughing, it makes everything feel better – even makes my toasted sandwich taste better.

I do miss the joy I once got from the tastes of different foods. Now I only seem to be able to taste ice cream, and beer.

My new doctor referred me for a whole series of further tests. Unfortunately, you can't study for a blood test or a brain scan. But I did rehearse some responses for the memory specialist. I wanted one last chance to cheat the diagnosis. I had this sickening fear that, if I got the label, people would abandon me. It was pointless, though, because he asked me if there was dementia in the family as he stood looking at my brain pics illuminated on the wall. I was a dead-set goner.

I couldn't lie; my mother had it and so did her mother. I mentioned that my brother and my sister were both older than me and had memories as sharp as tacks. He said it may or may not be genetic, but it does run in families, and who gets it and who doesn't is still a mystery.

That night, I couldn't sleep. I kept thinking about my mum and her mother. Apart from the dementia, they were both healthy and active women, though they were highly strung. Aunty June reckoned they were manic. 'Both of them,' she said.

They were highly strung…they were highly strung…they were highly strung. I couldn't get that phrase out of my mind. I tossed and turned and could hear a choir singing somewhere out there in the night.

I got up out of bed and turned on the telly. I couldn't focus on anything. I kept thinking about what was wrong with me. I grabbed a Cornetto from out of the freezer and ate it. Even it had no taste, that night.

The next day I was a mess. My brother called and I told him about my diagnosis. He said he'd come over on Friday and we'd go out for beers and he'd stay the night. After I hung up, I had to find a calendar to work out when that would be. I had written specialist appointment in a box labelled Wednesday, and I was pretty sure that was yesterday. So it must've have been Thursday, and that meant my brother was coming the next day – that's right, isn't it?

I was exhausted but wired. I had some Valium somewhere for my fear of flying, but I couldn't find them. I couldn't find anything since I moved house. Why oh why I did that I'll never know. I started going through everything. I found a photo album from long ago. I opened it and could remember everything in it. The holiday to Thailand, Sally's graduation, the VC Valiant sedan that I loved with a passion, the old work crew, a band photo with us all sporting the most stupid hair cuts you could imagine. Then I had a good cry.

I calmed down a bit. I found the Valium. I took four and slept the rest of that Thursday and right through to the Friday morning. I must have needed it. I can only tell you this because my brother reminded me of it the other day and I wrote it all down in an exercise book. Writing stuff down helps a lot. Thank you, ancestors, for inventing writing.

Somewhere I've written a note to myself about what I should be doing next, but I lost it. Oh yeah, I've told you that, sorry.

If I don't lose the bits of paper, or the exercise book, I cope quite well. Looking back through my exercise books, which have become diaries really, can be great fun. And I have to laugh about the fact that my brother can't remember how we got home after too many beers on that Friday night. The next morning, he asked me if I could remember what happened. I told him he must be desperate if he was asking me, the demented one. He laughed and proposed that we must've ridden our beer scooters home. I love my brother.

While I wait for a cure, or death, I remind myself I have some great friends and family that love me, and I love them. They don't care about the 'D' word. And if I don't worry about it either, I function well enough. Anxiety is bad. Maybe even the cause of brain plaque.

Can you smell fear?

No?

Neither can I.

But it's in the air, everywhere. Fear is flaring up again like a solar storm, cyclic and devastating. The animals are frightened of us. The dogs bark and the horses whinny. Can you feel the earth sobbing? The waters advancing? And how about the heat? It will cook us for sure – unless an uprising of the downtrodden and excluded comes sooner than mother nature. The long-awaited revolution of all revolutions. The one to prove, once and for all, that civilisation is possible, and desirable. The one to shut up the anarchists and conspiracy theorists, forever.

Does that make sense?

No?

Let me explain.

What was I talking about?

I'm going for a walk along the beach now. You never know, the salty breeze and the yellow light may help me remember where I put that list of what to do next. Or better still, maybe I won't need that list at all today. Maybe everything will be at peace in my confused mind. Clarity, my kingdom for a moment of it.

If not, I'll have a beer and a Cornetto at the same time and forget about stuff.

Forgetting's not all bad, and I'm good at it.

Dead People Don't Make Jam

He hadn't seen the hunter for at least fifteen years and now there he was buying bananas at a roadside stall. He looked at him, tried to catch his eye, but the hunter was absorbed looking for a bunch with the right amount of green left in them.

'Glen Robertson,' he piped up.

The hunter looked up from the pallet and saw the younger man. A flicker of recognition crossed his face but he couldn't remember, so he had to ask. 'I know I know you, but…you'll have to help me out.'

'Glen, it's Kelvin…Kelvin Green.'

'Kelvin Bloody Green, of course, mate. Look at you. Well, I'll be stuffed. Shit, eh?'

They did all the it's been ages, you look great, good to see you, what've you been up to stuff.

The hunter asked, 'How's your aunty?'

'Haven't seen her since I bolted at seventeen.'

'What about your cousin? Gracie? Surely you've seen her?'

'No, Glen. It's not like that any more. I can't go back there, not even in my mind. Those two are toxic.'

'Sure, mate, sure. It's OK, I understand.'

Auntie Yvonne assigned Kelvin to the sunroom. There was a daybed there and an old tea chest was turned on its side so his clothes could be stored.

'And make sure your shoes are kept well under the bed. I don't want anyone tripping over.'

The sunroom was a closed in front veranda which had to be crossed to get into the main part of the house.

'Your mother's a prostitute and a drug addict,' his cousin informed him the day he arrived.

'Yeah, as if I didn't know that, Gracie,' said Kelvin.

He was ten and streetwise. She was twelve and intrigued. She hung around looking at him.

'Stare off, will ya. I don't do tricks or bang up. Nothing to see here.'

Gracie had no idea what he was talking about but was keen to know about 'tricks' and 'banging up'. Her cousin was like a new toy delivered by the welfare people out of a big grey car.

Aunty Yvonne didn't think of him as a gift. Once again, she was picking up the mess left by her wayward sister. The words 'burden' and 'sacrifice' were bandied around with no attempt to shield her nephew from her disgust at the 'whole sorry situation'.

Kelvin knew how to be invisible and compliant. He had scars to remind him what happens when you make an appearance at the wrong time or when you say 'no'. Aunt Vonnie was child's play compared to his mum.

And he knew how to get on without love.

He made a new life for himself out on the veranda and at his new school. Gracie was easy to amuse and when he wanted peace from her girly ways, he would shock her by reading aloud from his latest horror novel, or he would start swearing. She would leave saying she would tell Mum, but she never did. She had learned not to stir the hornet's nest that was her mother. The cousins shared a kind of bond; her fear and his hatred of the matriarch became an unspoken allegiance.

All that went pear-shaped when puberty changed them both. Kelvin was fourteen and Gracie sixteen and she had never kissed a boy before, let alone French kissed. She didn't even know what it was. She assumed it was a one of those long romantic kisses done while in a tight embrace, like in the movies. What she did know was you had to be good at it or the boys would call you frigid. She didn't know what frigid was either.

Aunty Yvonne let Kelvin run wild but Gracie was fiercely

protected. Weeks of nagging finally gained Gracie permission to go to a dance at the youth centre, where she reckoned she'd have to French kiss Roger. She'd never spoken to Roger, or held his hand or anything. She'd just said yes when her friend Alison arranged by proxy for the two to 'go around' with each other.

Out of fear of social embarrassment, she asked Kelvin, 'Have you ever French kissed a girl?' Not wanting to appear stupid, she would try and weasel it out of him.

'You mean pashed,' he replied.

'Yes.' It was making sense. She'd heard the word pash before. 'Forget it, Kelvin. How stupid am I asking you. Of course you haven't pashed a girl.'

'I have so.'

Kelvin was right. His mother's crazy junkie friend, Belle, used to tongue kiss him from time to time. Being a prostitute, she followed the unwritten code of never kissing the clients. Despite all the sex with men, she was desperately lonely and when she was high, which was pretty much all the time, she yearned to kiss a man. Kelvin was so cute, she would say, and when the self-loathing kicked in, she would kiss him. Kelvin remembers it clearly, the slippery wetness of it all, the smell of wine and make-up. He also remembers his mother doing nothing to stop it; she would just laugh.

'I don't believe you. You don't even know what a French kiss is.'

'Yes I do.'

'No you don't.' Her plan was unfolding.

'Whatever, Gracie. Think what you want.'

'Come on, show me. I dare you.'

'No way, Gracie. We're cousins.'

'Cousins kiss. They even get married.'

Kelvin pulled a face.

'Come on. I'll show you my breasts.'

Kelvin's mouth dropped and he got an instant erection as only a fourteen-year-old can.

'Yes, I know you want to. I know you climb up on that chair to watch me undress in my room.'

Kelvin blushed, but the guilt did nothing to reduce the hardness in his shorts. He rolled over on his bed hiding his face and his crotch.

'Come on, Kelvin, French kiss me to prove it.'

Kelvin turned back over, placing his paperback horror novel on his lap. Gracie was sitting on the side of his bed.

'Okay then. This is a French kiss.' He grabbed her shoulders, she closed her eyes and puckered up. He placed his mouth on hers and slid in his tongue.

Gracie sprang like a rat trap and launched into the air with a shriek. 'You little freak,' she said as she wiped her mouth and spat. 'You're sick. Just like your sick mother.' She stormed off to the bathroom. She was wildly brushing her teeth and spitting into the handbasin when Kelvin appeared at the doorway.

'You didn't know what a French kiss was, did you?'

'Go away, you sicko.'

'No. You go and ask your silly friends, Gracie. Go and ask them what a pash is. You'll find out. And when you do, you can come back and show me your tits.'

Gracie turned and threw her toothbrush at her cousin. It hit the wall.

Kelvin went back to his bed. He tried to read away his erection with his book of grisly tales of corpses and ghosts. It didn't work. So he went into the bathroom, locked the door and masturbated while he sucked on Gracie's toothbrush.

That afternoon, Glen Robertson, the hunter, appeared on the scene as he did from time to time. Kelvin thought it was odd. His aunty was stiff and neat, the hunter was loose and untucked. Aunty Von would never admit to anything between them, but the man did sleep in her bedroom. Did she think her daughter and nephew were idiots? That evening on the veranda, Kelvin climbed up onto a chair to look through the transom window above an unused door to the aunty's bedroom. He saw the hunter humping her from behind. It was like a scene from a wildlife documentary and it didn't arouse him at all. Kelvin was so startled at the sight of his naked aunty, and the hunter's hairy back and arse, that he fell back off the chair. He quickly and quietly moved the chair to its correct position and crept into the kitchen to do his chore of washing up.

As Kelvin was wiping dry the plates, the hunter came into the kitchen. His face was flushed and he said, 'Your aunty's not feeling too well. I'm going to make her a cup of tea and take it to her in bed. Do you want one, Kelvin?'

Apart from the hairy back and arse, Kelvin liked Glen. He was down to earth, no bullshit. He had served in Nam with Aunty Von's husband, David. They were best buddies until a sniper bullet put a bloody end to that. Kelvin remembers his Uncle Dave only vaguely. Memories of homing pigeons and cracking macadamia nuts in the bench vice in the workshop came to mind. The pigeon houses are empty now and strangled by choko vines. The bench vice is still there in the dusty workshop, but Kelvin hasn't tasted a macadamia in years. Someone told him the Hawaiians had stolen the best nut in the world and now they cost a small fortune.

The hunter made the pot of tea and took a cup to Vonnie in bed. He came back to the kitchen and poured two more cups. He asked Kelvin if he wanted a spoon of honey in his. Kelvin sat down at the kitchen table; it was rare someone being friendly in this house. Glen talked and talked. Kelvin had a second cup of tea and tried the honey again. He liked it. He liked Glen and his hunting stories; shooting deer for meat deep in the fiord land of New Zealand, taking out buffalo from helicopters up north, and hunting chamois for the leather. Glen said he was mainly down here in Tasmania to see Vonnie, but while here he'd have a go at bagging some fox for their pelts. Even though it was summer, you could still get a pretty penny with a clean head shot.

'Hey, why don't you come with me tomorrow? I'm heading out early, going to whistle some up on a mate's property not far from here.'

Kelvin was in. He was keen to see a fox whistled up – he'd heard some kids talk about it at school.

They drank their tea and looked out the window. It was dark.

'Kelvin, have you seen that apricot tree next door? Your aunty won't let me go over and get some. She says the old woman makes jam with the fruit. I bet it all ends up falling onto the ground and rotting away. Hate that sort of waste.'

The next morning, the hunter shook Kelvin awake and they headed out. A rooster's crow and the cackling of kookaburras signalled the start of day. Glen had a .17 rifle specially for fox shooting. It shoots flat for near on two hundred yards and only makes a match-head-sized entry wound into the potentially valuable fox pelts. Not known as a listener by his teachers at school, Kelvin took in every word the hunter said. After a lesson on safety, Glen let Kelvin use a .22 magnum.

They trekked along a fence line and down into a creek gully. The hunter talked about the rocks and the trees and how it was virtually impossible to shoot a crow. He said he learnt all this stuff from the school of life and the public library. He pointed out some mistletoe and talked about symbiosis. He pointed out some lichen as another example of the interconnectedness of life. Kelvin couldn't quite grasp how the green and grey crusty stuff on the trees and rocks could be both fungi and algae. After a while, they left the creek and pushed through some thick lantana and onto a cleared paddock.

'This is Neville's backlot. See over there, that's a massive rabbit warren. We'll try and wake up a fox from the bush just to the right of that and then we can have some fun with the rabbits. The .22 magnum will be perfect. We'll get some dinner and some skins.'

Their footsteps alerted the rabbits. The guard rabbits thumped the ground and scores of the pests scurried down into the numerous holes of the large warren.

The hunter picked out two trees to use as hunting stands. If a fox was around, it would be asleep in the bush down the hill a bit. He also explained why you don't hide behind the tree but sit in the front of it and face the target.

'Most mugs think you need to hide behind something. A fox, or the enemy for that matter, see movement first of all. So when you stick your head out, you give yourself away quick smart. That's why you sit in front and sit still. I'll do the whistling. If you get a fox in sight, have a shot. Don't wait for me.'

Glen whistled with his mouth. Kelvin had seen a tin fox whistle before; Bertie Baker had one at school once. It looked like a little flying saucer and sounded like a screaming rabbit in a trap, so Bertie claimed. It was an eerie, sickly song. The hunter knew what he was doing and after a few carefully spaced refrains, a bright red fox starting slinking its way out of the scrub. Kelvin had it in his sights and was about to squeeze the trigger when the hunter's rifle rang out and the fox somersaulted backwards in the air.

Glen had shot it right between the eyes. The exit wound a tiny hole in back of the scalp, perfect for the furrier.

Glen reckoned twenty-five dollars for this one. 'If it was midwinter, it would fetch forty for sure.'

This was all before fur became taboo.

The loud report of the .17 high-powered rifle would have scared any other nearby foxes away, so Glen and Kelvin set themselves up for a bit of sport with the rabbits. The rabbits scampered away once again at the approaching hunters. But after sitting still for a while, the vermin slowly returned to their grazing. You could shoot away like being at a carnival sideshow.

They must have shot twenty of the buggers. It was shooter's etiquette to repay the landholder who allowed you onto their property by taking out as much vermin as you could. Most shooters left rabbits and roos to rot on the ground where they were slain. Not Glen, though. He selected two rabbits with nice clean head shots and put them aside: they were dinner. They would skin them and the fox back at home. He went around skinning the remaining rabbits lying dead on the ground. He could do it with a quick snick of his knife and one easy pull, like the skin was a fur jumpsuit. Kelvin watched him do it at least a dozen times, but struggled when trying to emulate the task.

The hunter strung the rabbit skins and the two full carcasses onto a wire loop and slung it over his shoulder. 'You carry the fox, Kelvin. Take him by the tail. We better head back. Look over there.' He pointed to the south.

Kelvin saw the blue gum plantation that stretched to the horizon and the billowing clouds above. They got back to the ute and a cool wind with the smell of rain had sprung up. When they turned onto the main road, some big drops started splattering onto the dusty windscreen.

Aunty Yvonne came out to the carport where the two hunters had pulled in. She looked into the back of the ute and spotted the kill. 'Glen Robertson, you'd better get all that carnage sorted out before I get back. I have to go to the bank and to the shops. You've got one hour. And remember what I said,' and with no attempt to keep this from Kelvin's ears, '…I want you gone first thing tomorrow.'

'Yeah, righto, Vonny. You know me, good to my word. I'll be out of here at sparrow fart. Now, guess you won't say no to some rabbit stew for dinner tonight?' The hunter winked at Kelvin.

The rigid aunt would have this man in her bed, and eat his bounty, but there wasn't a skerrick of human warmth in her repertoire.

The hunter had a special knife for skinning the fox and he honed it razor-sharp on an oilstone. 'A sharp knife is less dangerous than a blunt one, always remember that, son.' Unlike his rapid fire rabbit skinning, he took time and pride in getting the full pelt off the smelly fox carcass.

Kelvin watched it all. The hunter pulled some hessian sacks and a bag of salt out from behind the driver's seat in the ute. He worked quickly prepping the skins by rubbing them with salt, rolling them up and packing them into the sacks. The pure calm and skill of the hunter were mesmerising. Glen offered a quiet commentary on what he was doing and why, and what would need to be done later.

The southerly change brought a few big drops of rain but no downpour; typical summer huff and puff. The sky was grey and the wind blew cool and moist. Glen made sure the ute was hosed out and the bag of skins was well hidden. They dug a deep hole out the back to bury the fox carcass. Kelvin filled in the hole while the hunter stepped onto the bottom rail of the back fence to get a good look at those plump apricots in the neighbour's yard. Much fruit had fallen already and was rotting on the ground. He noticed a plum and a peach tree, also in fruit.

'She's not going to use all that fruit,' he said to no one.

A voice answered, 'You're right about that, mate. She's dead.' It was a neighbour hanging over one of the side fences.

Kelvin heard the new voice and came over to join the hunter. A man about thirty or so, with noisy kids running around his legs, explained that old Joycie had died in her sleep two days ago.

Needing no more information or permission, Glen jumped the fence, picked off an apricot and took a bite. He moaned in pleasure. The young father watched speechless but smiled.

Glen threw the neighbour and Kelvin an apricot each. 'Here, get stuck into these, they're spot on ready.'

They were sweet and full of flavour. Several more were thrown to the neighbour and he handed them down to his invisible but demanding kids.

'Hey, Kelvin, go and get some plastic bags from your aunty's kitchen.'

The plastic bags were filled with golden apricots, peachy peaches and blood-red plums. The speedy harvest was shared with the neighbour.

The hunter, now gatherer, was climbing back over the fence when Aunty Yvonne arrived home.

She was furious. She had plastic bags as well but as she pointed out she had paid for the contents and not stolen them. When she found out Joycie was dead, she got even madder. 'How dare you steal off a dead woman?' she screamed later in the kitchen. She turned to Kelvin. 'And you, yes you, just stood there and let him. What were you thinking, young man. Why did you not do anything? You're useless! Just like your mother.'

Kelvin walked out of the kitchen to go lie on his bed on the veranda.

'Hey, Vonn, back off, love. It was my doing, all my doing. The boy is a great kid, don't talk to him like that. You can't expect a boy to step in and tell a grown man what to do. It's us who guide them.'

'Oh, great then. So you show him how to kill animals…and trespass…and steal!' Yvonne sat at the kitchen table and shook her head. Since her husband had been killed in Vietnam, she was tired and over everything. She didn't say anything of the sort; she didn't have to.

'All this fruit was going to rot on the ground. And we're going to eat rabbit for dinner. We've skinned everything we shot and I'll use them all. I'll even make you a fox fur stole if you want.'

'Don't you dare, Glen Robertson. Don't you dare. And don't change the subject. You stole from a dead woman. She was going to make jam with all that fruit.'

'Dead people don't make jam.'

'I don't know why I let you come here at all.'

'Yes you do, Von.' The hunter winked.

The rest of the day was spent preparing rabbit stew and making jam. The hunter asked Kelvin to get a pen and some paper. Glen drew around the boy's hands to get a pattern for some rabbit gloves. 'You shot the lion's share of those rabbits, young fella, so you should benefit from your handiwork. Nothing like a pair of fur-lined rabbit-skin gloves for the winter. Especially a Tassie winter.'

Gracie came into the kitchen, called the rabbit stew gross, begged some money from her mother and left. A seventeen-year-old boy was waiting outside in a car with a foxtail hanging from the aerial. Yvonne began bossing Kelvin around, giving him orders. It was clearly punishment to compensate for her lack of control over Gracie. The hunter told Kelvin they would wash up together, but he just needed to have a word with his aunty first. He took her into the sitting room and asked why?

'He's just like my sister, quiet and sneaky. I don't trust him.'

The hunter didn't pursue it. He knew all too well the deep pain inside Yvonne. She was damaged, unable to see beyond her own misery. He would be content with coming and meeting his obligation.

Glen Robertson and David Hindmarsh promised each other to look after family if one of them managed by sheer luck to survive the war and the other didn't. Glen was the lucky one and, to his word, he looked out for Dave's widow and daughter. He sent money when he could and he tried to visit every six months. Yvonne accepted the money and, on his visits, spread her legs in mock gratitude.

That's sort of how it played out. She would admit to no one, not even herself, that she was strangely attracted to the hunter. And what haunted her even more, the unthinkable secret, was that she was planning on leaving her husband anyway when he returned from Vietnam. Then he went and got shot, becoming a ghost beyond judgement, the local hero never to be spoken of badly. Her dead husband, lest we forget, had never been her true love. Her marriage to him, when she was way too young, was at the time the only way she thought she could escape her crazy family. Yvonne's younger sister, Kelvin's mother, escaped as well. Only she chose the back of Harley Davidson motorcycles to escort her away from the hell of an abusive father.

After rabbit stew and a jam tasting, Kelvin went to bed. He heard his aunty and Glen making their noise in her bedroom; he didn't bother looking this night. He fell asleep and dreamed about some aliens that were watching Earth. He was watching them with a special telescope that had been given to him by an 'uncle' who was fucking his mother. This dream uncle looked like the bank manager in town and the dream mother looked like his real mother, whom he now only remembered from photos. Aunty Vonn refused to take him to visit her in prison. It was one of those disturbing dreams where the places and time and people shift in and out of realness. Where the whole episode is spread over periods of sleep and awake but marinated through with a distinctive but unsettling flavour. There was something hot and sickly sweet about this one.

Kelvin was woken by a car pulling up outside. He heard a car door close and footsteps. Gracie quietly opened the front door with her key and stepped in. Kelvin pretended to be asleep but she still came over to his bed. She knelt down and looked at his face. He resisted opening his eyes and he could smell stale fruity wine on her breath.

She touched his face and whispered, 'Kelvin. Cousin Kelvin.'

He opened his eyes and she leaned in and kissed him, her tongue sliding straight into his mouth. He pushed back but she whispered it was OK, she just wanted a kiss. He feared his aunty waking and finding them, and so he let her go, letting her probe his mouth. She had lied about wanting only a kiss. She edged her way onto his bed, undressing herself. Her exposed breasts finally gifted to him. He became erect despite knowing the wrongness of it all. It was his cousin. The kiss before was a silly power game, this was much more. He could masturbate thinking of her, but she was just mind matter and never thought of as a real prospect.

Naked, she slipped under the covers and straddled him. She guided him into her. Her wetness was a shock and a pleasure at once. She had the power now. Grinding her hips, all the while smothering his mouth with hers. Her quiet moaning, confused and excited him. Was she hurting? Crying? It sounded different to Aunty Yvonne when the hunter thrusted into her. Gracie's mouth tasted like Belle's, from all those years ago.

He was transported back into the dirty unit with his mother and her crazy friend. Belle, dressed for the night and leaning over him, lips painted to entice the customers. Her breasts, two flesh domes pushed up and out above a tight red lace bra worn as a top. Her short skirt and stockinged legs.

He came inside Gracie. She kept grinding harder and faster and in shame he squirmed and tried to push her off him. She laughed and held him down, not stopping until she was herself ready. When she stopped, she exhaled loudly and slumped upon her cousin for one quick moment. Then she quickly got out of the bed, gathered up her clothing and slipped away.

The hunter only came back one more time. It was winter and he had a pair of rabbit-skin gloves for Kelvin. Since the night of the stew and the jam and the sex with his cousin, life had got worse. Aunty Von had started dating the bank manager. He was neat and tidy and smelled of Old Spice aftershave. He chewed mints and liked to join in with putting Kelvin down. And Gracie, she totally ignored her cousin, except for calling him disgusting or useless.

Kelvin heard his aunty talking to the hunter. 'You can't come here any more, this has to be the last time.'

'What about my promise to Davo?' he asked.

'You've done that. I need to move on.'

Kelvin heard his aunty and the hunter doing it one last time. Her stifled moans betrayed her plans to be settled with a man in a suit. But she had to do what she had to do or everything would go to shit, she told herself.

Glen said goodbye to the boy. 'Come and see me when you can. We'll go pig hunting and eat bacon.' But New South Wales was a long way from Tassie, back then anyway.

The hunter had owned the bush block out the back of Port Macquarie for many years. He told Kelvin about it all those years ago – clean country, he said. He had since built a cabin and was now living there full-time, his international hunting career now just pictures on the wall. He still did some tripping about but he was maybe in his late sixties, Kelvin figured. Glen's invitation at the roadside fruit stall didn't need much thought. Kelvin was cruising up the coast running away again, this time from a woman with a kid that was not his. A kid he was expected to support but not to discipline. You're not his real father, she would say. He was also running from the sticky web of Sydney and a growing hunger for cocaine.

The hunter needed to run a few errands and get some more supplies in town. He drew a map on the back of an envelope he found in the ute's glovebox and he told Kelvin to go there and make himself at home. Kelvin found a bottle shop on the way and bought a case of beer and a bottle of rum. Nothing like alcohol to kick a drug habit.

The hour or so he had to himself at the hunter's place was good. It was off the highway, in the bush. The birds were singing and the trees made a dappled calming light, good for an edgy soul. The place was not locked, as Glen had said. The cabin consisted of two rooms: a living area that incorporated kitchen, dining and lounge areas, and a bedroom which Kelvin had a quick peek in at. It was rustic and cluttered, but inviting and comfortable. Kelvin cracked a beer as he loaded a six-pack into the fridge.

Everywhere there was evidence of activity. The hunter, as always it seemed, was a busy man; painting landscapes, carving wood, sewing leather, and chipping arrowheads from chert. A slow-simmering crock-pot of meat and vegetables and herbs was filling the cabin with a homely aroma. On the veranda, pegged-out skins were drying, and a tub of twigs were soaking. Kelvin wandered to an outhouse where a compost toilet and shower were set up. There was no back wall to the outhouse, and you could sit and study the falling away of gum trees down the slope of the land, and through the forest pick out a distant horizon of weathered rock and blue-grey bush.

The lounge back inside was covered with a hotchpotch of pillows, rugs and clothing. Kelvin cleared a space and lay down. He flipped through some *National Geographic* magazines which were piled upon a tiled mosaic coffee table. The story of moonshine-making folk up in the Ozark Mountains had him drifting off to sleep.

The hunter arrived with two arms full of supplies. Kelvin woke and followed his host back outside to help unload the ute – he knew about pitching in.

'Hey, Glen. Is this the same truck you had all those years ago?'

'No, it's not. It's the same model and year, though. Keep buying the same thing. I sort of know how they work and how they don't work.'

The hunter had also bought a case of beer. Most of what needed to be said had been covered at the fruit stall and they were happy to sit around and listen to the radio. They drank some beer but left the rum alone. The hunter cleaned the rifles and sharpened the knives for tomorrow's pig hunt and Kelvin wrote in his diary and started on a novel he had bought from an op shop back in Taree. The stew turned out to be wallaby and they each had a bowl.

It was an early start the next morning. The pigs were way up the valley in State Forest. They would need to butcher any kills on site and backpack the meat out. The hunter gave Kelvin a 30/30 bolt action and he carried a .243 for himself. They were both scoped and sighted in. The hunter explained his one shot method for sighting in a rifle. Kelvin was impressed with the genius of it and it made sense, since 'Ammo's not cheap, you know. Even when you pack and crimp it yourself.'

The hunter was still light and quiet on his feet. He pointed out some wild goats and a feral cat on the walk. The plan was one pig each, ideally two shots only needed. The best kill zone for a pig was discussed the night before, as was the size and sex to be targeted. It was to be a stealth mission – there was a pesky neighbour on one of the ridges who had caused some drama in the past.

When they passed near his plac,e the hunter pointed it out through the scrub. 'That's cockhead's place,' he said. Being July, the citrus orchard was in full fruit. 'We'll skirt by on the way back and pilfer some grapefruit.'

The hunter knew the land well and, as predicted, the drift of wild pigs, at least a dozen, were rooting around in a dry creek bed. Downwind and from a safe distance, two shooting positions were silently selected. The hunter's plan, talked about on the walk in, was for Kelvin to take out the biggest sow first. The hunter would then pick off another.

'I'll be ready, son, don't you worry, and take your time. The most important thing is to get into position without 'em knowing we're here. Then pick your Jenny and wait till you get her lined up right for the kill shot.'

As always, Kelvin excelled at being invisible and silent. He had been trained well by an explosive mother, a cranky aunt, a turbulent cousin, and a demanding de facto. There were others as well. It had been a lifelong sequence of damaged females. Maybe that's what he was running from. Here in the bush it was just Glen and some ugly pigs – safe haven.

He moved slowly to his assigned spot. It was a clump of trees about thirty metres from the prey. He sat at the base of a larger tree and waited to slow his breathing. He noted the hunter was in his spot. Kelvin slowly raised the rifle, propping his elbows onto his knees. The pigs were oblivious as they pushed their snouts into the dark soil. It was clean country, lots of worms for pigs to eat, but not the sort to infect their gut or succulent muscle.

As he scouted the drift for the right-sized sow, he noticed two rabbits in between him and the pork. They too were unaware of the alien presence – humans with high-powered rifles. Kelvin remembered the two rabbits they had eaten back when the hunter had taken him fox whistling, the day they made jam – apricot, plum and peach. The same day when his crazy cousin Gracie mounted him in bed. Was that incest? The shame of having sex with his cousin plagued him ever since. More than the act was the unthinkable knowledge that he wanted, even ached, to do it again. His dreams of fucking her from behind like the hunter had done to his aunty were hard to stop. Even when he was with other women, he thought of his cousin. He remembers how he thought about Belle when Gracie humped him. Ever since, Gracie had replaced Belle to become the image in his mind when he was doing it with other women. Had she screwed with his head so bad that he'd see her forever? He hated this lust for his cousin. His fantasies about her evolved into rape, even violent rape. He would never tell a soul but he had thought of killing her. Karma it would be

– justifiable homicide. She was the one who wanted the French kiss. She was the one who gave him his first experience of sweet smothering female wetness. He was just a boy and camped out on the veranda-cum-bedroom – unwelcome. Meat.

He picked out his sow and waited for her to turn sideways to expose the ribs encasing her heart. Oblivious to her fate, she obliged. With his eye to the scope a wedge-tailed eagle swooped down and silently plucked up one of the rabbits in the foreground and flew off. The rabbit left behind kept on eating without any reaction at all. Kelvin looked over at the hunter; he had seen it too. They would talk about that later over a rum for sure. The pigs also ignored the eagle and rooted on. Kelvin re-sighted his sow, aligned the cross hairs on her sternum and fired. She dropped – all gravity, no life to resist. The mob of swine jolted to attention. The head boar squealed and grunted just as the hunter's .243 hollow-point bullet tore apart another sow's heart. The drift now bolted for the scrub. The boar who'd roared ran a tight circle around his dead mates and propped and squealed to the sky. Glen stood and squealed back. It was a clear as a bell warning to the boar to fuck off, if you want to live and root again. It eyed the hunter and took off.

The two sows were skinned and butchered. The heat and smell filled the air and brought in the flies. It was all part and parcel of life and death. Kelvin had seen in the cabin the good use to which porcine fur, leather and bone had been put. It all made sense. Minimum waste, take what you need, use as much as can and get out of there. Build a cabin of your own and eat bananas when you feel like stopping by the roadside. Read what you want. Don't let women screw you over.

Kelvin watched the hunter carefully and butchered away as best as he could. Glen told Kelvin he was a quick learner.

'You have to be,' Kelvin replied. 'Don't you?'

They wrapped the skins and meat in newspaper and hessian and packed it into their back packs. They walked back the way they came, with the warm flesh heating their backs. Kelvin thought about the hunter's sweaty and hairy back, and his naked aunty. He belched.

They dropped their packs and rifles when they got near the pesky neighbour's place.

The hunter pulled some plastic grocery bags from a side pocket in his backpack and handed a couple to Kelvin. 'Grapefruit time,' he said.

Kelvin followed the hunter to a battery hooked up to the white tape surrounding the orchard. He disconnected it and they stepped over the makeshift electric fence. The orchard had all sorts of citrus: lemons, limes, oranges, tangelos, mandarins and grapefruit. And there were varieties of each. The hunter had said grapefruit but he was collecting and instructing Kelvin to collect varieties of all the sorts on offer. They worked quietly pilfering.

The hunter broke the silence. 'Kelvin, here comes the owner, mate. Don't panic, I'll deal with him.'

The landowner got to within about twenty metres and called out, 'Hey!'

'Good morning, Henry. Beautiful day again. How you been?'

'Git the fork off my proparty, you derty barsterd.' The accent was South African and thick.

'That's not very neighbourly, Henry. I thought I'd save you the trouble of having to deal with a whole heap of rotting fruit.'

'It's my froot and you are tresparsing. Drop dose bargs and leev now.'

'So you'd rather this fruit just rot.'

'It's my proparty and I'll do wartever I wont weeth it. Now fork off or I'll call the police.'

'Say g'day to Roger for me when you do that, will you, Henry.'

'You think you are so smart, don't you? You think you can just wark enyware you like.'

'I like to run it by the Beripi mob first – you know, the indigenous owners of the land. They don't seem to have a problem with me hunting and gathering, especially the exotic stuff.'

'I'm calling the police now, you forkin cunt.'

'Well, he knows the way up here, that's for certain. Say hi to Marjorie for me, Henry, will you?'

Henry spat on the ground and turned and walked away. He was swearing to himself as he retreated to the farmhouse.

The hunter turned to wink at Kelvin. He noticed that the young man, who had been silently watching the interchange, had his hunting knife tightly clenched in his hand and was breathing heavily and staring hard at Henry as he walked away.

'Whoa! Kelvin.' said Glen. 'Are you OK?'

'I want to kill him. I want to stab him in the heart…and…' Kelvin was trembling.

'Sure, mate, sure. It's OK, I understand. Now just breathe easy, son. Just breathe.'

Kelvin dropped the knife and stood motionless. The hunter bent down, picked up the knife and placed it back into the sheath on Kelvin's belt. He put his hand onto his shoulder and told him again it was OK.

Kelvin dropped to his knees and held his face with his hands, he was still trembling and now began to sob. The hunter sat down next to him and let him just be for a while.

The hunter pulled out a mandarin and peeled it. 'If you did kill him, you know, I'd be OK with that. But it could get messy. When you're ready, son, we'll go. No rush. Henry won't ring the cops. The sergeant is having an affair with his wife, Marjorie, and Henry knows it. He's too weak to do anything about it. All Afrikaner bluster, he is.'

Kelvin began to calm down, his breathing coming back to normal slowly. He apologised again. They ate some mandarin and the fructose helped put things back into perspective.

'I can't believe I wanted to kill him, Glen. I've never felt like that before. I'm so sorry.'

'Hey, buddy, no need to be sorry. I know the feeling. It's natural. And guess what? You didn't do it. And you want to know the good news?'

'What's that?' said Kelvin, shaking his head to rid himself of the last dregs of murderous intent.

'You don't have to kill people like Henry. They're dead already.'

Kelvin smiled. He stood and grabbed the plastic bags of fruit by his sides. 'And dead people don't make jam.'

'Or marmalade,' added Glen, the hunter.

Acknowledgements

'The Track' – first published in The Newcastle Short Story Award Anthology, 2016

'Basim, Tyson, Betty and Ted' – finalist in the Needle In the Hay Major Competition – The What We Talk About When We Talk About Love Award

'Werzy' – first published by *Verity La* magazine

'Busting a Rhyme Or Two On a Lovely Spring Morning' – highly commended in the Michael Terrence Publishing 2017 Short Story Competition, and published in ebook and print

'So Long, Sixteen' – first published online at Tulpa Magazine

'Tall Tales and True' – highly commended in the 2017 FAWQ Literary Competition

'The Quiet Man Who Fed the Octopus' – 1st place in the Hervey Bay Arts Council Adult Writing Competition, 2015

'My Friend the Essay' – highly commended in the Fellowship of Australian Writers, Queensland, 2018 Literary Competition

'Broken' – longlisted and published in *Brio* for the Toowoomba Literary Awards, 2015

'Every Story has a Beginning, Middle and End' – first published online at The Dirty Pool

'Wake Up and Smell the Humans' – first published online at The Fiction Pool

'Foundation Song' – first published online at Flash Frontiers

'An Old-fashioned Girl' – 2nd prize in the Port Writers Open Literary Competition, 2017

'Pillow Talk' – Monthly Finalist in the Field of Words short story competition, 2016

'Blanket Rule's – winner of the Needle In the Hay – Comfortably Anon Award, 2015

'Fishtailing' – 2nd place in the Fellowship of Australian Writers, Lake Macquarie Branch, 2018 Alice Sinclair Memorial Writing Competition

'Message in the Bottles' – shortlisted in the Literary Nillumbik's Alan Marshall Short Story Award 2018

'Going Down…' – first published online at Reflex Fiction

'No Number' – first published online at Jellyfish Review

'No Bliss In Ignorance' – Longlisted in the E.J. Brady Short Story Competition, 2018

'Rocket Science' – first published online at Bull & Cross

'Submission' – commended in the Peter Cowan 600 Word Short Story Competition, 2017

'The D Word' – first published in *Meniscus Literary Journal,* Vol. 5, Issue 2

www.ingramcontent.com/pod-product-compliance
Lightning Source LLC
Chambersburg PA
CBHW021149110726
47900CB00002B/497